The Watchers

To Andrew
Thanks for Being
a fan of the Books!

ALSO BY

Tony Acree

The Hand of God

The Watchers

Tony Acree

Hydra
Publications

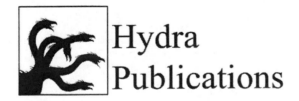

Printed in the United States of America

ISBN: 0996086714
ISBN-13: 978-0-9960867-1-4

Hydra Publications
1310 Meadowridge Trail
Goshen, KY 40026

www.hydrapublications.com

DEDICATION

For Lynn Tincher and Linda Goin.
Thanks for showing faith in a newbie.

And in memory of
Allie Thompson and Bob Beale,
two dear friends now on the grandest adventure.

CHAPTER ONE

Ruth Anne closed her eyes and took deep steady breaths, trying to slow her heart rate and not think about the mountain of rock pressing down on her. She'd never gone spelunking before, and after today? She never would again.

She reopened her eyes. Thanks to the light on her helmet, she could see the reason she agreed to come at all: the hunky figure of Jason Mueller snaking further down "the wormhole." That's what Jason called this part of the cave, a long very narrow tunnel through solid rock. They were both students at the University of Kentucky, he in pre-med, she still stuck on undecided while a member of the cheerleading squad. Her friends teased her she was after an MRS degree, and they weren't far off.

Jason was from one of Lexington's oldest and richest families and she had her eye on him for the entire semester. When he invited her to go cave diving, she all too quickly said yes, forgetting how much she hated being in tight spaces and was even more terrified of bugs. The thought of spiders climbing all over her kept her up at night. But Jason was into extreme sports and she was into him. She didn't dare say no once he asked her to join him on this underground expedition, for fear she might not get a second chance to go out with him.

So here she was, a billion miles underground, on her stomach, crawling through a space where the gap left only inches to spare in any direction. He promised, since this was her first time, that they would go to an "easy" cave for her first dive and brought her to a farm his family owned down near Mammoth Cave National Park in Edmonson County, Kentucky. Jason believed their cave had to hook up at some point with Mammoth Cave, and was convinced he could find that connection given enough time.

He told her Mammoth Cave was nearly four hundred miles long, the longest in the world, blah, blah, blah. She couldn't care less. She just liked his curly black hair, blue eyes and the way he looked in his faded jeans. Wearing a red, black and blue checkered flannel shirt, he looked like a lumberjack dream boat.

And up until about an hour ago, their trek through the cave was the easy trip he promised with fewer bugs than expected, thank God, and no bats. But after going through one very tight squeeze, Jason came to a complete stop. Looking up, Jason noticed an opening about six feet off the ground where a large boulder, matching the size of the hole, now rested at their feet.

"That's new," Jason said. "I'll bet those tremors earlier this year must have shaken that boulder loose and caused a breakdown. Let's take a look."

Jumping, he grabbed the edge of the ledge. Pulling himself up, he first glanced around and then climbed the rest of the way and disappeared from view. Ruth Anne nearly had a panic attack as she looked around at nothing but rock and a darkness that seemed to close in around her. She started calling for Jason, but he soon stuck his head out of the hole, his face lit up with excitement.

"You *have* to see this," he said. "Here, take my hand and I'll pull you up."

Every part of her being told her not to do it, but then she looked into those smiling blue eyes, jumped, grabbed his hands and climbed up beside him.

She crawled onto the ledge and could see another tunnel disappearing downward, further than the light of her helmet could reach. She was about to say something when she froze and goose bumps popped out all over her body. She could swear she heard what sounded like someone whispering. It was just barely audible and she closed her eyes and strained to make out the words. But it stopped and all she heard was Jason. "Think about it," he said. "No one in the history of the planet has ever seen what we're about to see. This passage goes out quite a bit, then there's a flattener and I came to get you before exploring that part. Is this awesome, or what?"

She voted for the "or what" and tried talking him into getting more people before exploring this new part of the cave, but he said he wanted to be the first one to see this area and to share it only with her. If she wanted to wait for him, well, that was up to her and she could stay here and he'd return later. She considered her limited options and decided splitting up and staying behind was a bad plan, so she reluctantly agreed to further explore the new area with him. She thought about mentioning the whispering and her growing sense of unease, but was worried he might think she was some nut job. But there was no way in hell he was leaving her in the dark by herself.

She breathed in the musty cave air and continued crawling on her stomach after Jason and thought to herself, maybe he isn't worth it. After a bit the opening widened, but the ceiling remained low. She bumped her head several times as she tried to scratch her nose.

Jason stopped. "Do you see that?" he asked.

"See what?" She inched closer to him, trying to look past him, but saw nothing.

"Turn your helmet light off for just a moment. I think I see some kind of glow up ahead."

"You *can't* be serious?"

"Just do it. It'll only be for a minute."

Ruth Anne hesitated, then reached up and begrudgingly turned off her helmet lamp. Jason did the same and for a terrifying moment, the darkness was total. She reached out and put her hand on his boot, but then she could see what caught his attention. Up ahead there was a soft red glow.

"Oh, Jesus. Do you think there's lava up there?" she asked.

"Don't be silly. There's no volcanic activity in this part of the country."

"Yeah, but what about the earthquakes. Maybe they did something and now lava is bubbling to the surface."

He switched his light on again and she did the same. "Think about it, Ruth Anne. If it was lava, it would be getting warmer. And it's not."

He was right. It was snowing when they entered the cave and it was down to about twenty-five degrees outside. But once in the cave the temperature stayed constant, in the mid-fifties, and it didn't feel any different the closer they got to the light.

He continued, "And we would smell sulfur. The smell would drive us out of here, but I don't smell any. Do you?"

No, not that she was aware of. They moved slowly on, towards the source of the mysterious light. They crawled another hundred feet or so where the ceiling rose to about sitting height and the bottom dropped off to a small ledge. Jason glanced over the side and said, "There's what looks like a fissure and the glow is coming down from one end. Hang on a sec'."

He swung his legs over the side and dropped down, then raised his arms up ready to catch her. But Ruth Anne, backing away slightly said, "Look, Jason, let's go back. I'm getting a bad feeling about this. I mean, what if you step into a sinkhole, or something like that, and get hurt? We're down here all alone and no one knows where we are."

He dropped his hands to his sides and didn't look happy. "Fine," he said. "How about this? I'll walk up the fissure a bit to see if I can tell where the glow is coming from. Then we'll head back and get a group in here to explore this new section more thoroughly. O.K?"

Ruth Anne looked down the cave fissure towards the glowing red light, her sense of unease growing. She nodded yes and said, "Be careful. And stay where I can see you. Please?"

"You got it." Jason moved quickly down the path and just to the end of her light's reach when he stopped and seemed to look off to his right, where the passageway made a sharp right turn. He shouted to her, "Just another minute," he paused. "I think I see something." He took another step and disappeared from view.

"Jason! Wait!" Ruth Anne shouted. But he didn't. She wrung her hands while counting the seconds, waiting for him to return. She could still see the glow from his helmet lamp and was watching it intently when it blinked out. The other end of the fissure was now barely illuminated by her own lamp and the same peculiar soft red glow.

She screamed his name several times, but there was no answer. A low moan escaped her body as she looked over her shoulder at the barely visible path that led them here. Her body began to shake uncontrollably and panic seeped into her bones. She wasn't sure she could remember the way they came into the cave without Jason leading the way. Frozen with fear, she was too afraid to go after Jason and too terrified to try to leave alone.

After several paralyzing moments, she knew she couldn't stay where she was. The terror of being lost forever in the cave trumped her fear of going after Jason. She jumped down and followed his footsteps, carefully.

When she reached the end of the fissure, the path made a hard right turn. She slowly peeked around the corner and could tell the red glow was stronger just up ahead. She inched forward, checking the ground for sinkholes or drop offs, but the path looked solid. Like Jason, she thought she could see something. But as she moved closer and strained her eyes for a better look, she came to an abrupt stop, her mind instantly in shock beyond understanding by what she now saw.

There, in front of her, was a really tall old man sitting on a stone block. She assumed he was old because his hair flowed down nearly to his waist and was as white as the snow falling outside the cave. Not only that, but the man was huge. As a cheerleader for the basketball and football teams, she spent a lot of time around some really big men, but this guy was as tall or taller than any of them.

Jason must be right, she thought. The cave on his family's farm must hook up to Mammoth Cave, and that's how he got here, from another entrance. There's *no way* he could fit through the "wormhole" like we did.

The red glow was emanating from somewhere in front of and below the man, as if he sat around a fire pit. The man turned his head and she could see he was eating something. Noticing her, he stood and began taking long strides towards her. He was wearing a long robe, like you see people in the Middle East wear, but without the headdress. Her shock intensified when she noticed shackles around his wrists, with short lengths of chain dangling from them. Was he an escaped prisoner?

As he approached her she saw he was chewing on something. Her terror exploded when she realized he was holding the end of a human arm. He casually raised it to his mouth, tore off another bite, then wiped his mouth with his hand. Blood dripped from his fingers. The arm still contained bloody shreds of Jason's checkered shirt.

The man smiled and Ruth Anne began to scream.

CHAPTER 2

When I was a kid, I always wanted to grow up to be a ninja. I got bit by the bug watching *Teenage Mutant Ninja Turtles.* I'd sit and watch that show for hours via the magic of a stack of well-worn videotapes. I figured, hell, if a turtle could be a ninja then I could, too. My brother Mikey and I would practice by running around the neighborhood, sneaking up on people and letting them have it with Nerf Swords, slashing and then dashing away.

But life was kinda funny. I kept growing, and before long being ninja-stealthy was out. You don't see too many six and a half-foot tall ninja fighters. I was still light on my feet, but hiding in shadows wasn't going to happen. Unless it's one big ass shadow. I can still remember working on ninja moves in the backyard and my mother yelling out, "Victor Riley McCain, stop that before you break something . . . or someone!"

As an adult I guess I got as close as I could to being one by joining Special Forces and then later becoming a bounty hunter. I still sneak up on bad guys and like to wear black—comes with the territory. But I outgrew the black ninja outfit, I don't carry a cool pretend sword and prefer my glock. You hit a bail jumper with a rubber sword and you're in for an ass kicking.

These thoughts were running through my mind as I looked through the peephole of the door in my room at the Jefferson Hotel in Richmond, Virginia. The Jefferson was one of the nation's finest four star hotels. It burned to the ground, was rebuilt, closed, and then reopened again. A dozen U.S. presidents have stayed here. At one point, they even had live alligators in the marble pools in the lobby. No, really. The history nut in me would have loved to explore every nook and cranny of the grand old building, but not this trip.

I was here to kill a man. A few months ago the thought of murdering anyone in cold blood . . . it never would have entered my mind. My job as a bounty hunter was to bust the men and women who murdered people, then cut and run when they made bail. Oh, how things changed.

A few months ago, I didn't know God and Satan were real—I mean, deep down, really believed they were real. I didn't know my only brother was one of Satan's top lieutenants and plotted mass murder on an unfathomable scale. I hadn't met, fallen in love with and then lost the most beautiful woman on the planet, Samantha, kidnapped by my scum-ball brother. I also didn't know about the Hand of God, God's own bounty hunter, named Dominic Montoya. And when Montoya was killed, Lord knows I never expected to take his place as the Hand of God.

Yet here I was, trying to finish the job Montoya died trying to complete: to track down and kill my own flesh and blood, Mikey. For nearly three months I searched for him and Samantha. The douche bag even sent me a Christmas card. I showed up at mom's house for the holidays on the chance he might too, but no dice.

A tip led me here to the Jefferson and to a man staying in the Governor's Suite who might have information on where Mikey was lying low. I managed to book the room across the hallway. With the dinner hour now over I stood watching for my mark to return to his room.

As I waited, I had time to think about God. If you asked ten people to define God, you would likely receive ten different answers. For example, the priest in the parish where I grew up said that, "God is everything you see and knows everything you think." Pat Robertson thinks God is a man with a long white beard and a Republican. The nuns in my childhood Catholic school were convinced God was a woman because a man could never get things so perfect.

My friend Bob believes God is no different than Santa Claus or the Easter Bunny: a fictional character made up to help us deal with the fact that when we die and become ashes to ashes and dust to dust, there's nothing more. And that terrifies us. So we created a fictional character to help us sleep at night.

I, on the other hand, knew God was real. True, I'd never met the guy, or deity, or whatever the hell you wanted to call him. But I had met the Ying to his Yang: Satan. The S.O.B. strolled into my office and changed my life forever. Hell, he caused me to lose my very soul. So, yeah, I was sure there was a God and now I was worried I would never make it upstairs when I died to meet Him.

Samantha Tyler, the woman Satan asked me to track down for him, was convinced there was a Devil, but emphatically believed God was dead and that's why the world hadn't heard a peep out of him (or her, thank you very much Sister Margaret) in nearly two thousand years. He just went poof in the night and left us all hanging here at the mercy of Satan and his minions.

But during my brief conversation with the fallen angel, I could tell he thought God was still up there, large and in charge. So if God was dead, his arch nemesis hadn't gotten the memo. Satan was doing all he could to regain his place in Heaven and replace the Lord Almighty. Fat chance, Satan ol' buddy. Every fiber in my body told me God was real and still sitting high upon his throne.

My contemplations were interrupted when I saw three men, all dressed in suits, and a young girl walk into view and stop at the door across from mine. The men were laughing and smiling, but the girl kept her eyes down and didn't join in the fun. One of the men took out a key card, opened the door and let the other three in the room. Turning and closing the door, he took up a guard position outside the room.

I gave them a few minutes before I made my move, wanting the hired gun outside the room to relax. When I could see him starting to look bored, I opened my door. When you're as tall as I am, sometimes it's hard to blend in, so I do the exact opposite. I was dressed in a nondescript green sweat suit, a workout bag slung over one shoulder, and carried a basketball. When you're a head taller than anyone else in the room, give them the illusion of what they're seeing: in this case, a cool dude basketball player. I dyed my black hair blonde and donned huge Ray-Ban aviator sunglasses. I had ear buds in each ear and rap music turned up to ear-splitting level. The things I do for my craft.

While shutting my door I bobbed my head to the music, nodded to the man, and started down the hallway. I began to twirl the basketball on my finger. Passing him, I almost dropped the ball, then batted it into the air, high above the other man's head. As planned, natural human reaction took over. From the time we're little kids we're taught if there's a ball in the air, then catch it. And that's just what he did. He reached up with both hands to grab the ball, which meant his hands were nowhere near the gun I could tell he kept under his suit jacket.

His head was also tilted up while he watched the flight of the ball. I shot my hand up and with the hard edge of my knuckles punched him hard in the throat. I could feel his windpipe collapse and his eyes bulged. The basketball dropped and bounced down the hallway.

His hands flew to his throat and I grabbed his gun from its holster and placed it into my bag. He tried hard to take a breath, but his crushed windpipe prevented even a smidgen of air to pass through. He gripped the front of my sweat suit, his eyes pleading. I opened up his jacket and took the room key from the inside pocket. Spinning him around in front of the door, I reached back into my bag and took hold of my gun, complete with suppressor already attached, and slid the key card into the door lock. All told less than fifteen seconds from start to finish. My luck held as there was no one in the hallway.

With a snick, the door unlocked and I opened it. The Governor's Suite was made up of multiple rooms. The door opened into a sitting room with a couch, several chairs and a flat screen TV on the wall. The door to the bedroom was closed and the other bodyguard was sitting on the couch watching an NBA game with the sound down low.

He looked up as we came in and shock froze him in place for a split second. It was all I needed. I pushed the door guard on top of him, shut the door, took two quick strides, and placed my gun against his forehead. I made a shushing motion with my free hand. He nodded he understood and rolled the other man off of him, who continued to make wheezing noises, his face turning red from lack of oxygen.

I removed his gun and dropped it into my bag, and took out plastic cuffs. I mouthed for him to lie down and face the back of the couch. He complied and I quickly cuffed his hands and legs in a hogtie position. I then took duct tape out of my bag, tore off a strip and placed it over his mouth.

The guy I hit in the throat was already passed out so I left him alone and moved to the bedroom door, and listened. I could hear music playing and a man moaning. I opened the door and stepped inside the darkened bedroom.

From the TV's glow, I saw the man was on top of the girl, who was barely a teenager, at best. Rage flared up inside me and it was all I could do not to pull him off and beat him to death with my bare hands. Instead, I strode over to the bed, grabbed a fist full of hair, yanked him backwards and off the girl.

Yelling in pain, he turned and came off the bed ready to fight until he saw me. Or, more to the point, my gun. Coming up short, he took a step back and put his hands in the air.

I looked at the girl. "Take your clothes, go into the bathroom and get dressed," I said. "Don't come out until I tell you to. Do it now."

Without a word she gathered up her things and quietly went to the bathroom and shut the door. The man said, "You are *so* dead. You have no clue—." He stopped suddenly when I closed the distance, struck him hard in the gut and then pushed him back onto the bed. The man was middle-aged with what was once a fairly good build, but now soft around the edges, and graying hair at his temples.

For the next few minutes I watched with satisfaction as the naked man rolled back and forth on the bed in pain. "Do you have any clue who I am?" he finally managed to say through clenched teeth.

"You're Tommy Spenoza, a member of the Spenoza crime family out of Philly. Yeah. I know who you are. You're a frickin' pedophile, Tommy. Your own family ratted you out. Guess you thought taking your child victims out of Philly would keep the family off your back. Well, here I am. They didn't even ask for money to spill the beans on you."

Tommy cussed a blue streak and then asked, "So. They sent you here to whack me, is that it?"

"Your family didn't send me. They just told me where to find you.

What I want from you is information. Where's Belial and where have they taken Samantha Tyler?"

At the mention of the name Belial, Tommy went pale. "I don't know who you're talking about."

I shrugged and shot the pillow right by his head. The gun made a loud pfpfpt sound, despite the silencer, and the pillow jumped. Tommy made a strangled cry and tried to get off the bed but I leveled the gun at his nose and he stayed still.

"See Tommy, if you got nothin' for me, you're useless. The only thing keeping you breathing is you might have something I want. If you don't . . ." I let the thought trail off shrugging a shoulder.

"Okay, okay. I get it. Yeah, sure. I know this Belial-guy. He's a customer."

"And just what is he buying from you? You're in the construction business, right?"

"Yeah. Mostly." Tommy started to relax as he was now in more familiar territory. I was starting to get more than a little weirded out interrogating a naked mob guy, but no one said this job would be normal. "He wants to buy equipment from me. Heavy equipment."

"What does he plan to do with the so-called equipment?"

He flashed me a shark tooth grin and said, "No clue. Don't know, don't care. In my business you don't ask those kinds of questions." He paused for a moment, laid back on his elbows, completely unselfconscious, despite all mother nature gave him in plain view. "You know, " he continued, "you got by my guys out there pretty easy and then got the drop on me. That took guts and balls the size of fuckin' Texas, you know what I mean? I can use a guy like you. I don't know what you're being paid now, but I can pay you more. You know my family. You know it's true. What do ya say?"

I ignored the offer. "When was the last time you talked to him?"

"I haven't heard from him in over a month. He placed his order and I filled it. We're not exactly texting buddies, ya know what I mean?" He laughed like he had just told the funniest joke in the world. Moron.

I moved closer to him and asked, "Where's Samantha Tyler?" I maintained a calm demeanor, but inside my stomach was roiling waiting for an answer.

"Like I know? I know who she is, sure. But it's not like I'm her appointment secretary. If you want to know where she is ask her dad, the Congressman."

I felt my heart sink, but it was a shot in the dark. "I only have one more question. The safe here in your room, what's the password?" I knew all the top rooms in the Jefferson had their own wall safe in the closet.

He spread his hands out and said, "Never use it. I mean, come on, who's going to steal from me? Am I right? Besides, you don't look like the thief type."

"You know, when you're right, you're right. I'm not the thief type. I'm the Hand of God. Do you think they have a special place in Hell for child molesters, Tommy? Well, you're going to find out."

Tommy's eyes widened and he raised both hands and started to say something, but he never finished. I shot him twice, once in the heart and once between the eyes. I stood there for a moment and watched the life ebb from his body. I wish I felt something, some twinge of regret at having taken another man's life. But I didn't. All my years spent overseas fighting for Uncle Sam, killing Al Qaeda and Taliban scumbags, nada. And the men I killed during the mini war with my brother, the same. And even if I was the kind to have doubts about killing a man? I don't think I would in this case. Tommy Spenoza had been trafficking in child sex slaves for years on the east coast and his death would put a real dent in the sexual predator pipeline. He deserved to die, which I guess is the point of why I was here in the first place. I put the gun back in my bag and went and knocked softly on the bathroom door.

The girl, now dressed, opened the door, looked up at me and asked, "Is he dead?"

"Yes. He is. He can never hurt you again."

I don't know what I thought her reaction would be. Joy. Relief. Fear. Something. But she showed no more reaction than I had at Tommy's death. She looked me in the eyes and I saw nothing. She asked, "Are you going to kill me now?"

I crouched down and sat on my heels which put us at nearly eye level. "No. I'm not. What I can do is take you to a place where you will never be hurt again. Where the people will give you a different life than you have here. Interested?"

She gave a tiny nod, but I'm not sure she believed me. "You said you're the Hand of God. What's that?"

"I'm kind of like God's bounty hunter. I track down evil people and stop them from hurting other people. People like Tommy."

"So you stop them by killing them?" She said this with a small voice, her eyes large in the bathroom lights.

I nodded. "When I have to. Guys like Tommy never change and sometimes I have no choice but to take them out. I don't like it or enjoy it, but in his case it had to be done so he wouldn't hurt any other kids."

Her brow furrowed as she thought about what I said. She gave another small nod of her own then said, “He lied to you, you know. When you asked about Belial?” She stood there, not moving. She seemed to be barely breathing.

“So you were listening to us? What part was the lie?”

“When he said he hadn’t talked to Belial. He was on the phone in the car talking to some guy and he used that name. And it wasn’t about any type of equipment. Mr. Spenoza has something the other guy wants and I could tell Mr. Spenoza was really scared. He told the guy he wanted more money ‘cause of all the trouble he’d been through to find whatever it is he got for the guy. Then the other man started yelling and Mr. Spenoza began sweating while the other man talked.”

“What’s your name?” I felt such heartache for this child because that’s what she really was. If she had any type of childhood, it had been ripped from her. Her eyes were not those of a young teenager, but of a woman seeing the end of the world.

She gave a shrug of her shoulders. “They call me Mary.” She paused for a second and then continued, “He lied about the safe, too. He put some things in there. He used his credit card to lock it. Bragged about his American Express card. Like I cared.” The last comment was the first time she said something that sounded like a real teenager.

“Do you think what the guy wants is in the safe?” She shook her head yes. “Thanks, Mary. Wait another second and then we’ll get out of here.”

I went and searched the room and found Tommy’s wallet and cell phone in the nightstand drawer. I took out his AmEx card and went into the closet and opened the safe. I took out a stack of papers and a small brown box with intricate writing on the sides in a language I didn’t know and what looked like stars on the top. I opened the box and found a sheet of parchment, yellowed and in a protective sleeve. It was in the same language as the box. I put it back and closed the lid.

I popped the battery out of the cell phone, to keep people from tracking it, then dumped the haul into my bag. Later I would go through the call list on Tommy’s Blackberry and find the one my brother used. I might be able to use it to track him down. I zipped up the bag and went back to the girl.

She remained exactly where I left her. “Like I said earlier, I can take you away from this life to a place safe—unless there’s some place else you’d rather go.”

She shook her head no. “I don’t have any place else. My parents sold me for meth a few years ago. Then I was sold to Tommy. Now that he’s dead, I got no one.”

I wanted to go back and shoot Tommy a few more times. I said, "You have my word, your life will be different from now on. I know people who will take you in and treat you like one of their own daughters." I offered her my hand. "Let's go. Don't look at Tommy and stay near me."

She stared at me a moment, then dropped her eyes to my hand. Taking a small step, she slipped her hand in mine and I blocked her view of the bed as we walked past and into the other room. I held my finger and motioned for her to stop as I knelt down by the man handcuffed on the couch. I slipped a knife out of my bag and cut the restraints and put them back in my bag. He sat up stiffly on the couch. I ripped the tape off of his mouth and he grimaced when it tore skin from his lips.

"Here's what's going to happen," I said. "You're going to call the Spenoza family and tell them Tommy got hit by three men who said they were there to get revenge for their sister who Tommy raped. You're going to tell them the men wore masks, so you couldn't see what they looked like. You're not going to mention anything about me. Not what I look like, how tall I am, or how pretty I am. I have a source in both the family and the police department. If anything ever leaks out about me then I'm gonna know. And when that happens, you and anyone you love or care about, they're dead."

I pointed to the bodyguard on the floor next to us, eyes open and unseeing in death.

"Understand?"

"Yeah," shaking his head. "Got it. I don't want no trouble." He swallowed hard a couple of times and I could see the fear racing across his features and smell it rolling off of him.

"You're gonna sit here for an hour and then call the family and get them out here to clean up this mess. Let them know the brothers said they would leak info about Tommy and his predilection for young children to the press. The Philadelphia Inquirer would have a field day." I nodded towards the door. "We're leaving now."

I didn't mean a single word I said about hunting down his family or any of the rest of it, but he believed it anyway, and that's all that mattered. The man sat ramrod straight and made no move to stop us. Out in the hallway I bent down and picked up my basketball, took Mary by the hand and left the hotel through the back exit. An hour later, after making a few phone calls, I dropped Mary off at a church on the outskirts of Richmond who promised to take care of her. Then I was in my red '69 Chevelle barreling down I-64 on my way to Louisville. One step closer to a family reunion with Mikey.

CHAPTER 3

I have an app on my smart phone which allows me to listen to police radios from different cities. As I made my way west I listened for any mention of problems at The Jefferson Hotel on the Richmond Police scanner, but fortunately there was no activity mentioned there. After a couple of hours, I turned it off. It started to snow, but I continued to drive through the night. My thoughts turned first to my brother and the fact that I was going to have to kill him.

When I agreed to be the Hand of God and to hunt down and kill my brother, it didn't sink in right away. The closer I got to actually punching his ticket, I wasn't sure how I felt about it all. There was no doubt my brother planned to murder hundreds, if not thousands, of children. I kept replaying the last time I saw him, hiding behind me begging me to protect him from Dominic Montoya. I thought that he was innocent. Then he started laughing and kicking Montoya as he lay dying. My brother deserved to die for his sins and it seemed I was going to be the instrument of his death.

I thought about Samantha, too, and my knuckles turned white on the steering wheel. I imagined all the unspeakable things the thugs with the Church of Light Reclaimed, soldiers for Satan, might be doing to her . . . if she was even still alive. I held out hope that her father, Congressman Cyrus Tyler, who was also the highest ranking member of the Church, could keep her breathing. Heaven help all of them if she was not.

These thoughts rolled around in my brain until I pulled in at the back of the Derby Mission around 5 a.m. You'd think being the Hand of God might grant me nicer digs, but it didn't. It did give me a safe place to sleep at night and that was enough. I parked the car, grabbed my bag, and entered through the back door. Heading towards my room, I glanced into Brother Joshua's office and was not surprised to see him working away at his desk.

A black man somewhere north of forty years old with just the first tinges of gray in his hair, he ran both the mission and me. I don't know exactly how to describe our relationship. Boss? Scheduler? Profit of Doom? I was God's hit man and he was the man who told me who to take out. I knew, without a shred of doubt, those orders were coming from a higher power. It didn't stop me from wondering, however, how that sounds and what I would do if ever caught by the police and forced to try and explain why I did what I did.

"Yes, Officer. I kill people for God. Really. I do. And this guy who runs a homeless mission tells me who to kill. I'm serious." An insanity plea would be easy.

But according to Brother Joshua—or just J, as I liked to call him—one of the perks of being the Hand of God was I never had to worry about being arrested by the fuzz. It's one of the two freebies that come with the job. The other one was I was safe from harm as long as I was in a Church which is why I moved from my really nice town home to a fifteen by fifteen foot room in the back of the Derby Mission. Thanks to there being a church sanctuary on the property, the forces of evil can't touch me here. That's it. Once I step off of church property, no magical protection, no aura of invulnerability. I can be shot and killed just like any other man. Just ask my predecessor about that one.

Walking into his office, I shut the door and plopped into one of the two chairs facing his desk. He took off his reading glasses and put them on top of his head. Placing his elbows on his desk, he folded his hands, rested his chin on top of them, and waited. I gave him a complete rundown on Tommy Spenoza. Then I reached into my bag and passed him the box.

"Ever seen anything like this?" I asked.

He studied the box, turning it this way and that, and then opened it and took out the sheet of parchment. "The language on the box and the parchment appears to be some type of Semitic language, which I don't read." When I shot him a what-the-hell look, he further explained. "This is a group of languages from around the Horn of Africa. I'll get someone to translate it for us. As for the stars, if there is a religious meaning, it could be any one of several things: it could represent the children of Israel, angels, princes and rulers on Earth. We'll know more when we get the translation."

"Makes you wonder why Mikey-boy is hot to trot to get his hands on this" I said. "After what he tried to pull with the bird flu virus, I'd hate to think what he has up his sleeve next. Robbing his bank account has to have put a real hitch in his giddy up, but it will only slow him down for so long. I also have Tommy's phone and since Mikey called him, I have a number I can use to try and track him, though I doubt he's using anything but a burner phone. But you never know." I used the same myself. If the bad guys were looking for me as much as I was looking for them, no need to help them along.

"I'll get Kurt working on the numbers in Tommy's phone." Kurt Pervis, major hacker and computer geek, played a large role in helping me shut down the plot by the Church of the Light Reclaimed to kill children during an academic tournament by having donated computers release a virulent form of the bird flu. When it was over, he and I hid the thirty million dollars Samantha had stolen from Mikey and the Church. They wanted that money back.

And when we took on the Church back in November, Samantha, Winston and I left fingerprints in spots where there was no shortage of dead bodies. It was only a matter of time before the cops matched our fingerprints with those on file with the state when we obtained our bounty hunter licenses. No problem. Kurt and his hacker buddies broke into the state databases where my prints were on file and changed them so when my prints were run, they didn't pop up on the grid. Somehow they got into the Department of Defense records and did the same thing. I didn't ask how. I was just thankful they did. They did the same thing for Winston. Samantha's prints were not on file anywhere, so no worries on her account. Kurt was now taking it easy in Hawaii, soaking in the sun and doing odd jobs for me.

Joshua said, "I'm not sure involving him the way you do is a good idea. You are after some of the most dangerous people, and things, on the planet. It's just a matter of time before they turn their attention on him. And from what you've told me, he is ill-equipped to protect himself."

"Look, J, I don't use him in the field. He helped me a few months back and stuck his neck out to help bring down the Church's plans. But now all he does is computer work for me. He's keeping his head down and I'm keeping him away from the dangerous stuff. He's back to being just a Geek. When I need muscle help I call on Winston. I told you about him."

"The former football player turned bounty hunter. Yes, you did. While I don't like you including him either, at least he can take care of himself." Changing the subject, he continued, "I thought you should know, the girl you brought to us in Richmond will be taken in by foster parents who specialize in child abuse victims. She will be well taken care of. You must have made quite an impression," he paused, "seems she asked them if she could be placed with you."

I felt my eyes tearing up. I managed to say, "I couldn't take care of a puppy. She's better off with a good family." I ran my hands through my hair. "I sure do hope the kid makes it. J, you should have seen her eyes. The poor kid had no joy in her."

"Well, thanks to you, now she at least has a chance. Why don't you get some sleep and we can talk in the morning about what's next." He pulled his glasses back down on his nose and continued on with mission business. Looking at him you would have no clue we were discussing death and destruction just minutes earlier.

With some effort, I picked my sorry ass out of the chair and made my way down the hallway, beyond the maintenance and storage rooms, to my monkish room. I was bone-tired and didn't even take my clothes or shoes off, just dropped my bag onto the ground, my phone onto the small night stand, and collapsed on a bed barely big enough to handle my large frame. I reached up and turned off the light.

It seemed I barely closed my eyes and spread my arms out when the phone rang. Picking it up, I glanced at the caller ID and answered it.

"Kurt, you're a dead man calling me this early in the morning. Dead. Man."

"Dude. It's morning here, but the middle of the afternoon back in the Bluegrass. Wake up. I found her."

CHAPTER 4

I sat bolt upright in bed, all weariness driven from my body.

"Tell me," I growled.

I nearly crushed the phone in my hand waiting for the details. I'd been searching for Samantha ever since she was taken by Mikey and his lapdog, Preston Deveraux, from his warehouse by gunpoint. I'd gotten close several times, but no dice.

"It's like this. My boys and me, we've been hammering at the Church in cyberspace, attacking them every place we can get a toehold. Then we came up with the idea to go after the guys who work for her old man, the Congressman. We love the challenge of going after government targets. That's where the real thrill in hacking is. Playing cat and mouse with Feds is a real high for a lot of them," he said unable to hide the enthusiasm in his voice.

"Anyways, we got into the email accounts and computers of several of the aides who work for that jack-ass and it paid off. One guy, a staffer named Ozzy Wheadon, sent an email to the Congressman complaining his daughter was bored and to send down a female staffer to keep her company. So, we backtracked the IP address and it came from the Naples, Florida area. We did more checking and ran everyone on his staff for property in Naples. Wheadon's family owns a vacation home in Naples. Dude, Samantha *has* to be down there."

He waited for me to respond. "When was the Email sent?" I said.

"Today. Dude, get your ass down there. We found her." I could hear the triumph in his voice as he read off an address. I turned my light on and wrote it down.

"Kurt, I won't ever forget this. I mean it. Ever. Even if it doesn't pan out. Ya hear me?"

"I do, Dude. Now make me proud. Go get her. Do you want me to fly back and get in on this?" For Kurt just to offer, for him, was huge. Danger was not his middle name. But I knew if I asked, he would be on the next plane.

"No, Kurt. But you still da man. I'll call ya as soon as we make it down there." I clicked the phone off and started to make my plans.

****

Kurt hung up the phone and grinned from ear to ear. Making the big guy happy and to do it by putting him on the trail of finding the lovely Samantha? Priceless. Kurt sat in a beach chair on Hanalei Beach on the island of Kauai in Hawaii. Wearing a wide-brimmed straw hat and a dab of sunscreen on his nose, Kurt looked the part of a surfer bum, with a well-toned body, reaching an easy six feet tall and light-brown hair he wore just the other side of long. His smile and chocolate brown eyes beat those of any male model, and the women loved him. The problem started when he tried to love them back.

Women paraded by him on the beach in an effort to gain his attention. Some walked back and forth more than once, but Kurt concentrated on his laptop. He was slowly trying to work up the nerve to talk to one of them. Whenever a beautiful woman talked to him he froze up and started to hyperventilate. Sometimes he even broke out in hives. He couldn't remember a time when he didn't react this way. But that was the "old" Kurt.

He spent his time in Hawaii watching videos and listening to hypnosis tapes until he fell asleep at night. And during the day he looked for the right opportunity to try out his new self-confidence. After nearly three months in Hawaii, he hadn't quite found it yet. The "new" Kurt was a work in progress.

Of course he *had* been busy, he told himself. As part of a loose collection of hackers, he had organized a systematic and relentless attack against the Church of the Light Reclaimed and those they did business with. They made it nearly impossible for the Church to conduct business and considering they were a bunch of Satanists? They deserved it. His buddies had a hard time believing they were really Satan-lovers, but they didn't really care. And when he sicked them on Cyrus Tyler, they had a field day. Now their hard work could pay off with the rescue of Samantha. Sweet.

He was congratulating himself again when he realized a woman was staring at him, a wicked smile on her face. She was around five and a half feet tall with sandy blonde hair which fell about her shoulders, and the figure of a dancer. She looked to be somewhere near his own age of mid-twenties, but it was always hard for him to tell. Her bikini was white and extremely small, with a beach towel over one shoulder and carrying a small bag. He swallowed hard, cleared his throat, and said, "Hello." Just as the videos told him, he was keeping it simple. He took slow, even breaths and kept a smile on his face, even if inside his whole body was screaming at him to get up and run.

She walked over and spread the towel next to his chair, then slowly sat down, stretching out long legs and crossing them at the ankles. He concentrated on keeping his eyes on her face and tried not to stare at her chest, which was ample and barely covered. She tipped her head back, letting her hair cascade down over her shoulders, catching the sunlight. She then turned her head to face him and their eyes locked.

She asked, "Why would a man bring a laptop to one of the most beautiful beaches on the planet? You're watching porn, aren't you?"

Kurt blushed a deep red and slammed the lid of his laptop shut.

"No! I would never—I mean, you can't really think I—I was just—"

She laughed and placed a hand on his arm. "Take it easy champ, I was just messin' with ya. But seriously, when you're here your eyes should be on the beach and the babes. Well, at least this babe, anyways."

Kurt took another deep steadying breath and actually felt O.K. After all, she was coming on to him, which meant she had to think he was at least a decent-looking guy. And she did have a laugh he enjoyed hearing.

"You know? When you're right, you're right." He put the laptop to the side and turned his full attention to the girl. "You sound like you're from my part of the world. Where are you from?"

She took a pair of sunglasses out of her bag, slipped them on and laid back on her towel, basking in the sun. He couldn't imagine a more beautiful woman. He thought about Vic and Samantha and wondered if he just met his own "Samantha."

"I was born in Tennessee, but now I live in Lexington, Kentucky," she replied. "How about you?"

"No way. Seriously? I live in Louisville, born and raised. Go figure. I travel a million miles from home to meet a girl from just down the road."

"That's really weird. I hope you're not a dirty Cardinal bird-loving kind of guy. What brings you to Hawaii? I was supposed to be here with a girlfriend, but she got sick the day before the trip and couldn't come. She wanted me to wait, but there was no way in hell I was spending February in Kentucky. So I flew on out. You with the wife and kids? Girlfriend? Boyfriend?" She said with a slight smile on her lips.

"Uh. No," he stammered. "I'm single. Heterosexually single. I'm not into guys. Not that there's anything wrong with that. And I'm not really into sports, so I don't really care for either the Cardinals or the Cats. As for why I'm here, I'm out here on business and that's why I had the laptop with me. I design computer software and figured I might as well do it on the beach than in my hotel room."

He had perfected the lie enough he could tell it without stumbling. He longed to be able to tell someone about the whole battle with Satan-thing, but who would believe him? Heck, he could barely believe it.

"Sounds interesting," she said in a tone of voice which sounded anything but. For the first time in the conversation the old doubts started to creep in again and Kurt clammed up. He stared out at the ocean and berated himself for coming off so boring. I mean, the way she asked the question, she had to be a Kentucky fan and he could have played along. But no, he missed a chance to keep the conversation going. And bragging about being a software designer? Most chicks don't dig geeks. Smooth move there, Ex-lax.

He was on the verge of a major sulk when she said, "Most men have already asked me out by this part of the conversation. What's the matter? Not pretty enough?" Her lips scrunched into a child-like pout.

"No way," he said. "I don't know how you can even think that. You're gorgeous. Beyond gorgeous. You're goddess like. I mean, it's not possible for a woman to be prettier than you are. Just look at you. Da Vinci would rather paint you than the Mona Lisa, I'm sure of it. When God made woman, he had to have made Eve to look like you. You're so pretty—"

She interrupted, "Excuse me?"

"Yes?" Kurt swallowed hard a few times, waiting to hear what she would say next.

She turned and looked at him. "Shut up and just ask me out. Will you please?"

"Um. Sure." Kurt cleared his throat. "Would you like to have dinner with me tonight?"

"I'd love to have dinner with you. Now why don't you tell me your name?"

He stuck his hand out and said, "Kurt. Nice to meet you. And your name is?"

She took his hand in hers and Kurt felt a jolt go through his body at her touch. He could feel the softness of her hand and the strength of her grip and found himself falling instantly in love. She pulled her sunglasses down to the end of her nose and he felt like he was falling into the depths of her gray eyes.

"Ruth Anne. And believe me, Kurt, the pleasure's all mine."

CHAPTER 5

After hanging up with Kurt, I thumbed through my contact list and punched up the number for Winston Reynolds and hit dial. After a moment he answered with a, "Your dime, your time."

"Winston, we have a lead on Samantha. A good one. Looks like she's in Naples, Florida. I'm going down to get her and I'm leaving today. I need your help."

"Alright, I'm in, but I need you to give me an hour or two. I have something to take care of here and then I'm good to go."

"You got it. Meet me at the mission around six, I'll fill you in and then we can hit the road."

"Works for me. Don't forget to bring your bottle of Metamucil."

Everyone thinks he's a comic. I'm cruising through my early thirties and Winston was still traveling through his mid-twenties.

"Kiss my ass. At least I don't have to ask my mother if I can stay out late. Besides, you may have youth on me, but I'm much better looking. See you tonight." We hung up.

I dragged out my laptop, fired up the ol'-Google Machine, and typed in the address Kurt provided me. I studied the Google Maps info on the house we were going to stake out. I then found a pen and notepad and started taking notes on exactly how I planned to rain Hell down on the people holding Samantha.

****

Winston hung up the phone and sipped his coffee. He took another glance around the room at the people in the diner. His eyes brushed past the young man in the corner reading *The Courier-Journal* who was pretending not to watch him. But Winston knew better. He picked up the tail earlier in the day after working out at Hwang's Martial Arts. Drinking some water after his session, he was looking out the second story window when he noticed the guy sitting in a silver Honda Accord watching the building. He paid no real attention, since people frequently waited for others attending martial arts classes or visited other stores in the small strip mall all the time.

But he saw the guy again when he came out of Kroger after he stopped to pick up a few things. Same guy. Same Honda, sitting and watching. To make sure he wasn't being paranoid, he drove to the Oxmoor Mall, parked and walked inside, stopping at several stores to window shop and check for the tail. Sure enough, there he was down the concourse, also window shopping and trying not to look obvious. Major fail. Winston now paid a lot more attention to his surroundings following his hook up with Victor McCain.

Life had changed since his former boss and mentor, bounty hunter J.B. Booker was murdered by the Church of the Light Reclaimed. They offered J.B. a million dollars to find and capture Samantha Tyler. During their search, they crossed paths with Vic several times and he always seemed to be just ahead of them. After the Church murdered J.B. and another of his helpers, Winston joined up with Victor for good old fashioned revenge. In the day that followed he saw and did things he never imagined doing, but damn, it felt good.

Since then, he helped Victor take out some very bad men as they tried to slow down the Church and find and kill his brother. He shook his head thinking about it because that's just messed up. Winston had four brothers and two sisters and didn't think he could kill any of them, even if God ordered it. But there could be no doubt Michael McCain was one evil mofo and needed to be stopped. But by his own brother? Man, that stunk.

Now he wondered who sent this guy to follow him. Not that it mattered. Truth be told, he got a charge out of it. A former All Big East linebacker for the Louisville Cardinals, he hooked up with J.B. because he loved the rush of taking guys down and sending them to jail. Now they were taking it one step further by sending them to Hell. True, Vic did all the killings and Winston was there to watch his back and help with tracking people down, but he felt he was doing God's work. And he was smart enough to know sooner, rather than later, the bad guys would come knocking on his door.

And now, it seemed, they were here. He came into the diner for some pecan pie and coffee and to see what the tail would do. The man entered a few minutes after Winston, picking up a paper on his way to a booth. He sat down and ordered coffee. A young black man, skinny and dressed like a member of the chess team, he wore gold John Lennon-style glasses. When Winston left Kroger earlier, he drove by the man's car and noticed a Bellarmine University sticker on it. He definitely looked the college-prep type.

Winston stared out the window of the diner, at the people shopping in the mall and in the reflection he could see his own black face looking back at him. In his mid-twenties, he managed to keep his playing weight and physique, at six foot two inches tall and around two-hundred and thirty pounds. Drafted by the New York Jets, he hung around for a couple of years on the practice squad, but only played in three NFL games before being cut. He just wasn't fast enough.

He returned to Louisville to work out and to try and get another shot at the NFL, but he fell into the life of a bounty hunter instead and loved it. It gave his life purpose and helped keep his community safer by getting some truly bad men off the streets. After throwing in his lot with Vic, even more so. When Vic asked Winston to keep helping him, and he agreed, Vic told him everything: about Satan, what it meant to be the Hand of God, and how he was doing this to earn back his own lost soul. He also explained how the danger would only ramp up as the Church started to fight back against the Can-O' Whup-Ass Victor was going to open on them. He didn't want Winston to have any false illusions. Amazingly to Winston, he believed him. Vic offered to pay him from the thirty million stolen from the Church of the Light Reclaimed, so money wasn't an issue. Winston asked for a couple of days to think about it. Helping a man commit murder, no matter the reason, was not something you do without some heavy duty thinking. And Vic said they would be hunting people for the express purpose of killing them.

The first thing he did was visit his favorite Great Aunt Julia. A large woman with an even larger heart, she never missed a Sunday singing with her church choir and quoted the Bible as easily as another would tell you the name of their children. He attended every church service with her when in town and had his own deep devotion to God. He didn't tell her all of it, but enough so she could tell him whether or not he was nuts.

"Child, the Lord has been delivering punishment to the wicked ever since Eve took a bite out the apple. The Lord is leading you down the path He wants you to follow. So do what your heart tells you is right," she said.

His heart told him to help Victor with that Can-O' Whup-Ass and they were doing quite a job. In three months they removed four men who held high positions with the Church—just not the two men highest on their list: Mikey and a real piece of work named Preston Deveraux. If they really could free Samantha then they may be that much closer to punching their tickets.

Winston tipped his cup back, downing the last of his coffee. It was time to deliver a message to whoever it was following him. Gathering up his trash and tossing it into the garbage, he left through the side door of the diner and down towards the sign pointing to the restrooms. He didn't bother to check to see if the man was following him, but as soon as he turned the corner towards the restrooms, he took off at a full sprint.

As a teenager when he was a "Maller" working for a toy store which closed years ago, he remembered the hallway emptied out by the storage areas, with a supply closet directly across from the men's room. Turning the knob and finding the door unlocked, Winston shook his head. Some things never change. Opening the door he quickly ducked inside, the smell of damp mops and bleach unmistakable, his mind flashed back to more nights than he cared to remember mopping the toy store floor.

Leaving the door open the barest of cracks, he watched as the young man eased slowly past the door, glancing at the men's room. He stopped at a pair of water fountains between the men's and women's doors, and waited.

When Winston didn't come out after five minutes, the man reached into his pocket and pulled out a cell phone. He tapped in a number and after a moment said, "It's Chazaqiel. Tell Samyaza I may have lost him. I'll contact you when I know more." He ended the call and put it back in his pocket. He looked up and down the hallway, pushed the door to the men's room open and stepped inside.

Once the door closed, Winston left the supply room and followed the man, stopping the door before it closed completely, coming in quietly behind him. He caught Mr. Bellarmine straightening up after glancing under the stalls to see if Winston was hiding inside.

Moving behind him, Winston reached out to tap the young man on the shoulder, but before he could say a word, the man attacked, launching his right elbow straight back, aiming to smash Winston's nose. Instinct took over and Winston pivoted, blocking the strike with his right forearm, while at the same time snaking his left arm up and under the other man's, grabbing his neck in a half-nelson. At that point, it became an issue of mass, as Winston used his greater body weight to lift the lighter man off his feet and slammed his face down onto the long sink counter. He heard the man's nose break and a fountain of blood streaked across the countertop and mirror. His glasses went flying into the sink basin causing the automatic water dispenser to turn on with the movement.

Winston lifted the man back up, kicked open the door to one of the stalls and threw him inside and on top of a toilet. Mr. Bellarmine immediately tried to get up, but as he straightened his leg, Winston kicked out and slammed his foot into the man's right knee, driving his knee cap backwards, shattering it. He followed that kick with another to the man's chest, slamming him into the corner of the stall. The man grimaced in pain, but didn't move and said nothing.

"Tell whoever sent you, this is what will happen to anyone else I see following me around. So back the hell off," Winston said.

With that he left the men's room, walked quickly out of the Oxmoor Mall, and to the main parking lot to his car.

Winston began to drive away when he noticed a commotion at the entrance. Mr. Bellarmine, blood still dripping down his face, stumbled through the door with his knee still bent backwards. People pointed and stared as the man passed them, his clothes soaked with blood. He had to be in an enormous amount of pain and looked like something out of *The Walking Dead,* but he kept limping down the pavement towards Winston.

He stopped when their eyes met. There was no expression on Mr. Bellarmine's face as he just watched, which sent a shiver down Winston's spine. No way the man should've been able to follow him with a knee so completely destroyed. Yet there he stood, glaring at him and Winston knew just what was on his mind: vengeance.

CHAPTER 6

I met Winston at the door to the mission and led him to J's office. I told him to have a seat while I went into the kitchen and asked the main man to join us for a few minutes. J always helped to prep the mission meals and then serve them. A real man of the people. I stood in the kitchen door and finally caught his attention. I nodded, pointing back down the hallway, he excused himself and followed me to his office.

After making the introductions, I gave the boss man the scoop on my conversation with Kurt, my plans to head south and if the information was correct, to rescue Samantha.

"You know it won't be as easy as it was the last time you did this, when you and Winston hit the house out in the country. Those guards weren't top notch and they didn't expect you to find them." Brother Joshua said. "This time they'll be watching, and may even be hoping you'll make a rescue attempt in order to get a shot at taking you out."

I shook my head. "You could be right, but I don't care. If I'd done more to protect her in the first place, she wouldn't be trapped with those scumbags suffering who knows what. I feel responsible for the fact they have her at all. The only real question I have for you is, will you sanction the trip or am I going rogue? These are bad men, J. I don't have to tell you that. I have to go down and try to pry her loose from the Church."

I knew to go down there kicking ass and taking names, without permission, would be breaking the agreement I made when I became the Hand of God. I agreed to only go after targets approved by J. I tried to keep my face a smooth mask of "I don't give a rat's ass." But inside I was turning into knots. Winston sat next to me, his hands folded in his lap, and kept silent.

J watched me for a few minutes before he spoke. I don't know if he was just running through his options or mind-melding with the Big Guy upstairs. Eventually he said, "You can go, but try not to kill anyone while you're down there if you can help it. You assume they will all be Church thugs, but you don't really know."

"And if I can't rescue her without killing the lot of them?"

"The Lord's will be done."

"You know what, J? Sometimes the Lord's will is a pain in the ass." This got a snicker out of Winston, which earned him the evil eye from J. But Winston just stared back. I got what I needed, so I stood up and left without another word. Winston was right behind me. We made our way to my room and I motioned for Winston to take the only chair, a battered old leather swivel chair parked in front of a small desk.

"So, are you good to go?" I asked.

He nodded back and he filled me in on his adventure at the Mall.

"This black on black crime is really getting out of hand," I said.

"Says you. Whitey been beating on 'my people' for centuries, down in the hood, we're just playing catch up."

"Hood, my ass. Your mother and father are both doctors and you grew up in the East End. Hell, your dad is a member of Valhalla Country Club and on the PGA's Board of Directors. Your hood is all ascots and beamers."

"True that. But have you ever seen an Izod wearing black man when his Mercedes won't start? Brutal, man. Just brutal."

"I take it you got the license plate number of the guy following you?"

"Yeah. I got it. When he made the call he said his name was Chaz-something and he called some dude and dropped the name Sam Yaza. You ever heard of any Satanist with that name?"

"Nodda. Doesn't ring a bell."

He gave me the license number and I called a cop buddy of mine named Rusty to get the lowdown on this Chaz-guy. Rusty put me on hold for a few minutes and when he came back on the line the tone of his voice told me I had stepped in it. "Uh, Vic? Why do you want information on this particular car?"

"It's a car that's been seen around the home of a jumper I'm looking for and I thought if I could get a line on the owner, I might be able to track down my guy. There's a chance they might be bunking together. Why? What's up with this guy?"

"The car is owned by an African American male, twenty-one years old, named Mal McGeorge. Here's the thing: he was just admitted to University Hospital. Seems someone beat the ever lovin' crap out of him down at the Oxmoor Mall. He then collapsed outside one of the entrances and when the EMTs arrived on the scene, he had no clue where he was and was screaming over and over about someone being in his head. Vic, the guy clawed his own eyes out of their sockets. What's the name of the guy you're looking for? Perhaps this guy is the one who assaulted Mr. McGeorge."

"Holy shit, Rusty, that's messed up. But come on, man, if I tell you and you get to him first, then I don't collect a paycheck. How about this? I'll check things out and if I find out my perp had anything to do with the attack, I'll call you personally. You know I'll play it straight."

He read off an address on Louisville's East Side. "Fair enough, Vic. You've kept your word in the past, but you'd best keep me in the loop on this one. Be careful now, ya hear?"

"Bingo, Ringo." I hung up and relayed the information to Winston.

"Might be a good thing you and I are headed south for a few days. No clue if they'll be able to link you to what happened, but being out of town for a while can't hurt. We can work on our tans."

He looked at the dark ebony of his skin, then back at me and shrugged. "Whatever works for you, man. Should we go back and tell J about all of this? If it's the Church, it's probably something he should know. And I'm telling you, when he walked out as I was leaving, he wasn't screaming and yelling. The man's shit was ice cold. I've taken down some real bad mofos and I'm telling you, Vic, none of them gave me the willies like this dude."

"Not just No, but *hell* no. We can tell him when we get back. I can't take a chance he'll want me to investigate this before we get Samantha. Once we have her, you and I can figure out who was following you and why. He sure doesn't sound like the kind of guy the Church has been using. But then again, I have no clue what it takes to be a card-carrying Satanist. Let's get our stuff into the car and hit the road. I'll fill you in on the way down. At least it'll be warmer down there. You sure you didn't have another tail following you over here?"

Winston gave me a dead fish stare as I threw on my coat and grabbed my gear. "The only tail following me I left barely standing at the mall. We're good," he said.

"Don't get your panties in a wad, I was just asking. Let's hit the road."

We made our way outside and over to a brand new Ford Flex I purchased a month earlier. After buying it, I dropped it off at Winston's uncle's house so he could make a few "modifications." A member of a local militia group, his uncle believed the government would one day come and take his guns away. He and some friends built an underground bunker with enough guns and ammo to hold off a good-sized rogue nation and knew a thing or two about hiding stuff you don't want the authorities to find. He took my Ford and built a hidden compartment to hold all my man toys—you know, the ones for which I never bothered to get permits: a couple of MPK5s, flash and concussion grenades and all the fixins' any hell-bent bounty hunter would need. A dark blue, it matched my University of Kentucky sensibilities while driving my University of Louisville sidekick nuts.

"I still can't believe you bought a soccer mom car," Winston said. "Man, next thing you know, your drinks will have little umbrellas sticking out of them, you'll be getting pedicures, and your eyebrows buzzed."

"Nothing wrong with the occasional pedi. Besides, this car blends in better than some of the others I looked at."

"It would if you were half your size and a woman. Might as well put a gorilla in a tux," Winston said with a laugh.

Winston grabbed a getaway bag from his car and we were off. The temp hovered just above zero with the wind chill factor. Where we were headed, down in Naples, it was clocking in at a balmy seventy-five degrees. I was always a fall-winter kind of guy, but even I was looking forward to spring. At least weather wouldn't be a factor when we took on the people holding Samantha hostage. The clock on the dash read almost straight up seven o'clock. It would take the better part of fifteen hours to make it to Naples with the two of us taking turns behind the wheel.

"Look in my bag on the seat behind you," I said. "You'll find a manila folder with satellite printouts of the home we're interested in." While he pulled out the folder, I continued, "The home sits off away from other houses and has several acres of land. There's a stone privacy fence around a large portion of the property with nothing but a well-manicured yard between the house and the fence. The only shots of the house are over head, so I can't tell how tall the fence is, but with no trees or any other places of concealment, it'll be hard to sneak up on them if they have sentries posted. We did get lucky, however, in that I searched for rental properties in the area and there's one a couple of houses down. I called the realtor handling the rental and managed to wrangle a month lease. So, we can take a day or two and case the situation."

"How much did that set you back? My folks have rented down there for winter trips and it ain't cheap."

"It's twelve grand a month, with an option for a second month. But we won't need it, 'cause I'm going to want to move quickly. There's no telling how long our intel will be good. For all we know, they move her every couple of days, but I doubt it. If she's been down there long enough to be bored, then I'm guessing she's been there awhile."

"Sounds good to me." He lowered his seat back to the full reclining position. "If I'm going to drive later, then I'm taking a nap now. Besides, I always like to take a nap after a good butt kicking."

And true to his word I heard light snoring noises before driving another ten miles down the road. Winston could sleep anywhere, anytime. I guess an honest man's pillow is his peace of mind. Me? I spent most nights lying in bed for hours and willing sleep to come with no luck.

I spent most of that time thinking of Samantha when I wasn't thinking about Mikey. I also had nightmares, dreaming about the death of Dominic Montoya, the former Hand of God. He lost his life because I refused to see what was right in front of my eyes. Montoya came to town looking for a man known only as Belial and in the end, everything pointed in Mikey's direction. But I just couldn't believe it and it cost Montoya his life, Samantha her freedom, and me my soul. Now I would spend the rest of my life—however long it would be—trying to fix all the damage I caused.

I merged onto I-65, eased the Flex up to a few miles over the limit, and hit the cruise control. I settled back into my seat and tried to relax as the miles melted away. If Kurt's info turned out to be right, then I would soon see Samantha again, one way or another.

CHAPTER 7

Since Kurt's idea of a great meal started and ended with a trip to Wendy's, he asked the concierge where he should take Ruth Anne for dinner and he suggested the Hanalei Dolphin, a combination restaurant, fish market and sushi bar. While just the thought of eating raw fish made his stomach do more flips than a cook at a pancake-eating contest, he called Ruth Anne and asked if it was O.K. with her. She said it sounded great and he made plans to pick her up around seven. She rented a villa just down the beach from his hotel and said she'd be ready at the appointed time.

It took him nearly an hour to decide what to wear, changing clothes about a dozen times, before choosing khaki shorts, a blue and white Hawaiian shirt and hiking sandals. Kurt stood and looked at his reflection in the mirror, and practiced his relaxation breathing but he still broke out in a light sweat. When the time came to call a cab, he almost dialed Ruth Anne back and canceled. He picked up and then lowered the phone several times before finally finding the courage in himself, saying aloud, "Screw it," and made the call.

Strolling out of the hotel lobby he found the cab waiting. He gave him the address and a few minutes later, they pulled into Ruth Anne's driveway. He told the cabbie to wait while he went to the door. Before pressing the doorbell, he leaned his head against the door frame and asked God for the strength to get through the night and prayed he would not break out in hives.

Please, Lord, he thought, no hives.

Following a few more deep breaths, he straightened and pressed the doorbell. He glanced over his shoulder to see the cabbie giving him two thumbs up. Kurt smiled weakly and turned back as the door opened.

When it did, his breathing stopped. He just plain forgot to breathe. Wearing a silk red evening dress, which barely made mid-thigh and her hair tied back in a ponytail, she appeared more a vision than reality. She carried a small red purse and nothing else. Doing a quick twirl with her dress rising and then falling, she said, "You like?"

When he didn't respond, she asked, "Kurt? Earth to Kurt? Come in please?"

He gave himself a mental slap and replied, "Hell yes. Wow. I mean, um, you look amazing."

He glanced down at his own clothes.

"Aw man, I feel really under-dressed. You must be embarrassed to go out with me looking like this. I can run back to the hotel and change. Give me a few minutes."

Before he could turn to leave she wrapped her arms around his neck and kissed him deeply. She broke the kiss off and purred, "You look delicious and no you won't go change. I'm starving, so let's go have dinner."

She slipped her arm into his and lead him, dazed and stunned, to the cab. He had never been kissed like *that* before and he felt light-headed from the experience.

He hardly spoke a word all the way to the restaurant as Ruth Anne talked about the rest of her day shopping and then swimming in the pool behind her villa. Kurt sat staring at her, watching the way her mouth moved, the way she breathed.

She stopped in mid-sentence and asked, "You planning on joining in the conversation, Big Boy?"

"No. I mean, yes. I'm sorry," Kurt said. "I love watching you talk. I could spend the whole night doing nothing but watching you."

"Well, I do need you to do your part. This is a date, after all."

Kurt got a reprieve as the cab pulled up in front of the restaurant. He paid the cabbie a generous tip and as they got out, the cabbie winked at him. Kurt smiled back, giving the cabbie two thumbs up and then escorted Ruth Anne inside. Soon they were seated at their table. They made small talk until after they gave the waiter their order and when he left, she said, "O.K. It's your turn. Tell me about this software you're working on."

Kurt swallowed hard. "There's not much to tell. I help design and test website security software. Most big companies are attacked daily by hackers and my job is to try and keep them out."

He knew he couldn't tell her about what he was really doing, trying to take down the Church of the Light Reclaimed, but it wasn't a complete lie. He had been working on security software, at the request of the cable company he worked for in Louisville, after hackers tried to bring their network down and Kurt suggested ways they could prevent such an attack. That all came to an end when he high-tailed it out of town and continued to help Victor put the big hurt on Satan and his followers.

"And you chose to do this programming from a beach in Hawaii?" she sounded skeptical.

"I can do the work from anywhere on the planet I can get an Internet connection, so why not on a beach in Hawaii?" he replied. He could feel the first itch start on his arms and he excused himself to make a quick trip to the men's room.

She touched him on the hand as he rose and said, "Hurry back, handsome."

Once again, he felt a bolt of electricity go through his body as her fingers trailed across the back of his hand. It took every ounce of willpower not to run to the bathroom. Inside the men's room, he reached into his pocket and took out the Benadryl he carried in case of emergencies and downed the two pills with a handful of water from the bathroom sink. He stared at the man looking back at him in the mirror.

"Keep it simple, Kurt," he said aloud to himself. "She digs you. All you have to do is keep it simple."

With restored self-confidence, he headed back to the table.

****

Ruth Anne watched him until he disappeared into the men's room, then opened her purse, took out a small flip phone, typed in a number and hit dial. After a few rings a man's voice said, "Were you able to make the exchange?"

She said, "No, I wasn't. He must be a true believer. He's not a very complex person, so I don't think there is any room for doubt for one such as he. He either believes or doesn't. I will have to get the information we need from him another way. It would be better if you let me do it my way. I promise you, he will tell us what we need to know."

"We still have time. The Spear is busy elsewhere and he is blind to our purpose. But if you move too fast he might be alerted, so be careful how you proceed. We don't want the Spear to learn of what we are doing until the time is right. Then it will be too late for him to stop us. You have the temptation of the flesh available to you. Use it. It has forever worked," the man said to her.

Her grip tightened on the phone. "I grow weary of this game. We must move more quickly," she said.

"You will do as I tell you to do." The connection ended and Ruth Anne put her phone away just as Kurt returned to the table. Inside she was seething, but she put a smile on her face.

"Feel better?" she asked.

****

"Much," Kurt said. "Who was on the phone?"

"Disgruntled ex-boyfriend," she said. The look on his face must have shown the fear he felt inside. "Don't worry. He's out of the picture and thousands of miles away. I'm footloose and fancy free. I'm all yours."

It shouldn't be a surprise she has an ex, Kurt thought to himself. Look at her. No way she wouldn't have one. And she was right. She was with him, not the other guy. He even managed to add some to the conversation over dinner, once the Benadryl kicked in and saved him from head to toe hives. She ate sushi while he enjoyed the Dolphin Salad. She offered him a bite of her sushi, but he didn't think he could eat food when he could tell what it had been while still alive. He had no problem eating meat, but his burgers looked nothing like a cow, so no worries. Now if they started making beef patties in the shape of a cow? He shuddered at the thought.

When they finished dinner, they took a cab back to her villa. She slipped her hand into his and lead him down to the beach as the sun glided slowly below the horizon. As they walked, hand-in-hand, the moon rose, full and bright. Then she dropped his hand and slid hers around his waist. After hesitating for a moment, he did the same and inside started congratulating himself on the "new Kurt" when the fragile self-confidence came crashing down in flames.

She came to a stop and turned him to face her, the ocean waves crashing behind them. Her hands finger-walked up his chest, snaked behind his head and pulled it down so she could kiss him. When the kiss ended she said, "I want you to spend the night with me, at my place. What do you say?"

The panic attack hit him hard and his body went rigid. The old Monopoly saying passed his thoughts: "Go Directly to Jail. Do Not Pass Go." He tried to talk, but found it hard to breathe. He would have taken off at a dead run, but his body refused to take any orders from his brain.

Ruth Anne's face went from playful to concerned. "Kurt? Talk to me. Are you O.K?"

He racked his brain, trying to come up with an excuse she would believe. How could he have not considered this possibility? Well, because it never happened before, he berated himself. He looked up and down the beach, hoping for inspiration. Finally he blurted, "Because I have a conference call. Later tonight. In my room."

Stepping back and crossing her arms, she asked, "A conference call? It's the middle of the night back in the states. You mean to tell me you have a business call this time of night? You're so full of shit."

She turned and started walking back to her villa. He trailed behind her hitting his forehead with the heel of his hand, saying over and over in his mind, idiot, idiot, idiot. A conference call? He bit his lip thinking as she continued to walk away. Then with a stroke of inspiration, "Yes. We have to do the tests in the middle of the night, after the call centers shut down. We can't test the systems during business hours. It has to be in the middle of the night."

She stopped and turned to look at him and raised her eyebrows. "You swear?" she said not completely convinced.

He swallowed hard and replied, "I swear."

It was all he could do not to cross his fingers and pray his explanation sounded plausible.

She closed the distance between them, smiled and leaned in for a kiss. But when he bent down to kiss her, she hit him hard in the arm and, boy, did it hurt. He clutched his arm and rubbed the spot where she tagged him. Wow. She was stronger than she looked!

"You should have told me about this meeting, Kurt. "

Kurt started mumbling an apology, but she cut him short.

"Learn something right now, Kurt. You're going to find out I'm not like most women. Now call your cab and I'll think about whether I want to see you tomorrow or not."

She left him standing at the end of the walkway as she stormed up to her front door, stepped inside, and slammed it behind her. He called for a cab and while he waited, he rubbed his arm where she slugged him and thought: she's right. She's not like most women.

CHAPTER 8

We were royally screwed. That's the conclusion I came to after two days of surveillance of the house owned by Wheadon's family in the Port Royal section of Naples. Using high-powered binoculars from the front room of our rental, we kept an around-the-clock eye on the comings and goings at Casa de Wheadon. The stone fence stood about seven feet tall with a solid iron gate at the end of the drive, surrounding the classic Spanish-style home you see a lot of here in Naples. The home sat right on the water with about two hundred feet of beach and two boat docks. The house featured balconies in both the front and back, and a wide veranda and pool in the back as well. Palm trees dotted the property, but offered no concealment.

A small security force prowled the grounds, both day and night, and they were good. Never falling into a pattern, they mixed up their routines. And there were dogs, Dobermans, both on leashes and running loose. The dogs never made a sound. Experience had taught me when dogs don't bark? It's because they're saving their energy to rip you a new one. Landscape lighting popped on with the approaching darkness and left little to no shadows to hide anything larger than a grapefruit.

As night dropped around us and the sun disappeared from view, Winston and I surveyed the scene from a rented Hydra Sports 3400 CC fishing boat, with a couple poles in the water and the anchor dropped. The boat cost me a small fortune to rent, but what the hell. I was spending money stolen from devil worshipers. So what did I care?

We turned the boat in such a way to keep an eye on the target while we contemplated a water assault. Thankfully, Winston knew his way around a boat because my expertise began and ended with, "They float you're good. They sink, you're not."

Swimming was something I did when I had no other choice. If a boat turned over twenty feet from shore, I can make it; thirty was a toss up; and fifty feet was a drag the river, I'm not coming up. I love the water, but I preferred to stay on top of it. For about the millionth time that afternoon, I pulled my life vest into a more comfortable position. I spent half a day going from store to store in Naples before I found one big enough to fit me.

I lowered the binocs, rubbed my eyes and then stared off to the horizon, the Gulf of Mexico stretching out seemingly forever, while the boat gently rocked with the evening tide. I let my mind go over all the possibilities and came to the same conclusion: we were hosed. I couldn't come up with a single possible way to get in and out in one piece. A two man assault was doomed to fail. Subterfuge wouldn't work either, as any delivery to the house was stopped at the front gate and the cars thoroughly searched. There are American embassies in backwater third world countries easier to slip into than this house.

We'd been watching from the boat for most of the early evening and going in from the water would be as suicidal as a frontal assault. We would need to cover several hundred feet of sand before we even made it to the property itself, and we'd be exposed the entire way.

I kept hoping we would catch a glimpse of Samantha, either walking the grounds or out on a balcony, but no luck. If she was inside they were keeping her on a short leash.

I said to Winston, "Storming the castle and trying to rescue the princess will only end up with you and me in body bags. We'll have to try something different."

Winston cranked his reel slowly, pulling in the line one last time and hoping for another hit. He caught and released several white trout. Me? I caught a sunburn.

He said, "I know a few guys I could probably get down here to help out. All you have to do is say the word and I'll make a few calls."

"Nah. We need a small army and there's no way to pull it off with any type of stealth. The amount of firepower we'd have to unleash would bring the cops down on us before we could even get in the front door."

"So, what. We just giving up?"

"Hell no. We're still getting her out. We'll just have to get them to bring her to us."

"And how do you figure to do that? Call up and ask?"

I sat there for a moment thinking. "Actually, not a bad idea. Let's get this boat back to its slip and I'll fill you in."

Winston and I stowed the fishing gear, raised the anchor and fired up the Hydra Sport. Cranking the wheel and opening the throttle, he guided us to shore, easing the boat in next to the dock while I jumped out and tied her off.

We got our stuff and hiked back to the Ford, rolling down the windows, and then cruised slowly by Samantha's gilded cage to our own rental. I went upstairs to take the first watch of our long distance surveillance, while Winston ordered up pizza from a local popular restaurant with the best reputation in town.

Once the pizza arrived, he brought it upstairs along with a couple of Millers. He popped the tops and handed me one. We clinked the bottles together and sat in the darkness of the room, watching for something, anything, to happen down at Wheadon's place.

"So, what bright idea do you have to get them to bring Samantha out?"

I flipped open the top to the pizza box and slid out a large slice of pepperoni, taking a huge bite and said around a mouthful of pie, "What they are relying on is no one knows where she is. They think they have her hidden away where no one can find her. So what if someone goes up and rings the bell and asks for Samantha? And if the people doing the ringing are cops?"

He pulled out his own piece of pizza and replied, "What? You and I dressing up like cops? Man, they'll be all over us in a heartbeat. You're kind of hard to hide, even dressed in blue."

"No. Not us. Real cops. We make an anonymous call saying a woman named Samantha has been kidnapped and is being held at the house. Then one of two things happens: the cops show up and demand they either produce her and the cops take her with them, or the bad guys demand the cops come back with a warrant, and when the cops are gone, they move her. If the first happens, then we show up at the precinct and whisk her away. If they do the second, we make our move and take them out. What do ya think?"

"Sounds like a plan to me. Better than sitting around on our asses all day doing nothing. The longer we stay here, the more you sulk."

"Kiss my ass. We're going to need a few things before we make our move. Does your uncle have any contacts down here?"

"Unc has friends everywhere. What do you need?"

I told him and his eyes went wide.

"Damn, Vic. You sure about this?"

"Hell and brimstone, Winston. Hell and brimstone. Think he knows someone who can help us out?"

"Let me call him." Winston pulled out his burner cell and called his uncle. After a few minutes he hung up. "He says he might know a guy. He'll pass along the request and have him call us. I told him to use your number."

We sat in silence for about an hour, taking turns watching the house, when the phone in my pocket rang. I pulled it out and the caller ID showed the name was blocked.

I answered and a man asked, "You the Hand?"

"That's right. And you are?"

"No names. Tomorrow morning at 8 a.m. I want you to stop and have breakfast at the Third Street Cafe in Naples. You know the place?"

"No, but I'm guessing it's on Third Street. I'll find it. How will I know who you are?"

"You won't. Order some breakfast, then sit outside at the table in front. Leave your friend at home. I see anyone else but you, and you won't live to regret it." And the call went dead.

Well, wasn't he a bundle of sunshine. I looked at Winston and said, "It's on. I have a meeting tomorrow morning. You, however, aren't invited. I need you to keep an eye on the house, anyways."

"I sure hope you know what you're doing. If this goes sideways? Wow."

All I could do was nod. Story of my life.

CHAPTER 9

The Third Street Cafe, as you can guess, was on Third Street, next to a 7 Eleven. I showed up just before eight and ordered a western omelet, hash browns and white bread toast. I chatted up with the cook and found out he moved to Naples from the Upper Peninsula of Michigan, where he toiled as a five star chef at several of the resorts there. Finally tired of the harsh winter weather, when the opportunity arose, he packed up and moved to the sun and sand of Naples.

Compared to prices at other restaurants in town, this one practically gave their food away. I watched as the cook finished preparing my breakfast, sliding the omelet and hash browns onto a plate with bacon and two slices of toast, and then set the plate on the counter. I snagged a cup of coffee and carried the food to a table outside and dug in. And damn, if it wasn't the best breakfast I'd eaten in ages.

As I shoveled the last bite of omelet into my mouth, a man strolled up and slid into a seat on the other side of the table. About six feet tall, the man wasn't any wider than a blade of grass. His clothes seemed to hang on his body rather than fit it and when he placed his hands on the table, one on top of the other, his fingers were just as thin and very long. Eyes the color of a muddy stream stared back at my baby blues.

"Can I buy you breakfast?" I asked.

"We're not staying," he replied. And as if to put action to his words, a white van pulled up to the curb and the side door opened. The man stood up and got in the passenger seat. I rose, gathered my trash, and dropped it in the can by the 7 Eleven.

"I guess I'm not following you then, huh?" I said.

"Nope." He gestured to the open door. "Get in, or not. Up to you. But we're leaving in ten seconds."

I shrugged my shoulders and got in, sliding the door closed. I had no idea where we were going, but it didn't really matter. I was the one who asked for the meeting and considering what I wanted from them, I knew the only way it would happen is if I played by their rules.

There were two other men in the van, a driver wearing a ball cap he pulled down low on his head, and next to me a very large man who looked like a grizzled Viking warrior with hair down to his shoulders and a beard reaching half-way down his chest. But truth be told, I didn't pay much attention to his looks. I focused more on the 357 Magnum he held, pushing it against my side.

"Look, if you don't want to be my B.F.F., fine," I said. "But you don't really need to use the gun, do we fellas?"

The Viking wannabe only smiled and pushed the gun harder into my side, while the others sat in silence. I settled in and went with the "Lord's will be done" attitude. We made our way out of Naples proper, heading north on Highway 41 until we were a bit outside of Cape Coral. The van turned into a commercial district and after a few blocks pulled into a parking lot and through an open garage door. After coming to a stop in the garage, the door closed behind us and we were shut off from the outside world.

The man from the cafe got out, opened the side door and stepped aside, nodding for me to get out. I stretched, loosening up the body for whatever came next.

"Time to move, asshole," the Viking said.

"And here I thought you and I had really connected on the ride over. Guess I'm losing my touch."

He shoved me with the gun and when he pulled it back, I shot my hand out, snatched his wrist, turning it up and back, forcing him to drop the gun. I got to it before he did and raising the gun, pushed the barrel against his forehead. His eyes blinked and I could tell he was holding his breath.

The driver never even moved his head, staring straight ahead. Tall-n-skinny stood by the side of the van, watching. I smiled at the now defenseless wild man and stepped out of the van. I reversed the gun, holding it by the barrel and handed it to the skinny guy who made first contact with me.

"I don't mind the cloak and dagger stuff," I said. "Your house, your rules. But don't think I'm some rookie you can intimidate. Not going to happen."

The wild man rolled out of the van and said, "Give me back my gun, Paulie, and I'll beat this son of a bitch to a pulp. Let's see how tough he is then."

Paulie said, "Shut up." He half-smiled and put the gun in the waistband of his slacks, while the other man stewed.

I glanced around the garage as Paulie walked to a nearby door. Large enough for several cars, workbenches lined two of the walls and were filled with various-type tools. I was good with guns and weapons of destruction, but I was hopeless with most everyday handyman tools. In fact, I can break down an MP5 quicker than most people can tie their shoes. But use a belt sander? Forget about it.

He opened the door and motioned for me to step through. I did so and walked into an office with furniture pushed against the wall and plastic covering gray shag carpet. I took a few steps and stopped. Looking down at the plastic I gestured towards the floor and asked, "You guys planning on doin' some painting?"

"With your brains depending on how the next few minutes go," Paulie said.

Before I could come up with a witty comeback, a door on the other side of the room swung open and a man somewhere in his late fifties or early sixties, stepped into the room. He wore a long-sleeved shirt, jeans, work boots, and a wary look on a deeply tanned face lined with age. He stopped a few feet in front of me and hooked his thumbs into his front pockets.

I offered him my hand and said, "Vic McCain. The pleasure's mine."

He didn't take my hand and replied, "Understand somethin.' You only made it this far because an old friend of mine asked me to meet with you. What you're a gonna do next is strip down to the suit the good Lord gave you when you came screaming into this world. Do it now, please."

"I hate to break it to you, but you're not really my type. When I strip down for someone other than my doctor, I want it to be a 'her' and a lot younger than you are."

"Listen funny boy, I ain't going to ask ya but one more time. Strip."

I glanced over my shoulder and Paulie now held the 357 down by his side with a lopsided grin on his face.

I reminded myself: their house, their rules. I unbuttoned my shirt.

"I'm packing, belt holster, so don't you guys go getting overly excited."

I dropped the shirt and held my hands out from my body as Paulie took my gun. I then lost the shoes and pants, and stood there in my briefs.

The old man said, "Them, too, hot shot. Don't worry. We ain't interested in lookin' at your pecker."

I slid down my boxer briefs and dropped them onto the pile of clothes.

"O.K. Now what?"

"This way."

He turned and went back through the same door he entered a few minutes earlier. I followed him into a large room filled with different types of air conditioning units, one wall taken up with what I could only assume were parts to fix them. More plastic covered the section of the floor where they told me to stop, and I wiggled my toes feeling the cold concrete underneath. I had a brief vision of me lying on the ground, a bullet hole in my head. I told myself to think more positive. If they wanted me dead, they'd have shot me already.

The door behind us closed and I stood there, the old man in front of me and Paulie behind me. The old man once again hooked his thumbs in his front pockets and just stared at me. I have to admit, I now had an idea how Tommy Spenoza felt lying naked on the bed while I held my gun pointed at him. It was really unnerving. And in this case, I guess that was the point. But I could guess another reason.

"You worried I might be wearing a wire?" I said.

"Crossed my mind. Stand still a minute while Paulie checks your hair."

I did as he asked while Paulie ran fingers through my hair, still blonde from my trip to Richmond and running a bit long. He found nothing and stepped back.

A minute later the Viking opened the door and said, "His stuff's clear." He sounded disappointed and left the room, closing the door behind him.

"Alright," the old man said. "Time to get down to business. You want a bomb. What're you planning on blowing to smithereens, Mr. Hand?"

"The name's Vic, and that falls under none of your damned business. The reason I need an I.E.D is my own. Besides, the less we know about each other, the better. Don't you think?"

I asked Winston's uncle to find me someone in his network who could supply me with an improvised explosive device. I didn't know how I'd use it. Not yet, anyways, but a few ideas kept bubbling to the top.

"Ain't nothin' improvised about my work. Everything I do is planned out to the millionth degree. I ain't used to providing things to strangers on short notice, but I go way back with our mutual friend and I kinda of owe him. So I'm going to give you what you ask for. But be warned. If you use it to kill children, I'll kill you. You attack a school or church, I'll kill you. The man who called me said you were a righteous man. I don't really give a shit. But you do any of the things I mentioned and you won't be able to ever sleep a peaceful night again. Do we understand each other?"

"We do. I would never do those things. I know you have no way to believe me, but it won't be an issue."

The man nodded and removed a small black remote control out of his back pocket.

"Here's a remote detonator. Place the bomb where you want it, flip up the switch guard and then press down. You can be up to a mile away."

I took the remote and said, "That simple?"

"Yep. That simple. Blowing things up ain't all that complicated. Get the right ingredients, put them together and there ya go. Who to blow up, that's different."

I nodded. "When do I get the bomb?"

"We put it in the back of your car. It's in a box wrapped with brown packing paper. Be careful and make sure you don't hit any big pot holes on the way home." He smiled then, but the smile didn't reach his eyes.

"Already in my car? What if I hadn't checked out? Why go to the trouble?" I asked.

"You were getting the bomb either way, Mr. Hand. The only question was if it would be you using the remote or me. You'd best be on your way. Get dressed and then Paulie will give you a lift to your car."

I've stared down a lot of big bad nasties in my lifetime, but the thought of me driving off into the sunset with a bomb I didn't know about in my car gave me the heebie jeebies. I went into the other room and got dressed. Paulie handed me my gun and I clipped it onto my belt and then followed him to the van.

The same man did the driving, but the Viking-dude didn't make the return trip. Paulie once again rode in the front and I hopped in the back. We drove in silence through town. When we reached the cafe, Paulie turned in the seat and said, "Good luck. I think he liked you."

Getting out, I slid the door closed behind me and stepped up to his window and asked, "How could you tell?"

"Because he didn't kill you."

He gave me another lopsided grin and a short wave and the van pulled away.

I walked over to my Ford and raised the lift gate. I found a small package under a blue blanket wrapped neatly in brown paper. I gently dropped the blanket over the bomb and a wild thought raced through my head: what if I hadn't passed the old man's test? I only had his word the remote he'd given me was *the* remote. I glanced around the parking lot, but didn't see anyone paying any attention to me.

Screw it. Like I said, Lord's will be done.

I shut the lift gate, but very softly. Then climbed behind the wheel. A plan began pinging around the recesses of my mind and it was past time to try it out and get moving. At least now I would get their attention. Boom goes the dynamite.

CHAPTER 10

It took me another day and a half to get things ready. I didn't want to use my Ford in the main operation, so Winston and I visited several used car dealerships until I found a Chevy S-10 with more mileage than a fifty-year old hooker with rust in several places and a couple of dents, but I didn't care. It ran fine for what I planned to use it for. I didn't need a looker.

Winston drove the Ford home while I took the Chevy for a spin out of town to a salvage yard where I bought a used tire. My final stop took me to Wal-Mart to buy another prepaid cell phone.

I could feel the excitement level building inside me. Before the day ended, if we were lucky, I'd have Samantha free and in my arms. I thought about the last time I saw her at Mikey's warehouse. She stood dazed with blood trickling down her temple from where Mikey's hired pit bull, Preston Deveraux, had slugged her.

We were together for less than a full day, yet her affect on me was life-altering. I was never a love-at-first-sight kind of guy. I thought it was a load of crap. But with Samantha and me? The attraction was immediate and, well, I'm pretty sure, mutual. My daydreams were haunted by my inability to save her. My sleepless nights lingered with the memories of the two of us in bed.

Finally, I now had a chance to get Samantha back. At the rental house, Winston and I split up the firepower between the Ford and the Chevy and moved the bomb from the Ford to the truck.

"Ready to get moving?" I asked.

"You got it. Let's do this."

I nodded and pulled out the new prepaid cell phone. I'd already looked up the number of the Naples Police Department. I typed it in and hit dial.

A dispatcher answered and said, "Naples Police, what is the nature of your emergency?"

I added a high whine to my voice and said, "I was in a house doing some work today and there's a woman there who said she's been kidnapped and they were holding her against her will. You have to help her."

"What is your name, sir? And what is the address where the woman is being held?"

I gave her the address."I can't give you my name. They'll kill me.

Help her, please! She's tall and has red hair. I think her name is Samantha. Please, you have to help her!" I disconnected the call. Now all we could do was wait.

Watching with the binoculars, ten minutes after my call, two blue and whites rolled up to the house. An officer got out and pushed the call button at the front gate and I watched as the officer carried on a one-sided conversation. Then the gate swung back, the officer returned to his car, and the two police cars drove up the driveway pulling into the circle turn-around in front of the house. Four officers exited the vehicles and then started up the front steps, hands on the butt of their guns.

Before they made it to the top of the steps a bare-chested man wearing swim trunks opened the door and walked outside to greet the officers with a cheery wave. He was of average height with dark brown hair cut short, sporting a news anchor quality smile. He appeared to be in his early twenties. The officers said something to the man and a look of confusion appeared on his face. He raised up a hand as if asking the officers to wait, while he turned over his shoulder and shouted back into the house.

The officers waited. A minute or so later, Samantha walked out the front door wearing a bikini top and shorts. My heart quickened. There she was. Picture the most beautiful woman in the world. Now that you have, realize that woman you pictured can't compete with the natural beauty of Samantha. Her auburn hair had grown since I last saw her. And in the Florida sun she was a bit more tanned.

Then my stomach dropped as she stepped up next to the man and slipped her arm around his waist, with him doing the same, in what looked to be a very familiar gesture. Winston moved the binocs an inch or so and glanced at me, but I kept my eyes on her.

On the day we met, we only talked about life in general for a few minutes at Molly Malone's before we hit Inspirational Global Software. Never once did she mention a boyfriend or being in a relationship. Not that she owed me anything, but watching her now with her arm around some yahoo hit me harder than a kick to the family jewels.

The officers talked for a while longer and then both Samantha and the man looked at each other and shrugged. After a few more minutes of talking, the officers waved goodbye, got back in their cars, and left.

Samantha and the man remained arm and arm as they watched the cops leave. When they drove out the front gate, Samantha dropped the smile and walked back inside. The man shouted something after her, and while I couldn't hear what was being said, I felt a surge of relief flood through me. The man raised his arm and looked down at his side where Samantha had dug her nails deeply enough into the skin to draw blood. He clenched his fists as he went inside and slammed the door. Two lovebirds they were not.

Winston said, “I don’t think she’s none too happy with studley. Think she’ll be O.K.? He looked mad enough to make her pay for what she did.”

“She’ll have to be. At least we know she’s there. I’m going to go get into position. If they do decide to make a move, I want to be ready. You keep an eye on them and if all hell breaks loose, call me.”

“Will do. You sure about this, man? You set that thing off, there’s no telling what will happen.”

“It’s the best I can come up with under the circumstances.”

The plan was fairly simple. Per my request, the bomb made by the militia guys came in on the small side. My goal was to disable any car they were in, not blow them to kingdom come. I would be in the Chevy in a line of trees just down from the bomb and Winston would be following in the Ford. When the bomb went off, I’d hit them from the front and Winston from the rear.

If they stayed put and didn’t move her, then I’d come up with something else. I had no clue what, but I’d find something to get her out of the house. And if Studley did hurt her, then he wouldn’t be long for this world.

I packed a cooler with food and a couple of water bottles, hauled them out to the truck, and took off.

I drove a couple hundred yards up the street and backed into a stand of red maples. I knew from the road I’d be hard to see. I turned the truck off and pulled out the bomb remote, setting it on the dashboard. I reached across the seat and rolled down the passenger side window and then did the same with mine. I then pulled the duffle bag closer and zipped it open, double-checking the contents. I removed a tear gas canister and put it next to me on the seat. As ready as I’d ever be, I leaned my head back to wait.

The late afternoon sun finally gave way to nightfall and the heat of the day changed to a comfortable chill. I did something I rarely did: I thought about God.

To say I was never a Bible thumper was an understatement. To be honest I could not have cared less about God. Even after the last few months, after becoming the Hand of God, I still avoided thinking about the afterlife, but for different reasons than before. Now I cared a great deal. It was knowing I could end up in Hell with Mikey that terrified me on many levels. I wondered if all that I now did would tip the scales back into a trip upstairs instead of the express elevator down.

My predecessor as the Hand, Dominic Montoya, had been a former Mexican drug cartel hit man, having killed dozens upon dozens of people before becoming God's bounty hunter. When he died I couldn't help but wonder if he'd done enough to take the stairway to Heaven.

Listening to the night sounds I tried to come to peace with my difficult situation. For the time being, I became resigned to my current circumstances and put thoughts of the afterlife in a back corner of my mind and shut the door. All I could do was try and do my best with whatever came next and let the rest take care of itself. I prayed it would be enough.

****

The wait ended just before 11 p.m. Winston called and said, "Yo, Vic. They just pulled two SUVs around to the front of the house. Hang on a sec." After a minute, he continued, "They just loaded Samantha into the back of the first car along with the pretty boy we saw earlier. One driver. Four hired guns into the second one." Another pause. "And they're off. How you want to do this? We planned on one car, not two."

"I'll use the bomb to take out the guns and improvise on the first car. Get in behind them and be ready."

"Roger that. I'll give you a shout when we hit the straight stretch. "

It was time to place the bomb. The main drag out of the area where Samantha was being kept had a long stretch of road bordering a canal where there were few homes and little traffic. I made sure I was alone, eased my way onto the road, then pulled into the middle of the straight away and stopped the truck. I got out and grabbed the old tire and dropped it in the grass at the edge of the road.

I then opened the passenger door and gently removed my gifted bomb from the floor board and set it inside the tire. I walked a few yards away, looked and could barely see the tire. The bomb wasn't visible at all.

I jogged back to the truck, hopped in and quickly reversed course, backing in underneath the trees, but staying close enough to see the cars coming for a good distance. I picked up the bomb remote, flipped off the trigger guard, and waited. I geared up mentally for destruction and mayhem, something I was very good at creating.

My phone rang. "Here we go. They just hit the straight away." Winston said.

"Roger that," I replied.

I could see the headlights of the two SUVs. Lucky for me the two cars were several car lengths apart. I cracked a few knuckles on the steering wheel and shifted my neck from side to side to loosen up.

I knew I only had one chance to get this right. Blow it too soon and I risked stopping Samantha's car or missing them entirely, while leaving the gunmen free to attack. Blow it too late and I risked missing both cars. I failed to ask the militia guys how long a lag time between pushing the button and the explosion, but I guess I was about to find out.

Samantha's ride passed the tire and I counted one, two and pushed the button. The bomb went up with a huge explosion in the night. *Damn!* If they made me a small bomb, I'd hate to see what a big one would do. The explosion roared like a huge shotgun blast and the second car was blown onto its side and sent rolling across the road. The rear end of the first car, despite being a dozen yards from the blast, was pushed into a skid. The driver hit the brakes, trying to get the large SUV under control.

I floored the truck, shooting out of the trees, on an interception course. The first car gunned the engine and took off, as the driver kept the pedal to the metal, trying to dart by me. He came up short and at the last moment cut the wheel as my truck crashed into his front left wheel. The collision sent a shock through my arms and I struggled to hold onto the steering wheel and maintain control of the truck. I could only pray Samantha had on her seatbelt. The old Chevy weighed in at just over two tons, the SUV about a thousand pounds more. But as a battering ram, the truck served its purpose well enough.

With the impact, the two vehicles left the road, our bumpers locked together as we flew side by side through a small chain link fence. I slammed my foot down on the brake, but it wasn't enough to prevent us from soaring down an embankment and into the canal.

I stiff armed the steering wheel as the truck and SUV smashed into the water, the impact tearing the two cars apart. My truck started listing to the left, and water poured in my open driver side window. I grabbed the duffle bag, zipped it closed and then shimmied my large body through the window as the water rushed in around me. I looked like a bear trying to slide through a doggie door. I gripped the top of the truck and pulled myself up and out, momentarily worried the truck would roll and trap me on the bottom.

I kicked away hard from the truck and hauled the heavy duffle bag behind me when the truck plunged completely under the surface of the water. The water must've been fairly deep as my feet didn't touch bottom. I struggled upward and finally broke the surface, sucking in the fresh Florida air. I took several strokes to the shore and threw my duffle bag onto the bank.

Panic hit me when I turned and watched the SUV sink below the surface of the water with no sign of Samantha or anyone else making it out of the car. What if the electric door locks or windows didn't work? What if they were all unconscious from the impact?

Swimming over, I dove and followed the swirling whirlpool down with the SUV settling onto the bottom of the canal. I couldn't see anything in the dark muddy water and only found it when I banged my hand on the rear of the car. I felt my way to the back doors of the vehicle which landed nose down, the weight of the engine causing it to sink quicker than the rear compartment.

Most deaths from car submersions happen because people panic. The water pressure makes opening the doors impossible unless the inside of the SUV floods completely, but I found a back door and pulled on the handle to check. Nada. I felt a thump as someone started to kick out the door's window. On the second kick the window exploded outwards. I took hold of the edge of the remaining pieces, pulled hard, and dislodged them from the door frame, slicing my hand in the process.

With my lungs screaming in protest I once again made my way to the surface. I popped up and took a deep breath. Winston was out of the Ford and standing at the edge of the canal, the car's headlights bathing the surface of the water in light.

"Samantha's still down there," I shouted.

He kicked off his shoes and dove in. As he did so, I heard another splash, this one from the other side of the canal, but I couldn't see anything.

I took a deep breath and prepared to follow Winston down when Studley came splashing to the surface about two feet away from me. We locked eyes and the weirdest sensation hit me, a sense of wrongness. If you asked me to explain why I wouldn't be able to, other than to say looking at him made my skin crawl.

I would worry about him later, I thought. I took another deep breath and dove down after Samantha. But Studley had other ideas and snagged my ankle to stop my descent. He yanked up hard, but my momentum dragged him under water with me.

I kicked out blindly with my other foot, doing my best to break his hold. I connected and he loosened his grip on my ankle, only to try to grab the other one and then tried to pull himself up my leg to get behind me.

I twisted in the water in time to circle my arm around his neck as he reached my waist, and then punched him in the face, over and over. He returned the favor, wrapping one arm around my waist, all the while hitting me with his other hand, using my mid-section for a punching bag. The water slowed our blows, but one landed solidly in my solar plexus, causing me to exhale the breath I was holding.

My focus changed from beating the ever-loving shit out of Studley, to needing to break his grip in order to find the surface. My lungs burned. In desperation I dug my thumb deep into his left eye, pushing as hard as I could as the amount of oxygen in my bloodstream decreased and carbon dioxide skyrocketed. Once the carbon levels reached a critical point I knew I would not be able to stop my lungs from trying to drink in every ounce of water in the canal, leading to a quick and painful death.

Finally, Studley yelled in garbled pain, losing his own breath and the grip on my waist. I pushed him away, kicking and straining for the surface, my head banging with one hell of a headache. It was only seconds that I was under water, but it seemed an eternity before my face broke into the cool night air and I opened my mouth and gasped for breath. A moment later Studley surfaced, doing the same about ten feet away from me. He glared in my direction with his one good eye, his left one already swelling shut, my other punches seriously ruining his pretty boy looks.

He snarled at me and spoke in a language I never heard before, but I didn't have to know the language to understand his meaning. He wanted to kill me and that was O.K. I planned on killing him first.

Before I could close the distance and find out which of us would be right, I felt a large object slap me in the side, and instinctively reached out with my hand, feeling something rough and bumpy go swimming by me.

Studley screamed incoherently at me, took one long stroke in my direction, but that was as far as he got. The alligator, which side-swiped me, burst out of the water and lunged forward catching Studley right where his neck joined his shoulder. His scream of defiance changed to one of utter terror. The gator turned over into a death spiral, taking Studley under, his screams dying as he did. Sucked to be him.

I heard a commotion behind me and saw Winston carrying Samantha out of the water. I swam to the edge of the canal and dragged myself onto the bank as Winston gently laid Samantha on the ground.

I moved to her side, gasping from the effort. Winston put his ear to her chest. His eyes squeezed shut for the briefest of moments and then they opened and he looked at me.

"Ah, man," he said, shaking his head. "I'm sorry. She's gone."

CHAPTER 11

All my anger and rage exploded inside me, I looked heavenward and howled at God. Samantha claimed God was dead, but I knew he was all too real and he continued to punish me for coming up short in the faith department. How much was enough? How much blood did God need from me?

I'd done everything He asked of me since becoming the Hand of God. I'd given up any semblance of my former life to live like a freakin' monk. My only friends were the two men who helped me hunt down and kill people. All I wanted was to see Samantha free from the clutches of the same people God wanted me to put down. And what was my reward? The death of the one woman I can say I ever loved. I picked her up and held her to my chest, too angry to cry. I brushed wet hair from her face, the face of an angel.

Winston stood and picked up the duffel. "Man, we have to get out of here. That bomb will bring the cops down on us and we've already spent more time here than we should've."

I knew he was right, but I just didn't give a damn. I just sat on the edge of the canal bank, and held Samantha. Winston threw the duffle in the trunk and opened the back door.

"You want to give up and let the shit roll over you? Fine. But not here. Get up and put her in the car. Let's go."

He put one hand under my arm and helped lift me to my feet, and I then picked up Samantha and gently carried her to the car. As I laid her on the back seat, her head rolled sideways and a little water trickled out of her mouth. I shook myself from my pity party and realized there was still a chance.

I dove inside and Winston threw the Ford in gear and we took off away from our rental and back towards Naples. I lowered the seat completely flat and stretched Samantha out with her head tilted back. I then checked her mouth to make sure there were no obstructions and started CPR. So help me God, if she dies because I didn't start CPR in time, because I was too busy blaming God for something I'd done? I wasn't sure what I would do.

Winston took the first right into a residential section of town just as the sirens could be heard rushing towards us. Another quick left and then a right took us away from the bomb scene and out of Naples.

I laced the fingers of my hands and began chest presses, all the time talking to Samantha. "Listen to me. You listening? Wake your ass up. You die on me now and you won't believe how pissed I'll be. You hear me? Come back to me. Wake up, dammit!"

Winston watched from the rearview mirror as I continued to press. Tears streamed silently down my cheeks. I'm not sure how long I did this, but between one press and the next, she began to cough out enough water to fill a swimming pool. I rolled her on her side. She continued to vomit up water and anything else in her stomach. She started to choke and then breathe in deep, ragged breaths. But dear Lord, breathe she did.

"Hot damn. She's back!" Winston shouted, and beat the dashboard with his fist.

I picked her up and held her close. Tears dropped down on her still damp face. I closed my eyes and said a quick prayer of thanks to God. I didn't know how long it would take for God to pound his message into my brain. But this time I felt blessed, as her fingers clutched my shirt, weakly at first, and then with more strength.

Finally, she opened her beautiful green eyes and stared up at me. How I missed getting lost in those eyes. Her breathing evened out and after a moment she closed her eyes again and fell asleep.

I wanted to shake her awake, with so many questions bouncing around in my head like a pinball machine. There were so many things I wanted to tell her. But I let her drift off. I could feel her heart beating against mine and, for now, I felt almost normal. She was safe.

Winston and I planned our exit from Naples in advance. He drove on through the early morning hours, staying on the back roads for about an hour. Then he caught Interstate 75 and headed north. When we hit Gainesville, Winston pulled up hotels on the GPS and decided on a hideaway motel off the beaten path. He found the place, parked, and then went inside to pay for two rooms.

I was looking out the front window waiting for his return when I felt someone watching me and looked down to find Samantha awake. I stroked her hair and a hint of a smile turned up the corners of her mouth.

She sat up and coughed a couple of times, then wrapped her arms around my neck and kissed me. If it was possible for my heart to jump through my chest, it would have at that very moment. After a minute she broke off the kiss, leaned back, smiled at me, and then hit me with a hard left to the chin.

"You goddamned son-of-a-bitch. You let them take me? How could you?"

I rubbed my chin. "I seem to remember a man had a gun to your head. What was I supposed to do? Let him put a bullet in your brain?" I replied.

I pictured our reunion many ways, and while I never thought it would be like running towards each other in a field of clover, I never expected this kind of reaction.

"A bullet to the brain would have been better than letting them kill Montoya and take me. Do you have any idea what the last three months have been like for me?"

"Oh. I'm sure. Sure looked like you and Studley were having a *terrible* time, arm and arm, when the police showed up, weren't you?"

I knew this wasn't true, but my anger was starting to boil over and I couldn't control myself.

"Don't even start with that, Vic. You don't know what you're talking about. Let me tell you something—"

She stopped when Winston opened the door and looked in the car at both of us.

"Uhh," he hesitated. "I only got two rooms. Do I need to go and get another?"

I said, "No," the same time Samantha said, "Yes."

"*No*," I repeated. "We'll be fine. We have some catching up to do. Don't we sweetheart?"

She glowered back at me, but didn't say anything. I got out of the car and retrieved a travel bag containing a change of clothes, along with the soggy duffle.

"You sure you guys are O.K.?" Winston whispered. "What did you say to her that pissed her off so much?"

"Not a frickin' thing. All I did was kiss the girl." There were times trying to figure out a woman was like trying to understand quantum mechanics, where particles can do different things all at the same time. It's just not meant to be.

He tossed me a room key, laughed and said, "You're in number eleven down on the left. I'm next door. Feel free to knock if you need a place to sleep." He headed to his room.

Samantha got out of the car and I reached inside and hit the door locks. Then she followed me to our room. I held the door open for her and flipped on the lights. She went straight to the bathroom and slammed the door shut.

I closed and locked the door and tossed the duffle on the floor. After a moment I heard the shower start and my mind went back to the last time the two of us were in a hotel room. That time I'd taken a shower and Samantha joined me, and we got to know each other in a very intimate way. I got the feeling if I tried to join her this time I could lose parts of me I value a great deal, if you catch my drift.

I removed my soggy clothes, grabbed a spare towel and dried off. I flopped down onto the queen sized bed. I was on the verge of falling asleep when the bathroom door opened and Samantha stepped out wearing one towel around her hair and one around her body. She padded across the room and sat on the edge of the bed next to me.

"You never should have let them shoot Dominic," she said in a small voice, staring at the floor, the sadness of recalled memories coloring her words.

"Yes. I know." I sighed.

"And your brother? He's evil. You know that, too, right?"

"To my eternal ruin. Yes, I know." I wanted to reach out to her, to touch her, but I knew now was not the time.

She finally looked at me, her hands clasped tightly in her lap. "If you'd stepped aside, Mike would be dead and maybe Dominic would still be alive. Why didn't you?"

"Because I thought I could save him. I knew it was true, that he was Belial. But I still thought I could save him. If it had been your dad Montoya was sent to kill, would you have let him shoot him down?"

She looked away again. She was silent for a long time, but I waited.

"I don't know," she said finally. "I really don't. I just wish it had turned out different."

"So do I. But it didn't." I thought about that afternoon in Mikey's warehouse, Montoya being shot by Deveraux and how my brother kicked him when he fell. I pushed the memory away. "What happened to you over the last three months?"

Tears slowly rolled down her cheeks. I put out a hand and rubbed her arm. In one quick motion she turned and laid down beside me, putting her head on my chest, and began to cry.

"I . . . I don't want to talk about it," she stammered. "Not now. I need some time. O.K.?"

"Sure. No worries." I held her until the crying stopped.

I thought she might have fallen to sleep when she said, speaking into my chest, "They told me if I tried to leave, they'd kill you . . . that they knew where you were. And all it would take is a phone call, and you'd be dead. I went to sleep every night wondering if they had already killed you and just didn't tell me."

I let out a short laugh. "I told you. I'm a lot harder to kill than you think. I'm fine."

She raised her head and turned to look at me. "So was Dominic. But he's dead." She laid her head back down. "What will the world do now with no Hand of God."

"Well, about that. Turns out when one Hand of God dies another takes his place. Kind of like how they replace James Bond in the movies. Another guy steps into the part."

"Steps into a death sentence, you mean. Taking that job is suicidal. I wonder how long it will take them to find his replacement?"

"Not long at all. They found Montoya's replacement pretty quick." I paused, then continued, "I'm the new Hand of God."

She sat up as if jolted by electric shock. "What? You can't! You can't be the Hand of God. It will kill you!"

"Samantha, I didn't really have a choice. When I let Mikey kill Montoya and then escape, I became one of the damned. When I die, I'm headed straight to Hell to keep Mikey company. I was offered a chance to redeem my soul by taking over for Dominic. I need to make things right."

"What? God talked to you? God told you that you were going to Hell? This is insane!" She started to tear up all over again.

I told her about Dominic Montoya's dying words, my meeting with Brother Joshua and about what I was doing as the Hand of God for the last three months.

"I've been trying to find both you and Mikey."

"So when you find your brother, you have to kill him? I told you before: God is dead. Vic, let someone else do this. What's God done for you? For me? You don't *have* to do this. You and I can take off, if you still have the money I gave you. We can hide anywhere in the world. Let God and Satan fight it out themselves. We've given enough."

Now it was my turn to shake my head.

"I can't. God is very real. Deep down, you know that. I need to do this to get myself straight. It doesn't mean we can't still be together. But first I have to take care of Mikey. I don't know what happens after that, but you said it yourself, I'm responsible for him being on the loose. And in my gut, I know Mikey is planning something else. He told me as much, so I have to stop him. What if Mikey decides to kill another group of kids. Do you think I could live with myself knowing the only reason he's alive is me?"

She slid off the bed and looked into my travel bag and pulled out a T-shirt. She took off both towels and put the shirt on.

"It's just not right," she said, lying back down beside me.

I didn't say anything in reply and after a couple of minutes, she said, "Do you mind just holding me tonight? I know you want more, but for tonight, all I want is to sleep."

"Sure."

She was right. I did want much more. But I could sense she'd been through the ringer over the last three months and with the night's rescue, what she needed most was to rest and recover. We both got under the covers and though it took awhile, she finally fell asleep.

I laid there, feeling the warmth of Samantha's body next to mine and smelled the motel shampoo scent in her hair. I thought about life, in general, and then about the future. I had two major goals. One goal I accomplished by freeing Samantha from Satan and his minions. But Mikey remained elusive. I knew I was closing in on him, but he managed to stay one step ahead of me.

When the Church discovered Samantha was no longer their hostage, it was going to be a major blow to them. With any luck, it might force them to stick their heads out of the holes they're hiding in. When they do that? I'll be ready to bash them in again.

CHAPTER 12

Bill watched through the heavy falling snow as the ghost walked deeper into the woods. He tipped back the last of his Budweiser and tossed the can into the corner of the deer blind with the other empties. He felt a long belch coming and let her rip. I mean, who was around to complain but the snow and the ghost.

He blinked his eyes several times and looked out again at the ghost. It took a moment for him to remember he didn't believe in those damned things. But there it was, a white shape moving quietly, sometimes disappearing from view and then reappearing as it moved in and out of the trees. Huh. Don't that beat all.

Then he remembered he brought a pair of binoculars with him, along with the twelve pack of Bud. He wouldn't be here at all if it wasn't for his whiney-ass girlfriend. When he told her he wanted to go and check out his deer blind and see if it needed any repairs, she said he loved it more than he did her. And if he loved it so much then maybe he should move out of her place and into the goddamned blind.

With two beers already making their way through his system, he told her, "Fine, I will."

So he gathered up his gear, his guns and his pride, and stormed out of the house, slamming the door behind him. All he ever heard was, "Nag, nag, nag."

On the way out of town he stopped by the Party Mart drive-thru and ordered up the twelve pack and a couple of cans of Skol. He drank another beer on the way and made a pit stop at a Thornton's gas station to take a piss and change into his hunting coveralls and hat—the one with the big gray UK emblem on the front. Good thing, because out here in the blind it was colder than a witch's titties. But hell, it kept the beer cold.

He pawed through his hunting bag and found the binoculars and after a few tries, got them focused in on the ghost.

I'll be damned, he thought to himself. It weren't no ghost, but a girl. And one damn good lookin' one, too. If the way she filled out her winter coat was any indication.

He nearly had a heart attack and almost dropped the glasses when the girl stopped and looked right in his direction. With her nearly a hundred yards out, there was no way she could really see him. But here she was staring right back at him. Long, wavy black hair spilled out from inside the hood of her coat and framed one of the most beautiful faces he'd ever seen. And Lord Almighty, but her breasts pushed the fabric of her coat out in a way which made a carnal desire blossom despite the beer.

He licked his lips a couple of times and then his brain finally caught up to what his eyes had been showing him as the girl started moving again: she was dragging a body behind her. Under each arm she gripped the legs of some guy who was either unconscious or stone cold dead. He offered no resistance and his arms trailed out behind him. Bill laughed a bit at that one. Stone cold. Damn if it wasn't.

He fought past the beer fog and decided dragging some poor fool through the woods, in the snow, was beyond peculiar and needed checking out.

He hung the binoculars around his neck and picked up his Dakota 76 Safari rifle he always hunted with. Even though it wasn't deer season it didn't mean he might not shoot one out here on the farm. Then he climbed slowly out of the deer blind, making sure to place each boot carefully on the next rung of the wooden ladder. Last thing he needed to do was stumble and fall and break his frickin' neck. He wouldn't give his girlfriend the pleasure.

Once on the ground, he took a moment to orient himself and headed in the direction where he last saw the girl. At ground level it became harder to see through the snow, but he finally caught sight of her and picked up the pace.

The voice of Elmer Fudd ran through his mind. "Be vewy quiet, I'm hunting wabbits," and he began to laugh so hard he nearly stumbled. When he straightened up, he could no longer see the girl.

He looked around through the falling curtain of snow, but no dice. He couldn't see her anywhere. He shrugged his shoulders and kept going forward, and after a moment found her trail. He started following it while thinking about who she might be. The owners of the farm lived in Lexington and paid him to keep the place up, but they hadn't been out in a few weeks. The old man and his wife only came out when the weather turned nice. They had a boy who visited more often to go traipsing through a cave on the back part of the property, but there wasn't much to do when the weather got cold. He didn't think the man being dragged was the boy, but he'd know soon enough. If the guy was hurt and needed help, she was headed in the wrong direction. The farmhouse was the other way. There weren't nothin' this way but more woods and the cave.

His thoughts were interrupted when he nearly stepped onto the man's head where he was left under the snow covered branches of an ancient oak.

Man, hell. Boy more like it. If the boy was out of his teens, he'd stop drinking for a year. Then again, maybe not. That'd be a long time without a brewsky. He knelt down, resting the gun against the trunk of the tree, and felt the side of the poor guy's neck, just like they do in all them TV doctor shows. He didn't feel nothin', so he slapped his cheeks a couple of times, but still nothin'. Huh.

He glanced around and could see the tracks stop just beyond where she let go of his legs and two things struck Bill at about the same time. The first was a thought. If you are followin' someone and the tracks stop under a tree, then maybe they climbed it. He looked up and the second thing hit him was the girl as she dropped out of the tree and he took two boots right to the kisser, and they went down together in a heap. He tried to reach for his gun as blood burst from his busted lip, staining the pristine white snow with a streak of bright red blood, but the girl was all over him.

The girl straddled him, and any other time he'd be thrilled to have a woman this hot on top of his chest. But not this one. She began to hit him in the face, over and over. Bill raised his arms to try and protect himself, but God Almighty, this girl pounded the hell out of him. He could feel himself losing consciousness.

The last thing he thought before darkness overtook him was something some actress said a long time ago: there are no good girls gone wrong, just bad girls found out.

Seems he found one of those bad girls and then his world went black.

CHAPTER 13

Samantha slept fitfully, often moaning in her sleep. If I slept at all it was only in brief spurts. When the sun managed to slip through the curtains early the next morning, I called over to Winston and asked him to find some place to pick up clothes for Samantha along with some breakfast for the three of us.

I got up, hit the shower and shaved. When I came out she was sitting on the bed watching the coverage of the bombing. She was still wearing my T-shirt. I plopped down next to her to see what the newsies were saying about my late night raid.

The local Gainesville TV stations were covering the event non-stop, as were all the major cable news shows. According to the reports, of the four guys in the first SUV, which took the brunt of the blast, two had to be hospitalized overnight. The other two were treated and released. It was also reported they were part of a private home security force and were heavily armed at the time of the attack.

The people in the second SUV which plunged into the canal, they were not so lucky. The driver drowned, never even getting his seatbelt unhooked. As for Studley, the gator did a real number on him. They never showed the body, but reports indicated the head remained attached to the body, but only barely.

We watched transfixed as the station played a video of the gator charging out of the water directly at the police and rescue crew, only to be gunned down before it could reach any of the people involved. Normally gators shied away from that many people, but this one had a hard-on for anything walking on two legs. I shuddered at the thought of the thing slapping me in the side on the way by. Close call. They said the names of the two dead men were being withheld until notification of next of kin.

According to a spokesman for the security firm, there was no one else missing and they could not speculate as to the motive for the attack. Guess the Church and Mikey didn't want the world at large to know Samantha had been in one of the cars. I had hoped as much.

There was no news on what happened to the driver of the Chevy. The police were still searching the canal, but so far they found no body. There was much speculation the driver had escaped the scene. You bet your ass, he had.

There was also much discussion on why the bombing occurred. The radical right blamed Al Qaeda and the President for not being tough on terror. Local experts speculated it was part of an on-going turf war between drug cartels in the southern Florida area. Then a call came in from a radical militia group claiming responsibility for the bombing, saying they did it as a blow against those who would take away their rights to bear arms.

The phone call was part of the deal I made with the bomb makers. For whatever reason, they disliked the rival militia group and wanted the Feds taking a harder look in their direction. The bomb was built in such a way as to point to them directly. I didn't care, since it muddied the water for investigators, which could only be a good thing for us.

"The guy I had the knock down drag out with in the water, the one the gator got, what was his name?" I asked.

"John." She quick glanced up at me, then back at the TV, engrossed with the news coverage. "That's what most people called him. And he was from Kentucky. You know him?"

"Nope. Never seen him before."

She turned the sound down on the TV and continued, "But like your brother, he had another name he used for some of the phone calls he got. He called himself Baraquiel." She shuddered. "He only showed up on the scene a few weeks ago, but he was a really bad guy. Really bad. I'm glad he's dead."

I watched as she sat, hands clasped together so tightly her knuckles turned white. I asked, "What did he do to you?"

She only shook her head No. I got off the bed and knelt before her, taking her hands in mine. "I'm here for you. Did he hurt you?" I could feel the anger bubbling to the surface, but the man was dead. The fact I couldn't find him and pound him some more disappointed me to no end.

"Vic, I said I didn't want to talk about it. O.K.? Please?" A single tear tracked its way down her cheek and so I dropped it. For now.

"Tell me about Mikey. What happened after you left the warehouse?"

"There's not much to tell. For the first few weeks they kept me drugged up. I wasn't exactly compliant and they wanted to control me easier. Once they were satisfied I no longer had the money, they eased up on the drugs and moved me around a lot. They told me if I tried to escape, they'd kill you. They showed me several pictures taken of you in different places."

"Really?" This surprised me. I would have thought they'd kill me in a heartbeat if they had a chance. The fact they hadn't kinda surprised me. I wondered if Mikey was showing brotherly love in leaving me be, but somehow I doubted it.

"Did you overhear anything which might point to what Mikey and the Church is planning next?"

"Sorry. Not a clue. They never talked about those kinds of things when I was around. And I wasn't allowed anywhere near a phone or computer or I'd have gotten in touch with you. I did see my dad once."

"He came to see me the first week we were in Florida," she said softly. "When I asked him about the Exodus Project, he laughed and told me to stay out of his business. Then he talked as if nothing had happened."

"He didn't deny it?" She shook her head in a small no. I thought about her father, one of the most powerful men in the country, hell, the world. And when his daughter took off with thirty million dollars of the Church's money, he sent one of Satan's twelve undead minions, a vampire named Eamon, after her.

My heart ached for Samantha. When she found out her father was a Satanist, she didn't think much of it at the time. She didn't believe in God or Satan. But then she found out not only was Satan real, but her father conspired to kill thousands of school children in his name? Can you imagine finding out you're Hitler's daughter? Same kind of thing. Then the son-of-a-bitch sent Eamon, a vampire, to track her down. Eamon was a serial killing child murderer back in the time of the great potato famine in Ireland. After his death, Satan gave him an opportunity to come back to Earth for a second chance at being a monster.

Samantha, with a little help from me, sent Eamon back to Hell where he belonged. But just the thought that her dad sent such a creature after her was devastating.

I stood, bent and kissed the top of her head. She wrapped her arms around my waist, pulled me close and cried. When the tears stopped, I kissed her again and began to pace the room. Then I got my phone out and used the Google Machine to try to find out more about Baraquiel. It took me several tries at different spellings and found nothing of interest. Then I hit the right spelling and my blood froze.

Winston knocked on the door and I let him in. He put bags of clothes and a sack of Krispy Kremes on the bed and I closed the door behind him. He turned to me smiling, but it faded when he saw the look on my face.

"What?"

"We have to get back to Louisville. *Now.* I think I know what Mikey is planning."

CHAPTER 14

Bill woke up and his face wailed in agony. He gingerly reached up and ran his fingers over puffy skin. It felt like he was hit in the face with a baseball bat—not once, but about a hundred times. Damn if he didn't need a drink.

Then he breathed in and nearly gagged from the odor which assaulted his senses. One summer, in his younger days, he picked up road kill for the county. Wherever he was now? It smelled like the bed of his truck after a hot summer day of picking up dead dogs, possums and raccoons. That's what it smelled like to him.

He managed to open one eye, while the other refused to cooperate and was completely swollen shut. He laid on his back and above him he could see a rocky ceiling bathed in a soft red glow. After a moment, he realized he must be in the cave Jason spent time exploring. How the Sam Hill had he gotten in here? And who turned on a red lamp? God, he needed more than one drink.

He slowly turned his head to the side, his neck protesting, and saw two people talking. One was one heck of a pretty girl. Black hair, angel face, and great ass. Man, what a body. Then the memory came rushing back of her on top of him beating the ever-loving daylights out of him and her hotness dialed back a few notches. She was talking to a tall, skinny dude with long white hair.

They both turned to look at him and for the first time in a very long time, Bill felt fear. Glancing away from them, he trembled, but it only surged inside of him when he saw the source of the smell: body parts and rotting flesh were scattered throughout the cave. He could make out several skeletons and what appeared to be teeth marks in the flesh.

The two of them walked over and stared down at him. "You said you wanted someone older and he is that," the woman said.

The man responded, "It is needed to command respect. People pay more attention if they think you have the experience of years. You are sure he's available?"

"Yes. He's yours." She said this with a smile that chilled Bill to his very soul.

He tried sitting up, but was overcome with dizziness and he collapsed back. "If you so much as lay a finger on me, I'll kick yer ass, Old Timer."

The man laughed and the sound was . . . beautiful. It reminded him of when his mom and dad took him to see *A Christmas Carol* at Actor's Theatre when he was a child, and the laugh of the Ghost of Christmas Past. Bountiful and joyful. And for the briefest moment his fear subsided and he was in awe.

Then the laughter stopped and the feeling left him and the stench once again assaulted his nose. The man knelt before him and said, "You are injured. I'm sorry my friend felt the need to do such things to you. Please, let me put you at ease."

The old man placed a hand on either side of his face, gently, and spoke in a language Bill had never heard before. It was lyrical and soothing. Miraculously, the pain and swelling in his body receded. He could fully open both eyes now and he stared up into the eyes of the old man. They were dark black and he could swear he saw stars falling in them. The fear was replaced by a calm which warmed his whole body.

Bill smiled up into his eyes and the man smiled back and everything was right with the world. But then, in an instant, it wasn't. He could feel the man's hands pressing tighter against his skull and in a rush, another being entered his mind.

Bill thrashed on the ground as his body fought the alien presence, but the "other" crushed his will and shoved what remained of him into the deepest recesses of his mind, cornered and cowering.

And this was no man. As the being took control, he sensed a presence as old as creation, with a power he could barely comprehend. As their minds blended together, he felt what the "other" felt: hunger, pain and anger. Anger so deep there was no bottom.

"Who *are* you?" Bill asked.

The presence responded, "I am Samyaza, captain of the Watchers and you have been chosen to help free my brothers. Once that is accomplished and we once again walk upon the Earth, we will take what is rightfully ours. As it was before, so shall it be again."

The woman smiled and nodded, repeating, "As it was before, so shall it be again."

And Bill knew he was powerless to stop them.

CHAPTER 15

It took the rest of the day for us to drive back to Louisville. Arriving at the mission around nine p.m. road-weary, the three of us trudged down the hallway to Brother Joshua's office. We found him staring out the window at the night with the box I'd taken from Tommy sitting on top of his desk.

I knocked on the door and the three of us filed into his office. He turned around and said to us, "I see you were successful in freeing Ms. Tyler." Bowing his head slightly, he continued, "Welcome to the Derby Mission."

She crossed her arms and stared at him for a moment. "So you're the one who pretends to talk to God and will be the one to get Victor killed. How many men have you sent to their deaths?" So much for a pleasant greeting.

J moved to his desk and sat down, placing his hands on the desk, one on top of the other. If he was upset at Samantha's accusation, he didn't show it.

"Ms. Tyler, what we do, the Hand of God and I, we do to make the world a better place. Everyone dies. Everyone. The only question is what happens after we die. Victor, and those who came before him, all make a choice. None are forced into God's service. From the time of Adam, men and women have the freedom to choose their fate. Victor has chosen his."

Samantha snorted. "Like he had a choice. You tell him he will burn in Hell if he doesn't and what's he supposed to do?" I gently placed a hand on her arm, but she shrugged it off. "How do you even sleep at night?"

"I sleep perfectly fine, I assure you." He changed the subject. "Now that you are free, Ms. Tyler, what are you plans?"

She looked at me and I responded, "I was hoping she could stay here for a bit, until we can figure that out."

He pursed his lips. "Fine. We can provide you a room for a time. But you must work while here, Ms. Tyler. Also, you must sleep in your own room. We do not allow cohabitation here at the mission." He followed this with a pointed look in my direction.

"I understand." After a brief pause, she added, "Thank you." From our conversation the night before, I knew just saying thank you was hard for her.

Brother Joshua picked up the phone on his desk, punched a couple of numbers and asked, "Could you come here, please."

A few moments later, a young lady with short curly blonde hair and an easy smile stuck her head in the door. "Yes?"

"Samantha Tyler, this is Lisa Crain. Ms. Crain will you show Ms. Tyler to a room in the women's dorm, please? And make sure she has what she needs when it comes to personal items. Then work with her to find a volunteer schedule she is comfortable with."

"Sure. No biggie." She stuck out a hand and Samantha took it. "Come on, I'll give you the grand tour. It will take all of five minutes." she chuckled.

Samantha left without a word and Winston and I took a seat.

"We have a problem." I said.

I filled him in on what happened in Florida, then had Winston tell him about what went down at the Mall.

"Does the name Baraquiel mean anything to you?"

"It does." He tapped the box in front of him. "You should have told me about Winston and what happened. If you had we could have moved sooner on this. The name you overheard, Winston, was not Sam Yaza, but Samyaza."

"By sooner, you mean instead of freeing Samantha, right?" I replied.

"You must remember, Victor, as I told Ms. Tyler, you agreed to be the Hand of God and all that it entails. Once you made the decision, then God chooses your course of action. Not you. Withholding such information can have dire consequences."

He was right. I made the choice freely. But Samantha was also right in that I didn't have much of a choice. Serve or go to Hell. I wasn't bitter over the decision. Mikey wouldn't be walking around wreaking havoc if it wasn't for me. But it didn't mean I had to like it.

"I didn't think it was overly important at the time. We've known the Church would eventually try and come back at us, and I planned to tell you as soon as we got back. Now we're back. Now we've told you. As for this Baraquiel character? I looked him up and it doesn't look good, if he's the real deal. And let me guess, this Samyaza guy and Baraquiel are connected?"

He nodded. "Yes. Do you know anything about the Watchers?"

I didn't, but Winston did.

"They're fallen angels, right?" Winston asked.

"Yes. Back in the early days of Man, God sent two hundred angels to watch over the affairs of men. But they began to lust after human women. After a time, they slept with women of their choosing and their offspring were the Nephilim. Great giants who preyed upon the Earth. The Watchers began to give men knowledge in mass that they were supposed to learn gradually: how to make better weapons, the art of mining, among others."

I knew it was just my imagination, but it seemed to get darker outside

J's window and the light in the room dimmed as he continued to speak.

"Then God decided to punish the Watchers and rid the world of their seed. So he sent the Great Flood to drown the Nephilim. First, he sent an angel to warn Noah and his family in order to preserve the human race. They were the only ones free of the Nephilim genes. Then God sent the rain to end their existence. Once the Nephilim were destroyed, the archangel Raphael and others chained and bound the Watchers in the valleys of the Earth, to be kept there until Judgment Day."

"Wait," I said, "I've heard of them. They're called the Grigori. Right?"

"Yes. That is another name which has been used for the Fallen, angels who rebelled against God and were punished."

"So you're saying they've managed to slip free of their chains and are loose again? How's that possible?"

"Both yes and no. No, their physical bodies are still chained. If the Watchers had managed to free themselves, in whole, you would know, for they would be a plague upon the face of the Earth. So no, their physical bodies remain chained."

Winston said, "I get the feeling there is a really bad 'but' coming next."

Brother Joshua nodded, "Are you familiar with demonic possession?"

Once again, Winston's knowledge of the Bible was much better than mine. He said, "Then Jesus asked him, 'What is your name?' 'My name is Legion,' he replied. Then Jesus cast the demons out into a bunch of pigs which ran into a lake and drowned."

"Very good. You know, Victor, spending time with Winston could have a positive effect on you."

"You can both kiss my ass. So you're telling me they're out possessing people? Why now? How's that possible? And what does that box have to do with all of this?"

"I believe they are," Joshua said. "As for why now? My guess is they've been found by someone. Most demonic possession takes place via touch. For the Watchers to possess someone, they need to be in physical contact with that person. Their powers would be limited, as they can only do so much while in someone else's body, but they would still be formidable—if only because of the knowledge they possess."

"And the box? How is the box and Mikey connected?" I asked.

"If a person knew where the Watchers were being imprisoned and knew the right words to say, they could free them from their chains. This box holds a document almost as old as the written word. It's a vision of a follower of Lucifer, and it contains portions of the proper words needed to unleash the Watchers. The language is ancient Ge'ez, a South Semitic language which originated in Ethiopia. It seems your brother means to release the Watchers and set them loose on the planet once again."

Winston let out a low whistle. "And once free, they will again produce children. The Nephilim will walk the Earth. And with God's promise to never flood the planet again, there is nothing to stop them."

Holy crap. Giants? I remembered watching old B-movies with rampaging Cyclops pillaging the countryside. Seeing them in person was not something I wanted to deal with.

"Well, if that happens, wouldn't God just send Raphael and a few of his best buds to bust their asses back into whatever dungeon they were put into in the first place?"

Brother Joshua shook his head no.

"I'm afraid not. The fate of Man is now in their own hands. If the Watchers are to be stopped, it will fall to *you* to do so."

Great. All I need to do is kill a bunch of giant-making divine beings who've been chained up for thousands of years, who could end life as we know it. No problem. I could probably get it done before breakfast in the morning. Yeah, right.

"What do we do next?"

"Find your brother. In the meantime, I'll make a few phone calls. You may need help with this one."

Ya think? I thought to myself.

"You know what? This job needs a better benefits package. Especially since there are no retirement perks."

"You're wrong. In your case, it's the best retirement plan you could ask for. Your soul."

Then Heaven help us.

CHAPTER 16

I woke up the next morning, showered, threw on a T-shirt which said, I Hope Your Life is As Good as You Portray On Facebook, my old Wranglers and boots and shuffled out with the down trodden who came in every morning to eat breakfast at the Derby Mission. Thanks to the snow, the place was packed with many of Louisville's homeless trying to find a safe, warm place to ride out the bad weather.

I was surprised to find Samantha standing next to Lisa in the serving line, spooning out scrambled eggs onto the plates of the young and old filing into the cafeteria.

When I stopped in front of her she offered a small smile and gave me a larger portion than the others. Lisa winked at me and added several pieces of bacon. An old geezer right behind me looked at the amount she spooned out for him and then at my plate and said, "I want what he's got, if you don't mind."

"You've only been here one day and already causing chaos in the food line." I said to Samantha.

She stuck her tongue out at me. I grabbed a cup of coffee and moved to a table in the far corner of the cafeteria away from everyone else. I noticed most of the people who came into the Derby Mission were not thrilled to be in my company. Perhaps they were intimidated by my size or the weird vibes they sensed from me. Maybe they simply didn't like my aftershave. I don't know. It worked to my advantage this morning.

After a few minutes, Samantha excused herself from kitchen duties and sat down across from me. She held a cup of orange juice in her hands, twirling the cup around in circles, but rarely took a drink.

I kept spooning in mouthfuls of eggs and bacon, and let her get to where she needed to be. After a moment, she sighed deeply. "I never said thank you for rescuing me. Again. You seem to be making a habit of that. Thank you."

She reached out a hand, tentatively, and covered one of mine.

"No worries," I said. "I just figured you like presenting me with a challenge."

"Hardly. Look, I know this has been hard on you as well. And I'm sorry for the way I've acted since you freed me. The last three months have been really tough."

"Ready to talk about it?"

"No. But I will be. Thanks for not pushing me. We do need to make some decisions, though. Like where I'm going to go?"

"If it's all the same to you, I'd like you to stay here for a bit. It's not exactly the Hilton. But with Brother Joshua, you'll be safe here."

She lowered her voice, "Speaking of Joshua, what do you know about him?"

"Truthfully? Not a lot. He's not the kind of person to talk about himself. Mostly he tells me who needs killing and I make it happen," I paused. "But one thing I do know, and I don't know how I know this, he is one man you don't want to mess with—kind of like when Lucifer walked into my office. I knew he was the Devil, no doubt about it. And when it comes to Joshua, kind of the same thing. I just know if you stay here, you'll be safe. Once I get this whole Mikey-thing taken care of, then we can talk about what to do next."

She nodded and glanced back at the line which was getting longer by the moment. "I guess I better get back to it. At least here I'm doing something worthwhile."

She squeezed my hand and then stood up, but before she left she asked, "Vic, will you do something for me?"

"Sure, gorgeous. Name it."

"Be very careful when it comes to Joshua. Please? For me?"

"Sure. No problem. But I think you're just upset at him over the whole Hand of God-thing."

She gave me a half-shrug and went back to the serving line. I watched her go, relieved she was safe, but worried about her nonetheless. I could understand why she wouldn't necessarily trust Brother Joshua, but I never picked up on anything I should be worried about—other than he kept sending me on extremely dangerous situations against foes who would like nothing better than to send me to the other side. But that came with the territory and I accepted it, more or less. There was always someone wanting to take me down.

Which raised an interesting question. I finished up my breakfast and asked Lisa if she'd seen Brother Joshua this morning. He almost never missed his time in the serving line.

"Oh. He was here in the cafeteria for a bit, but had to leave. I think he has a visitor and is in his office."

I thanked her and went in search of our fearless leader, and she was right. He was both in his office and not alone. A very large man wearing an orange workout shirt and black shorts, downing a Gatorade, was visiting with

Joshua in his office.

Muscles rippled as he raised the bottle and drained the rest of the purple liquid, then heaved the empty bottle into the trash can on the side of J's desk. His raven black hair, long and wavy, reached past his shoulders. I knocked on the doorframe and J waved me in.

"Victor McCain." I stuck out my hand and introduced myself.

He took it with a firm grip and said, "Andrew Colton. It's a pleasure, finally, to meet the Hand of God."

I looked at J and raised an eyebrow.

"I told you that you needed help. I've asked Father Colton to assist you in dealing with the Watchers. If they are, indeed, possessing people, and it seems likely, then you may need to have exorcisms performed. Father Colton is the best. I told him who you are and what you are facing."

"Father Colton, you're a priest? Father Brick, more like it." I said with admiration. "Wow. Let me guess: you're a member of the ball-busting clerical order?"

He laughed. "I'm not, though I am from a parish not too far from Venice Beach, California. I caught the red eye as soon as Joshua called. I've found when dealing with demonic spirits, it pays to be in shape. Things can occasionally get . . . a little physical. And if we really are dealing with the Watchers, then I have no doubt it will get extremely violent when we try and cast them out."

"Huh. I guess just putting a bullet in the body of the person they're using wouldn't be a good thing for the possess-e."

He turned serious. "No, it wouldn't. The only thing the host body has done wrong is not have a strong faith in God. Most are decent human beings who happen to be 'available' for the taking because they have lost faith in God. If you kill them to kill the demon, then there's not much chance for them to accept the Lord God Almighty before they die."

"Yeah. I get that. But as a last resort, it will kill the bad guy, right?" I asked.

"Matthew Chapter 12, verse 45, 'When an impure spirit comes out of a person, it goes through arid places seeking rest and does not find it.' They can be forced out by the death of the host or through an exorcism. If they leave voluntarily, they must have another host to transfer to for this to happen."

"Huh. Another question. You have to be touched to be possessed, is that right?"

"In most cases, no," Colton replied. "A person can be possessed simply by having lost faith in God. Demons look for empty vessels to fill. A soul filled with the light of our God Almighty, cannot be possessed. So I, for instance, could never be possessed."

I scratched at the stubble on my chin. "You're saying the Watchers are different?"

"Yes, the Watchers are not most cases. Because of how they are imprisoned, they would have to be near enough to be touched. I know it doesn't make much sense, but it's often like that in the world of demonic possession."

"All I really care about is if we track them down, do you think you can kick their asses out of the bodies they're in?"

With a smile as broad as it was confident, "If I can't, no one can. But yes, if you can keep them still long enough, I should be able to cast them into oblivion."

"Sounds good to me."

I turned to Brother Joshua and asked, "I want to get your opinion on something I thought of while eating breakfast. Samantha told me one way they kept her in line was by showing her pictures of me in different situations, telling me they could take me out any time they wanted to. Which begs the question, why didn't they?"

"Perhaps there is a reason why they chose to keep tabs on you instead of killing you," Brother Joshua replied. "When the Hand of God dies," he continued, "we never know who the next one will be. Your brother knows who the current Hand of God is. And as long as you're alive, that remains the case. If you die, he will not know where the next threat is coming from."

I nodded. This made sense. "Then I need to start mixing things up. How many people do you think we're going to be dealing with? How many of these Watchers are there?"

Joshua replied, "There are two hundred total, with twelve captains and one leader, Samyaza. So at the most, two hundred, although the total is likely much less than that."

"*Holy shit!* Two hundred? There could be that many fallen angels running around? Why does that not sound good?"

I've never lacked for confidence, but I mean, come on, two hundred of them? I started to think of what Samantha said about the Hand of God being a death sentence.

"Actually, I believe that total is already down to one hundred and ninety nine," Father Colton replied. "Brother Joshua filled me in on what happened in Florida. Like most Americans I've seen the video of the alligator charging out of the water, trying to take a hunk out of the rescuers on shore. I believe when the alligator bit into the young man, the fallen angel Baraquiel transferred to the alligator and then attempted to make contact with someone on shore. But they shot and killed the alligator before he could pull it off. With the alligator's death, he would be cast out into the arid wasteland." He stood up. "But take heart," he continued, "they probably haven't all made it to the surface, yet. So have faith, my friend."

Yeah, as if that made me feel any better.

"Faith I have," I replied. "Lives I have but one." I stood up as well. "Time to get to work."

"What do you suggest we do first?" Colton asked.

"Well, if the person has to be touched to be possessed, I suggest we start with the man Winston took out at the Mall, Mal McGeorge. If we can talk to him, then perhaps we can find out when the fallen angel took control of his body."

"Great," Colton said. "Let me get changed and we can head out," and he left the room.

"He's good, huh?" I said to Brother Joshua.

"The best. You will need him before this is done. Move as quickly as you can, Victor, for you can rest-assured the Fallen are doing so."

I let out a bone weary sigh and responded, "Aye, aye, Captain. Your wish is my command. Time to kick some fallen angel butt."

J shook his head as I walked out of his office. I got that a lot.

CHAPTER 17

Father Colton joined me, dressed in a traditional priest's frock. He still looked like a brick. On the way to McGeorge's house, he said, "I'm glad we're doing this. It's important I see this young man."

"Why's that?" I asked, as I drove down slush covered side roads. The snow had finally stopped. Nearly seven inches of snow had fallen while I was in Florida, a-typical for the Louisville area. I was already missing the warmth and sunshine of Naples.

"Once a demon is forced to leave a person's body, as I said, they must wander in an arid wasteland for a time. But eventually, they find their way back to the body they were in before—if that person hasn't had a change of heart when it comes to God. And when they come back, they can bring friends with them. Other demons they meet while wandering. It's not a good thing."

"I would think not."

We remained silent, lost in our own thoughts until I found the right house. I parked in the street and we walked up a freshly shoveled drive to a small but well kept home. I knocked on the door and after a minute a woman answered. She was what my mother would call "plump" and looked as if she'd been run through the ringer.

When she saw the two of us, she eyed us suspiciously and asked with hesitation, "Can I help you?"

"Mrs. McGreorge?" When she said yes, I continued, "My name is Victor McCain and this is Father Colton. I understand the police haven't caught the person who attacked your son and I would like to help. It's what I do for a living and I want to make sure the person who did this to your son is brought to justice."

"And you're, what, a private investigator?" While she hadn't closed the door yet, she still had not invited us in. "And you brought a priest, why?"

"Not exactly. I'm a bounty hunter. And I'm very good at what I do. And this would be at no cost to you. I just want to help. As for Father Colton, I heard what your son told the police about there being someone in his head. Father Colton is good at counseling people who feel they've been possessed by someone or something. He came with me in case he could offer your son help. How is he?"

With some reluctance, she opened the door and allowed us in. "Come in. My name is Evelyn. Let me get my husband." She motioned for us to sit in the family room and then she walked down the hallway and to another room. A door opened and she shouted, "Robert. We have visitors."

She closed the door and a conversation ensued in low tones. Footsteps came back in our direction and both Colton and I stood. Robert McGeorge, middle-aged and fit, came into the room, his wife right behind him.

He didn't waste any time. "My wife says you're a bounty hunter, that right?"

"Yes sir, I am. And I'd like to help. I think the person who did this to your son is mixed up with people I'm tracking. I'd like to see to it they pay for what they did to your son."

"What people?" I watched as he clenched and unclenched his hands several times.

"I can't tell you that. At least not yet. But I promise you, Mr. McGeorge, I will find them."

"If you know something, we could tell the police and they can make you tell who you're after," she said.

Robert McGeorge shushed his wife, raising a hand. "You look like you can deal out some punishment. You give me your word you will find whoever did this and hold them responsible for hurting our boy?"

"With a priest as my witness, you have my word."

I could make the promise because I was looking for the person who did this to their son, in a roundabout way. Winston would not have put the beat down on the kid if he wasn't possessed by a fallen angel. And when I found Mr. Bad Wings, I did plan on putting the hurt on him.

He nodded. "Good. What do you want from us?"

"I'd like to speak to your son. I want to ask him some questions, if that's alright."

Robert dry washed his face with his hand a couple of times. "If you can get him to talk to you. Mr. McCain, they really messed up my boy. We keep him sedated. He keeps wailing about voices in his head. He says they're gone, but he's afraid they'll come back."

Colton and I shared a look and I thought to myself, you bet your ass they'll be back.

The priest walked to Mr. McGeorge, putting his hand on his arm and said, "I believe I can bring peace to your son, so that he will rest easy. I would also like to help."

Robert, choked with emotion, said, "We would appreciate anything you can do. Please. Help my boy."

Evelyn led them up a flight of stairs and down a hallway to a darkened bedroom. Heavy curtains were pulled across the window to keep the morning light from intruding. Mal McGeorge was lying in bed, bandages covered where his eyes should be. He was sleeping but not soundly, and he mumbled as he dozed.

Father Colton whispered to me and Mrs. McGeorge, "Please give me a few minutes to speak with Mal. I will come get you when he and I have had a chance to talk."

Evelyn looked at me questioningly. I nodded and we walked down the hallway a bit. Colton closed the door.

"You plan on hurting the people who did this, don't you?" Evelyn asked.

"I only use violence when I have no other choice. But I don't plan on being gentle. The people behind this are as evil as it gets, Mrs. McGeorge. I plan on putting a stop to them."

"Call me Evelyn, please."

She didn't say another word as we waited. About five minutes later, Colton opened the door and motioned for us to come in.

Mal was sitting up in bed, propped up by several pillows. The curtains were open and light flooded the bedroom. He had his face turned towards the light, even though he couldn't see it. A silver cross now hung from a chain around his neck and he was rubbing it, back and forth, with his thumb.

When his mom saw this, her hands flew to her mouth and then she rushed to her son's side. "Mal, where did you get that cross?"

He turned towards the sound of his mother's voice, opened up his arms, and hugged his mother. "The Father gave it to me, mom. He said I can keep it."

She looked at Father Colton and mouthed, "Thank you."

Father Colton smiled and said, "It's my pleasure. Victor, I think Mal is ready to talk to you now. Mrs. McGeorge, why don't you and I let them talk while I speak to you and your husband."

He led her out and pulled the door shut behind him. I sat on the edge of his bed

"Did Father Colton tell you why we were here?" I asked him.

Mal replied, "He did. He explained what happened to me and how I can keep it from happening again. He said there could be others who are going through what I went through." In a weak voice he continued, "How do you think I can I help?"

"When the demon took control of you, do you remember where you were? We're trying to get a line on who the first one was."

Mal thought for a minute. "I . . . I was at a coffee shop down near campus. It's a place where students go to hang out, chill, get some work done, ya know? Place called DJ's Perky Brew."

I nodded, then realized he couldn't see it and said, "I do know. So tell me about what happened?"

"Well, I was studying for a big statistics test I have coming up and I saw a girl I went to high school with at Ballard, Ruth Anne Gardner. I waved hello and she came to my table and sat down." He paused at the memory. "We talked for a bit and then she put her hand on top of mine."

He stopped again and I watched his Adam's apple race up and down his throat a few times. He rubbed the cross a bit faster.

"They can't hurt you anymore, Mal. You're O.K," I reassured him.

"I know, I know. It's just . . . when she put her hand on mine, I felt this charge shoot through my body and then he was just—there. In my head. I tried to fight back, but, man, he was like nothing I've ever even dreamed of."

"Did he tell you his name?"

"Yes. Chazaqiel. He kept telling me how blessed I was." He paused again. "Look at me, man. Do I look blessed to you?" He turned his face towards the window and the light.

"It might not seem like it, but yes, you are. You have a mom and dad who love you. You're still alive and the demon has left your body and if you listen to Father Colton, it can never return. Considering how it's turned out for at least one other person, you're ahead of the game."

He said, "I don't even want to know." After a moment he continued, "Can you stop them? The demons?"

"That's my job. Kicking ass and takin' names. Father Colton will be helping me. Along with a couple of others."

"Father Colton is cool. Good luck, Vic," his voice trailed off. "I think I'd like to be alone now, if you don't mind, and think about things."

"No worries, man. You heal up. It gets better from here on out."

He didn't reply, just kept facing the window. I made my way downstairs and found Evelyn and Robert speaking in the family room with Father Colton.

Evelyn said, "Rob and I have tried to get Mal to church, but he always blew us off. We made him go on Sundays when he was a kid, but when he started college he never went. Said he didn't really care much for God." She looked right at Colton, "But now. Maybe there's hope. He's not looked that peaceful since he came home. Thank you. Oh Lord Jesus, thank you."

Robert said, "And I thank you, too. But what I really want is for you to keep your word. And when you have, you let me know, you hear?"

"I do. I won't stop until I have. When I give my word, I keep it."

"Be sure you do." He shook both our hands and we left.

When we were back in the car, Colton asked, "Learn anything useful?"

I spun the wheel on my Ford and goosed it at the end of the street, sliding back and forth in the snow and slush as I made the turn.

"Yes. I did. I have a name. Let's get back to the mission so I can check it out. When you were with McGeorge, you weren't in the room with him very long. Did you have enough time to do your hocus pocus thing?"

Father Colton laughed. "No need for an exorcism. The demon left the body voluntarily. All I had to do was sever the connection so the demon won't be able to come back. Then it was simply a matter of convincing Mal of the existence of God. He was very open to my words of counsel."

"I bet. Do you think he's safe, then?"

"From demon possession? Yes. But he will have a long road back to being whole. What he experienced is rare and leaves a lasting impression. I gave him the name of a local priest he can talk to if he starts to doubt. But he won't. So what's next for us?"

"Time to go hunting."

CHAPTER 18

Winston kept his strides short as he made his third trip around the Louisville Water Company Reservoir in Crescent Hill. On most nice days the place was packed from dawn until dusk with walkers and runners, enjoying the serene view of the water and historic design of the gatehouse. The gatehouse was built in 1879, back when even water treatment plants were made to look beautiful, like a quaint old stone church. The path around the water basin was conveniently marked so people could keep track of their miles and there were plenty of benches to relax on after their exercise was over. It was an awesome place to work out.

But today, with the temperature barely reaching twenty degrees and several inches of newly fallen snow on the stone pathway, he was the only one brave enough to venture out to the reservoir. Back when he played for the Cardinals, his teammates would start to bitch and moan when the weather turned cold, but not Winston.

Being outside when every breath sent a shock to the system made him feel more alive than working out on a hot summer day ever could. And today, he needed the peace and quiet of a good workout. Despite the cold, he only wore sweats and a hooded shirt as he put in his miles.

Earlier he received a call from Vic telling him how it went with Mal McGeorge and what they learned from him. By all accounts Mal was a good guy and it bothered Winston more than he wanted to admit about what he'd done to the young man. Granted, if he hadn't kicked his ass, the Watcher would have continued to control McGeorge. But that was small consolation considering the physical damage Winston inflicted.

He let his anger at being followed get the better of him, he admitted to himself. He should have handled the confrontation differently. He shrugged off the thought and decided live and learn. There was nothing he could do to rewind time and try a different solution. So be it.

He picked up the pace of his jog. While on the backside, a man walked up the snow-covered steps of the reservoir, looked around and then stopped. He rested his hands on the black iron railing and gazed down into his reflection in the water. The man was dressed in jeans and a heavy winter coat, so it was doubtful he was there to work out. But many came to the reservoir for the view, so his presence was no big deal.

Winston rounded the corner and began to make his way down towards the man. The stranger turned around, leaned against the rail and put his hands in his pockets. He appeared to be a little over six feet tall and solid. Even from this distance, Winston could see the steam from his breath rising into the still morning air.

When he was almost even with him, their eyes met and Winston gave a short nod and the man nodded back. There was a slight smile on the man's lips, but not his eyes. Winston realized he'd seen the same dead fish stare before: on Mal McGeorge at the Mall.

If this thought was even a fraction of a second later, he'd be dead. But as soon as it registered, he was spinning in defense and the knife meant for his back struck a glancing blow, tearing his hoody and slicing open skin across his rib cage. Winston grunted with pain, but continued the spin, his foot slamming into the side of the man's head in a circle kick, knocking the stranger sideways.

The man recovered and began tossing the knife back and forth between his hands circling Winston. "A little different this time, huh boy? This time, I picked a body to match yours. I'm going to enjoy killing you."

"Chazy-Q, I figured it had to be you."

Winston could feel blood dripping down his side, but he pushed the thought and the pain away and concentrated on the Watcher.

"Your weak ass couldn't carry my piss bucket. You should've stayed buried in your hole because I'm going to send you out of this body, too. And when I do, you got nobody to return to. We done took care of that. You're going wandering. I know that section of the Bible and I bet your ass you do, too. No water, forever thirsty, never finding rest. You have so much to look forward to."

After what he'd done to Mal McGeorge, Winston didn't want to hurt this man, but looking at the hatred on the other guy's face, and the knife in his hand, he wasn't sure he could avoid it.

When Chazaqiel made his move, Winston had to admit, he was fast. Very fast. But not fast enough. The Watcher stabbed quick and low, aiming to gut Winston. Instead of dancing back and away from the attack, Winston pivoted and stepped forward, wrapping the man's knife arm with his and lifting up, while pressing downward on the man's shoulder in a quick motion, dislocating the arm from its socket.

The man dropped the knife and swung hard with the other hand, firing several quick jabs, pounding Winston's wound. Winston, grunting with pain, reversed his motion, hooked the man and tossed him off his hip, sending the man crashing into the fence. Winston stumbled and fell into the snow, but quickly regained his feet.

Winston kicked the knife into the water and held his side, the pain intensifying. He decided trying to stop the man without severely hurting or even killing him wasn't an option. Winston glanced around to see if anyone else was at the reservoir, but the weather had kept all sane people inside their homes. He was on his own.

The man bounced up, his right arm hanging to his side. Winston retreated a few steps.

"Looks like you're taking the same ass whipping you took at the mall. Here I thought you angels were supposed to be kind of tough bad ass types. You've lost your touch."

The man snarled and in one quick motion, slammed his shoulder into the side of the fence, popping it back into joint.

Damn, that had to hurt, Winston thought.

The man/fallen angel growled and then charged Winston again and over the next five minutes the two traded blows, turning the snow under foot into dirty bloody slush. As the fight continued with neither of them gaining an advantage, Winston had to admit to himself, he was losing.

The longer the fight continued, the more weak he felt duc the blood loss from the knife wound. The other man didn't seem nearly as tired as he should have been. Perhaps having a fallen angel deep inside you had its benefits after all. He knew that if he didn't end this now, it would be the end of him. While Winston had no doubts as to where he was going after his mortal coil gave up the ghost, he was in no rush to get there.

Backing up a step, he slipped on the slush and fell to one knee. Seeing an opening, the fallen angel once again charged. But the slip was a perfectly timed ruse and Winston was ready for him. Years and years of football training paid off. From the time he was a little kid he was taught in order to take a man down you first must get low, get under the other man's defenses, and then come up hard. And that's exactly what he did. As Chazaqiel began to come down with a hard right, Winston shot forward underneath the blow, one arm going under the other man's crotch, the other around his waist. He lifted him high off the ground and then flung him backwards onto the rod iron fence.

As the man ricocheted off the fence, with all the power he had left in him, Winston grabbed the man's head in both hands and slammed it straight down onto one of the iron spikes.

The man's eyes bulged and his mouth opened into a silent scream. Winston let go of him and allowed the man to slide to the ground. His eyes found Winston's and the anger he'd seen in them earlier was replaced with sheer horror.

Winston sagged to his knees, breathing as if he'd just run a marathon, and began to pray. The man reached out weakly and Winston took his hand. The man/fallen angel tried to speak, but blood poured from his mouth.

Winston continued to pray for the man's soul, if not the angel's, and a moment later felt the man's hand relax in his grip and he knew he was gone. Winston felt tears fill his own eyes, for the life stripped from this man, as he was nothing more than a victim. He had no idea if the man believed enough to make it to Heaven, and the doubt gnawed at him.

Winston reached into his pocket, slowly pulled out his cell phone and dialed 911. He told them he was attacked while running at the reservoir and to please send police and an ambulance. The dispatch operator was asking for more information when he ended the call and then dialed Victor. He gave Vic a quick rundown on what happened and then told him he would call him later and hung up before he, too, could ask a lot of questions.

He looked again at the lifeless man and the grim scene surrounding him. He knew what he'd done would forever damn the man he killed, but he had little choice. The security cameras around the reservoir, no doubt, recorded the whole attack.

He turned off his phone and, with a shaking hand, put it back into his pocket. He looked around the reservoir a final time before slipping into unconsciousness on the blood-stained snow.

CHAPTER 19

"Winston? Winston?" the phone disconnected right when Father Colton and I pulled back into the Derby Mission.

"Problems?" Father Colton asked.

I muttered a profanity under my breath and threw the phone onto the dash.

"Yeah. Seems we're down both a fallen angel and a bounty hunter." I relayed what Winston told me. "He said he's been knifed, but didn't think it was too bad. He called an ambulance. When they arrive, they'll probably take him to University Hospital, downtown. I better get down there."

Colton laid his hand on my arm and said, "Why don't you let me go. You won't be of any use sitting in a hospital. You need to stay focused on the investigation. That means tracking down Ruth Anne Gardner. Winston will understand."

He was right and I knew it. It still pissed me off. "We shoulda been more careful. We knew they were following him before and we should have expected they would again."

We got out of the car and made our way inside. "Stop beating yourself up over it. He's a big boy. Joshua told me about him and what a help he's been to you. Look, I'll go tell Joshua what happened and then head down to the hospital. You go do what you need to do."

I ran a hand through my hair, which I was sure was starting to thin out as often as I pulled it these days.

"Yeah, yeah. Thanks. You're right. Call me as soon as you know something about Winston, O.K?" I gave him my number and we parted ways.

I went to my room, turned on my computer and ran "Gardner, Ruth" through my databases and found one the right age enrolled at the University of Kentucky. At least her school choice was on the side of the righteous. I found a listing for a previous address over off Crossmore Lane, not too far from Ballard High School where both she and Mal McGeorge attended high school.

I wrote down the address and headed back out into the late morning cold. As I made my way to the east side of town, I plopped in an old Bonnie Raitt CD and mulled my options. I considered the connection between Mikey and the Watchers. If my body was chained in some deep dark valley and I found my way to the surface, then I'd want to find someone to set me free.

This made me wonder about Tommy Spenoza. He shipped out construction equipment to Mikey. To dig them out? Possibly. The Watchers could end up being a backdoor way of finding Mikey if they were working together. The fact my brother was trying to track down things like the box with the parchment with the incantations to set them free, then you'd think they were in cahoots. There was always the outside chance Mikey wanted the stuff to try and keep them from not getting free, but who was I kidding?

Mikey and his slave master, Lucifer, wanted chaos in the world and releasing a group of two hundred pissed off fallen angels would certainly be enough to put the world into a tailspin. And I needed to make sure it didn't happen.

My mind drifted to Samantha and what our future would be like. But again, I was kidding myself. What type of future could the two of us have? As long as we were together, she was a target, like Winston. As the Hand of God, I'd never be able to reach old age with grandkids bouncing on my knee. At least I couldn't see how that would ever take place. Dominic Montoya, the Hand before me, died in his mid-thirties—early forties, at the latest—and he was one of the best contract killers on the planet. All his skills were not enough to keep him alive to become an AARP member.

Which begged the question: what did I want from Samantha? I loved her, wanted a future with her, all of that was certain. That I would never have one with her? That was nearly as certain, too. With an effort I snapped out of my minor funk. Time to concentrate on what was going on in the here-and-now, I reminded myself, and let the future take care of itself.

Gardner's home was a one-story brick ranch with an older model Toyota Camry in a driveway still covered in snow. There were no tracks in or out. So, whoever owned the car hadn't left in the last day or two.

I parked in the street and made my way to the door, ringing the bell and rubbing my hands to keep them warm. I hated to wear gloves because, in my line work, you never knew when you needed to pull your gun out and shoot the hell out of something. With my luck? The fabric would catch in the trigger and I'd never get a shot off.

I was about to ring the bell again when I felt the icy cold of a snowball explode on the side of my head. I turned towards the direction of the attack with my hand instinctively going under my coat to the butt of my gun, only to see a kid at the corner of the house laughing his ass off.

"Oh, man, I got you good." The kid was about twelve years old, dressed in snow pants, a coat, and a double-eared green knit cap with black snowflakes all over it which he pulled down tightly over his ears. In his other hand he held another snowball.

"Don't you dare throw that thing at me." I warned him.

And then he did. The kid had a pretty good arm and the snowball was heading straight for my face. But in one motion I snagged the snowball out of the air and hurled it back in his direction, hitting him in the right leg.

"Ow! Not fair!" he yelled, and started making a couple more of them. I did the same, scooping up snow from the porch. I spent the next couple of minutes reliving my childhood with the kid, trading shots back and forth. Most of them missed wildly, but it was fun.

Then I realized the front door was open. On the other side of a storm door an attractive woman somewhere north of fifty, dressed in pajamas and a robe, stood there watching me.

I raised my hand at the kid and said, "Enough, enough. Adult alert." I nodded towards the front door and the kid waved and took off again for the backyard.

I brushed snow and ice from my hair and coat and asked, "Mrs. Gardner?"

"Ex-Mrs. Gardner. It's Huffman now. What do you need?"

"My name is Victor McCain and I wanted to talk to you about Ruth Anne."

A hand went to the top of her robe and squeezed it shut.

"Have you found her? Do you work with Mr. Clifford?"

"May I come in? It's bloody cold out here."

She unlocked the door and opened it, standing back to let me in. "I'm sorry. Come in, please."

The air carried the scent of fresh baked cookies. She lead me into the living room where I took a seat on a sectional couch and she opted for a wingback chair across from me.

"No, ma'am. I don't know Mr. Clifford. Who is he?" I said.

"A private investigator I hired to find Ruth Anne. Why are you looking for my daughter?" She rested her hands in her lap, and kept rubbing one thumb with the other.

"One of her friends was attacked and I'm trying to find the ones responsible. I think she may know the people involved. So I was hoping to ask her some questions. Do you know where she is?"

"Not exactly. She dropped out of school and took off. I know she really didn't like college, but this isn't like her." She paused and then asked, "I'm sorry. But do you have some form of ID?"

I got my billfold out of my back pocket and took out my bounty hunters license. She studied it for a moment and then handed it back.

"What's the name of her friend?"

"Mal McGeorge. They went to school together at Ballard."

"I saw the report about what happened to him on the news. Can you wait here a minute?"

I said I would and she left the room. She returned a short time later with a sheaf of papers in her hand.

"Ruth Anne and I always talk every couple of days. When several days passed and she didn't answer, I called and talked to some of her friends at U.K. and they said they hadn't seen her for days. So I filed a missing persons report. The police in Lexington looked into it and had a video of her taking money out of her checking account at an ATM machine. The fact she looked normal, not under any duress, suggested to them she'd just taken off."

"Has she ever done this before?"

"Never. She's not the world's greatest student, but she gets by. That's why I hired the private investigator." She handed me the papers. "Looks like she's not the only one. A number of college kids in Lexington and here in Louisville have all gone missing. It's like they all dropped off the face of the Earth."

I started reading the report.

"How many of them did she know?"

"At least ten. But the news isn't all good. Did you hear about that bombing down in Florida?"

I kept a neutral look on my face and said, "Yeah. I've heard a bit about it. Why?"

"The guy killed by the alligator, the one that ended up in the canal? His name was John Gabriel. He was one of the missing students. Mr. Clifford says his parents had no idea where he'd gone, and then he turns up dead. It's horrible."

"Aw, man. That's really unfortunate. Did they ever learn why he was down there?"

"I don't know. But I've contacted the parents of several of the other missing kids and they're like me. All good kids who've dropped out of school and out of sight and we have no idea why." Her voice cracked and she pulled a tissue from a pocket and began dabbing her eyes.

I knew why, lady. They were infected with the seed of a fallen angel. And ten of them. When I learned about Mal McGeorge and Ruth Anne, I had hoped they would be the only ones, but I should have known better.

"Where does Clifford think Ruth Anne is now?"

"That's just it. He tracked her movements to Hawaii. He flew out there a few days ago and I haven't heard from him since. Neither has his office. All of our calls go straight to voicemail. Mr. Clifford was worried they were mixed up with some kind of cult. Do you think she's in danger?"

Holy crap. Hawaii? I could see the helplessness and fear on her face and I wish I could have put her mind at ease, but I couldn't. Because now I was worried. Kurt was in Hawaii. They'd sent someone after Winston, put one with Samantha, no doubt waiting on me. And one in Hawaii? That couldn't be a coincidence.

"I don't know. But I intend to find out. Do you have a way to make me a copy of this report?"

"Yes. I'll be right back."

She gathered up the papers and left the room. As soon as she was gone I got out my phone and called Kurt. It rang several times and then went to voicemail. I left a message for him to call me. Right away.

Kurt wanted to spend his time lying low in paradise. Now it seemed Hell had come calling.

CHAPTER 20

Kurt sat in the dining room of the hotel, moping. Ruth Anne was still mad at him and refused to see him for the last couple of days. She said she would call him if and when she wanted to see him and he would just have to wait by the phone. And so far his phone refused to ring.

He was on his second helping of pancakes when the call from Victor came in, but he let it go to voicemail. He didn't have the heart to talk to him. All he wanted to do was drown his sorrows in blueberry pancakes and maple syrup. The bad guys of the world would just have to wait.

He was debating on whether to add an order of biscuits and gravy, knowing he would have to run a lot of extra miles just to break even with the calorie count, when Ruth Anne scooted onto the seat next to him in the booth, bumping his hip so he would scoot over and give her room.

"Miss me?"

She wore a blue sundress with her hair pulled back into a ponytail and it was as if the sun had returned from a month's absence.

"Miss you? You have no idea how much. I mean, I called you every day and you just ignored me. I figured you'd met someone else, or gone back to the mainland or, hell, I don't know what. But miss you? It was like someone had removed all the music from the world. Like all my food lost its taste. Like—"

"Uh, Kurt?" she interrupted him.

He stopped. "Yes?" He looked into her eyes and for a moment he had the weirdest sensation of watching stars fall, but it passed. "Yes, Ruth Anne?"

"Shut up, will you? I want you to take me out on the island shopping. Then we're going back to my place and I'm going to fix you dinner. And you are not, I repeat, *not* allowed to leave. You're spending the night. Can you handle that?"

He swallowed hard a couple of times and realized he could. It was time to make the final jump into a real relationship. He got his phone out saying, "Let me just make a couple of phone calls. A buddy just called and I should—"

Once again she interrupted him as she snatched his phone out of his hand and dropped it into her purse.

"Not a chance, Big Boy. I can't have you called into an emergency software meeting, now can I?" She smiled coyly.

"But it will only take a minute, I'm sure."

She began to pout. "Kurt, it's like this. Today you're either mine, or you're not. If you want your phone back, then fine. You can have it. But I'm out of here. Today I want you to disconnect from everything else. Today is all about us. Can you do that? For me?"

Kurt thought about it and decided she was right. He did need a day all to himself. Free from the Church of the Light Reclaimed. Free from thoughts of Satan. Free from Vic, Winston and free from all the stress their life had become. Free to let his hair down and have fun.

"I can. Sounds great. You know what? Keep the phone the rest of the day. I don't need it. Where do you want to go first?"

"I think we'll wander a bit and see what we come up with. I promise you, Kurt. This will be a night you will never forget."

****

Huffman came back and handed me a copy of the P.I.'s report. I took a card from my inside coat pocket and handed it to her.

"Here's my card. My cell number is listed at the bottom. If you hear from Ruth Anne, I'd appreciate you calling to let me know. If I find out anything, I'll do the same."

We both stood. She offered her hand and said, "Mr. McCain, I don't know how to thank you or pay you for that matter. All the extra cash I had to my name I spent on Mr. Clifford."

"It's Victor. And don't worry about it. I'm doing this pro bono. Something's going on and I plan on getting to the bottom of it." Like banishing several fallen angels to the abyss, but somehow I got the feeling honesty would not be the best policy right at this very moment.

"Please, it's Rose Mary. Is it alright if I have Mr. Clifford contact you? When I hear back from him?"

"By all means, please do. Was that your son I was trading shots with outside?"

She smiled and said, "Yes. His name is Timothy. He and Ruth Anne are almost ten years apart. I haven't told him what's going on with his sister because I know he'd worry. He should enjoy just being a kid." The smile vanished. "Victor, please do what you can to bring my baby back to me."

I assured her I would and headed back to the car. I called Kurt again, but with the same results. I began to get a bad feeling about what was going on way out west, but couldn't do much about it at the moment.

Thanks to the work of the private dick, I had a lot more information to digest. Since it was lunchtime I decided to drop by Molly Malone's, an Irish pub, for a bite to eat. I parked across the street in the PNC parking lot and walked to the corner. When the pedestrian crosswalk sign turned in my favor, a black limousine pulled up next to me and a burly bald-headed man in a black suit and tie got out of the front seat, went to the back door and opened it.

"Get in," he said.

"I bet the chicks really dig that type of intro, Big Guy, but you're not my type. It doesn't really do anything for me."

He pulled back the edge of his suit jacket so I could see the gun he was wearing in a shoulder holster. I laughed and pulled back my coat.

"Mine's bigger, and in this case, size really does matter."

I think he was getting ready to actually find out the truth of that statement when a man leaned across the back seat and said, "That's alright, Brad. Mr. McCain, all I really want to do is talk. You have my word. Brad is ex-Marine and thinks in a very straightforward manner."

I glanced into the car. "I'll be damned, Congressman Tyler. What a surprise. As far as your handyman goes, what else would you expect from a jarhead? Tell me, what brings you to the great Commonwealth of Kentucky?"

My tone was light, but my senses were on high alert. I was standing in a very exposed position talking with one of the most dangerous men on the planet, Satan's Pope, no less. The chances of me getting into a car with this man were about the same as me being named a Victoria's Secret lingerie model.

"I think you know why I'm here. Please, get in. You have my word you won't be harmed."

Cyrus Tyler looked great for a sixty year old. His face showed nary a wrinkle and his hair, while going gray on the sides, was still a dark brown. Granted, his smile would look better on a great white shark, with about as much warmth, but his voice held the timber of a professional baritone.

His brand of politics would make the most extreme Tea Party candidates look timid: a far right-wing nut job who thinks homosexuals should be shot, Liberals should be jailed, and anyone who doesn't think the way he does should buy a ticket on the next boat back to wherever in the hell they came from. As the current majority leader in the House of Representatives, many think he's in line to be the next Speaker of the House.

I looked over to Molly Malone's inviting front door and said, "I tell you what. I was just about to have lunch across the street. Why don't you find a place to park your chariot and join me. Leave the jarhead at the door, though. He might scare any women and children inside."

Brad flexed his neck muscles, but like the good pit bull he was, stayed in place until his master told him to move.

I didn't wait for an answer but crossed the street, using my well-developed peripheral vision to try and watch every place at once. I pushed my way inside and breathed a bit easier when the door closed behind me with no one putting a bullet in my brain. Yay me.

I moved to my regular table where I could watch all the entrances at once and waited. After a few minutes Congressman Tyler strode into the restaurant as if he owned the place walked over to my table and joined me. The former marine stayed outside. I wondered if he was house-broken.

A waitress walked up to us with two menus and handed one to Tyler and offered me one, but I waved it off. She stared at the congressman.

"You look familiar. Are you from around here?" she said.

He smiled at her and replied, "I get that a lot, but no, I'm not from around here. I'm here on business and decided to stop and have lunch with a friend."

I bristled inside at the thought of this man calling me "friend," but kept a calm exterior.

"Janice, I'll have the usual, please." She nodded and made a note on her pad.

Tyler handed the menu back to her and responded, "I'll have whatever he's having. Thank you."

She smiled and went to place the order. If he was curious as to what the "usual" was he didn't ask.

"So, where is she?" he said.

I knew who "she" was but said, "I'm sorry, could you be a bit more specific?" He gave me his best steely glare which I'm sure intimidated most of the people he dealt with on a daily basis. But I'm not one of those folks. I stared back, trying not to blink. After a minute or two, I couldn't help it and blinked anyway. Damn. I hated losing the staring game in grade school. Still did. Before one of us could break the silence, Janice stopped back by the table, and dropped off a couple of Guinness Dark Lagers.

He waited for her to leave again and finally said, "Let me explain something to you, Victor. I love my daughter very much and when someone steals her from me, it upsets me. Greatly."

I nodded. "I can only imagine. But she's, what, twenty-four years old? I believe she's old enough to make her own decisions. And being kidnapped and stuck in whatever basement daddy wants to hide her in is not what she wants." I didn't mention she hadn't exactly been thrilled with me either the night of her rescue, but why bring up the bad stuff.

Sitting and talking to the man was beyond surreal. If Samantha and I ever tied the knot, he would be my father-in-law. A father-in-law from Hell, almost literally. I honestly believed if I lived long enough, at one point, I would be asked to hunt down this man and drive a dagger through his heart. Love makes for strange family arrangements.

"Let me explain the situation to you more clearly. When my wife died, many years ago, the only thing left in my life was Samantha."

I laughed. "Well, that and a deep hatred for God. After all, you did sell your soul to the guy who finished a distant second."

He ignored my barb. "I kept her close, perhaps too close. She was too involved in what I was doing with the Church. I thought she would feel the same way I did, but I guess not. When she ran a few months back, I panicked. I knew there were people who would hurt her, just to get at me, and I did everything I could to find her and bring her back home, where she'd be safe."

I pursed my lips. "She ran because she discovered her father was one mean son of a bitch who planned to murder thousands of innocent children. And you wanted to protect her? So let me get this straight. To protect her, you sent a vampire to hunt her down? Eamon? That's your idea of safe?"

"Eamon had a way of getting things done. He would do what it took to find her, no matter the cost. I was desperate. So yes, I asked him to help find my daughter. She'd taken something that didn't belong to her and there were some of my associates who wanted her dead. I would not allow it."

"You sure have a strange way of showing fatherly love, you know that?" We took another break as Janice brought over two bowls of shepherd's pie. The bowls were piping hot with steam curling into the air and the smell beyond good.

"Hot shepherd's pie on a cold day is good for the soul," I said. "And Lord knows yours needs all the help it can get."

Tyler continued to ignore my barbs and took up the previous conversation.

"And you think she will be safe with you? You're a dead man walking and I want my daughter nowhere near you when this blows up in your face. As hard as it may be for you to believe, I do love my daughter. If she stays with you, she will die."

I picked up a spoon, lifted a large helping of the stew to my lips, blew on it and began to eat my lunch. Tyler did the same and for a moment we ate without saying anything. I was stalling because I knew he was only saying the same thing which kept me up at night. In one nightmare, Samantha and I were lying in bed, asleep, when I awoke to find Eamon sitting on the edge of the bed, blood dripping from the vampire's mouth from where he ripped out a side of Samantha's neck. When I woke up the next morning, the sheets were wet from sweating through them during the night. The fact her father was an evil bastard didn't make him wrong on this score. I picked up my napkin and wiped my lips.

"Perhaps you're right. But the choice is not yours or mine. It's hers. And unlike you, I'm letting her decide on her own. Who knows? In the end she may tell both of us to kiss her ass and disappear."

Tyler downed a large portion of his Guinness and then set the glass on the table, staring into what remained of the dark liquid as if it held the answers to all of life's problems. He nodded to himself and then looked me in the eyes.

"One day, I'm going to kill you and I won't make it quick. It will be as long and painful as I can. I will make you scream for mercy which will never come, and you will realize the same thing I did a long time ago and that is God doesn't give a damn about you, me or anyone else. But until such time, please make sure she's safe. I couldn't bear it if she was to die. She is so much like her mother. Headstrong, beautiful, and in the end, I fear she will be the death of me. She means everything to me."

No, I thought, I'll be the death of you. But I could tell he meant what he was saying about Samantha. He really did love his daughter.

"You have my word, I'd give my life to save hers. As long as I draw breath, I will keep her safe."

He stood, tossing his napkin down, and offered me his hand.

"Thank you. I know you will." I looked at the hand for a long moment, but then took it. He reached into the breast pocket of his coat for his wallet and took out a fifty and dropped it on the table. Without another word he turned and walked out the door.

When Janice came back I ordered another Guinness and pulled the report out of my coat pocket. I placed it on the table and took a few more sips of my beer, thinking about Samantha, her father, and how we were all really royally screwed. In the end, either her father or I would die. Maybe even both of us. And if we weren't careful, Samantha could end up being collateral damage.

CHAPTER 21

Kurt was having the best day of his life. After breakfast, he and Ruth Anne spent the first part of the day shopping. They picked up a few knick knacks, then stopped by a grocery store to buy steaks and vegetables for the two of them to grill later that night. Dropping the food off at her place, they headed back to the beach. For the first time in his life, Kurt spent the day with a beautiful woman and was happy.

True, he did have some apprehension when it came to how the evening would end, but he put it out of his mind and worked on trying to enjoy the moment. He never even needed the Benadryl in his pocket. He got a big kick out of other people watching the two of them strolling down the beach, hand in hand.

They made one fine looking couple. Kurt spent most of the time daydreaming about what life would be like if they got married. Surely they would have the best looking children on the planet. Well, if they looked like their mother. And if they got his brains, then the sky would be the limit for any offspring. Mom's good lucks and dad's brains? There would be no stopping them.

When it came time for dinner, they went back to her place. He got the grill started and threw on the steaks while she prepared the veggies. They'd picked up a Shafer Vineyards red wine to go with the steaks. It cost him sixty dollars and he nearly choked over the price, since his idea of an expensive drink was buying a sixty-four ounce bottle of Diet Dr. Pepper, but she insisted so he plopped down his card. Nothing but the best for his girl.

They ate dinner on the patio, with the mid-eighties high for the day having cooled into the mid-seventies. A soft breeze blew in from the ocean. Kurt uncorked the wine, poured two glasses, and raised his in a toast.

"To the two of us. May every day forward be as much fun as today."

She clinked her glass to his and they both drank. He decided it was time to ask the questions he'd been avoiding all day.

"So, where have you been the last couple of days? I was beginning to think you headed back home."

She took a long sip of wine and replied, "I was here, but I had my own business to take care of. There were things going on back home that needed tending to."

Kurt's frowned. "What type of . . . things?" He cut up his steak and took a bite. It was grilled to perfection but could have used a little steak sauce. She slapped him with a spoon when he suggested it earlier saying it would ruin a good steak.

"Well, you know, school-type stuff. When you drop out of college and take off for Hawaii, sometimes mothers aren't happy about it. So I had to spend time filling out forms for school, so I'd have incompletes, then move some money around. That type of thing."

"And that took three days?" He found it hard to believe there was that much paperwork in the world.

She raised an eyebrow and gave him a wicked smile. "No. It didn't. I was also punishing you for leaving me alone the other night. Do you realize how long it took me to get off that night all by myself?"

Kurt choked and nearly snorted wine out of his nose when she said this, which made her giggle.

"Sorry. It was just, well, I had that call, you know, and I didn't know you wanted me to stay, I mean, that night, so I wasn't prepared for it and, well, I had to work, and—"

She kicked him hard under the table. "Will you stop it? I was only teaching you a lesson. I'm not the kind of girl you leave hanging. So tonight you're mine. All mine."

They made small talk the rest of dinner and then carried their plates inside, washed them off and put them in the dishwasher. Kurt felt downright domesticated as he and Ruth Anne worked side-by-side. When the kitchen chores were finished, he walked into the TV area, plopped on the couch and turned on the big screen.

She walked over, took the remote from his hand and turned it off. "Oh no you don't. No TV. Get your ass in the bedroom, mister."

Kurt smiled weakly, got up and followed her like a submissive puppy down the hall to her bedroom. His palms began to sweat and he brushed them against his shorts to dry them off. He contemplated taking the Benadryl, but the medication sometimes made him sleepy and he thought that would be a very bad thing to happen.

"I'm going to go into the bathroom and freshen up," she said. "Take your shirt off and make yourself comfortable." She gave him a long, slow kiss and then turned and disappeared into the bathroom, closing the door behind her.

Kurt gulped a couple of times and did as she asked, taking his shirt off and sitting on the bed for a bit, then lying down. He tried to look natural, crossing and uncrossing his legs, and then his arms. Then he flopped to his side and watched the bathroom door. Then he sat up again. He finally laid back down with his head on the pillow and stared up at the ceiling and silently repeated all the self-help techniques he learned.

He licked his lips and thought about what he was about to do. He was still a virgin, but knew enough to know how things worked. He'd heard his guy friends talk about how to please a woman often enough. He was in the middle of planning what he should do first when the bathroom door opened and all thoughts flew from his mind.

Wearing a light blue teddy which showed off her curvy tanned body to full effect, she sauntered over to the bed and climbed slowly over to him. She gave him another kiss, and ran her hand down his bare chest and to his crotch.

He nearly jumped out of the bed at her touch and he tried to sit up, but she pushed him forcefully back down and then straddled him. She kissed him all over his chest, then up to his neck. At first, he ran his hands stiffly up and down her back, occasionally patting her shoulder. But when she reached his neck, thousands of years of evolutionary genetics took over and his body began to respond.

She kissed him and slid her hands up his arms, stretching them above his head, while her hair fell across his face. This must be what Heaven was like, Kurt thought. Her fingers entwined with his as she raised them to rest against the headboard made of metal and painted white in the shape of tree limbs covered in ivy.

She took his right hand, then the left, and wrapped his fingers around the bars of the headboard, and kissed her way up his arms, pressing her breasts against his face. He closed his eyes and enjoyed her kisses. Returning the favor, he started to kiss her chest when he felt something cold around one wrist and then the other, and heard a loud snick when the handcuffs closed.

His eyes flew open with surprise as she sat up, still straddling him. "There. Now you can't leave."

He licked his lips a couple of times and said, "Ruth Anne. I'm not going to leave. Honest. Let me out of these things."

"Not a chance. I've been trying to get you into my bed and now that I have you, I'm not taking any chances." She smiled down at him, but Kurt felt more like a trapped rabbit.

All of a sudden he heard a noise coming from her purse on the nightstand and realized it was his phone with the Vic McCain ringtone. He used the song *Bounty Hunter* by Molly Hatchet.

Ruth Anne raised an eyebrow, reached into her bag and pulled out his phone. She slid the bar to answer it, put it on speaker and placed the phone next to his head. He could hear Victor asking, "Kurt? Where've you been?

I've been trying to reach you all day."

Kurt swallowed a couple more times before answering. "Uh. Hey Vic, I'm kind of tied up at the moment. Can I call you back later?"

"What the hell's going on? You pick up a couple more blow up dolls?"

"Very funny. Actually, I've been on a date, if you must know. I've been busy. I do have a life, you know."

"Kurt, your date. What's her name? It's not Ruth Anne, is it? Kurt, you could be in danger—"

Ruth Anne hit the end button and tossed the phone onto the nightstand.

"Well, he got that part right. Guess the jig is up, eh Kurt?"

Panicking, Kurt pulled hard on the cuffs, but they weren't budging and neither was the headboard.

Ruth Anne rolled off of him and the bed, and stood up. She walked over to a chair in the corner, picked up a T-shirt and pulled it on.

"Look, Ruth Anne. I thought you and I were a couple? You don't have to do this. Let me go. Please? I promise I won't take off."

She laughed, "Fat chance." Raising her voice, she shouted, "You might as well come out. The Spear knows about me."

Kurt heard a door open down the hall and footsteps approaching the bedroom. When the man entered the room, Kurt closed his eyes and groaned. He tried to keep his heart from galloping out of his chest, but it was no use. He knew he was in really big trouble.

"Long time no see, Kurt. How the hell are you?" Michael Christopher "Mikey" McCain said.

Kurt knew how he was: dead.

CHAPTER 22

I stared at the phone and thought about what Kurt hanging up on me meant. I could tell our conversation was on speaker and Kurt wasn't known for using that function on his phone, paranoid about other people listening in on his business. My guess was someone was listening in on our conversation.

I sat back and rested my head against the hospital waiting room wall. Father Colton called earlier to tell me Winston would soon be released. I drove down to University Hospital to relieve him so he could get some rest and to wait for Winston.

Now I needed to add Kurt to my worry list. With a fallen angel in the big islands, and Kurt with a girlfriend, I couldn't help but feel he was in some serious trouble. I promised to protect him from the dangerous side of my work. It seemed I wasn't able to keep my end of the deal.

I didn't have long to wait before Winston walked out to join me. He looked good, if a little stiff. We shook hands and I led the way back to the Ford. Once we were both inside I turned the heat on full blast.

"Let's hear it," I said as we took off. "Tell me, how did a wimpy fallen angel get the drop on you?"

He spent a few minutes telling me exactly what happened at the reservoir, up until the time he passed out.

"I woke up in the recovery room with two Louisville Metro detectives wanting to talk to me. I told them what I told you, minus the whole fallen angel part. They'd already looked at the security camera footage from the main building camera. And since it went down pretty much as I indicated, there wasn't much they could shake out of me. They kept asking why the guy attacked me, that I must have known him. Were we involved in a drug deal gone bad, regular old shit."

"Did they know the guy's name by the time they came to see you?"

I kept an eye on the rear view mirror as I drove a random path through the early morning Louisville streets. If someone was following us, they were going to have a very difficult time doing it. We were virtually the only car on the road at this time of night following a heavy snow.

He shook his head in the affirmative. "Linville Pierce. Worked out at the G.E. plant, but hadn't shown up for work in a few days. Wife hadn't seen him either. Wouldn't answer his cell phone, completely dropped off the grid. Guess he's been hunting me."

"Yep. Damn. Sure does suck for him, doesn't it?"

"Man, in the worst way. The dude had two kids. And now he'll be remembered for trying to murder a man, and for no reason. Cops said they'll look into it more, but I think I'm in the clear. Video don't lie." After a brief pause, he said, "Vic, I did everything I could not to hurt the guy, but I didn't have a choice. I guess the knife wound was worse than I thought. It was either him or me." Winston just stared out the window at the passing street lights, shaking his head back and forth. "This stuff is really messed up."

"It is and it was you or him," I agreed. "You did what you had to do. Believe me, I feel the same way. That guy in Florida would have drowned my ass if I hadn't taken him on. True, the gator killed him before I could, but I promise you, if the gator didn't? I would have. And there's more." I told him what I learned about Ruth Anne Gardner and the other missing college students and how Ruth Anne was reportedly in Hawaii. "I'm betting Ruth Anne is the date and Kurt's in real trouble."

"Well, at least there's now only one hundred and ninety-eight of them left. That settles it then. Let's go by my place so I can pack a few things. Then you can drop me off at the airport."

"Like hell. You're in no shape to fly to Hawaii."

I watched Winston as he tried to get comfortable in the passenger seat, an occasional grimace crossing his features. I got the feeling the knife wound bothered him a lot more than he was letting on to me.

"Shut up, old man. I'm fine. At least fine enough. Let's face it, you can't go. There's too much going on here. Besides, I'll have the plane ride to the coast and then across the ocean to rest up. By the time I get there I'll be O.K. We can't leave Kurt hanging out there by himself. You and I both know he's got no chance against a mugger with a banana in his pocket, let alone a Watcher."

Despite how frustrating the truth was, he was right. I couldn't leave here. And Kurt would definitely need help. Kurt was a geek who wouldn't even watch a scary movie without the lights on and the doors locked.

"Besides," Winston continued, "at least this time I know what I'm up against. They won't catch me again like they did today. Payback's a bitch. If I can track them down and subdue her, then your new buddy should be able to find me a guy on the islands who can perform an exorcism."

"O.K. I'll ask him to be ready. You won't be able to take any of our toys with you, so you will have to improvise. You sure you feel up to it?"

"Damn straight. And don't worry about me. I'll work it out. The hard part will be finding them."

"Thanks, Winston. I appreciate all you've done to help me. I mean it." I stuck out my fist and he bumped it. It paid to have friends who are bad asses in their own right. I finally made it to his place and kept watch outside while he got a few things, then dropped him off at Louisville International Airport in order to catch an American Airlines flight to Hawaii. I handed him a printout of Ruth Anne's driver's license, so he would have an idea of who he was looking for.

After he waved goodbye and entered the airport, I put the car in drive and once again made a random path through the city. But I didn't go back to the Derby Mission. Instead I ended up at the Red Roof Inn over off of Hurstbourne Lane. I wanted to keep off the bad guy radar for another day, in case they were watching the mission. Studying the report I narrowed down another possible fallen angel possession, who, if his credit card charges were any indication, was still in Louisville. I planned to drive out to his parent's place in the morning, with Father Colton in tow, to see if I could track him down.

I had a pretty good idea who pointed the Watchers in our direction. I knew Mikey had to be behind this. The sooner I snapped his ever lovin' neck, the better the planet, as a whole, would be.

****

I managed to get a few hours sleep, and not much more, before my phone alarm went off with the sunrise. I took a quick hot shower, grabbed some coffee and a couple of Egg McMuffins at McD's, and then made my way into town to pick up Father Colton.

He got into the car, tossing a bag into the backseat, and I handed him a copy of Clifford's report, opened to the fourth page. "There's a photo of the guy we're looking for. His name is Charlie Sutton. He's a student at the Speed School at the University of Louisville. He went missing about the same time Mal McGeorge did. I called out and spoke to his parents yesterday afternoon, but they were reluctant to talk to me over the phone. I got the impression they might know where their son was hiding out, so I thought we might as well pay them a visit in person and impress upon them the gravity of the situation. At least with the two of us we can do good-cop-bad-cop."

"Do I get to be the bad cop?" Colton asked with a grin.

"Do I get to wear a priest's smock?" I responded back. "No? Then no, you get to be the good guy."

The Sutton's lived on a family farm in southwest Oldham County and it took us the better part of a half hour to get there. After checking several mail boxes we found the right one next to a long gravel road leading between a grove of trees.

Father Colton pointed to the sky and asked, “Are those vultures?” I looked up to where he pointed and there were dozens and dozens of them flying in a huge circle off to our right.

“Yes, but we call them buzzards. Same difference.” I couldn’t recall ever seeing that many in the air at once and it bothered me. They also usually waited until the day warmed up to take to the skies. But on this winter day, it was as warm as it was going to get and perhaps they somehow knew it.

We passed several tobacco barns on the way to the main house and pulled up in front of a two-story clapboard house in need of a paint job. There were a couple of trucks parked under a carport. As we got out of the car, I noticed the buzzards were flying over a part of the farm a short walk away.

The driveway was shoveled clear of snow. We went up to the front door and I knocked loudly. No answer. I peered through the front window and could see the living room and into the kitchen. A couple of straight-backed chairs were toppled onto their sides and dishes were scattered across the floor. I reached under my coat and pulled my gun out of its holster.

“Father, here’s what you’re going to do. You’re going to go back to the car.” I handed him my keys. “I want you to start it up, turn it around and point it in the other direction. I’m going to take a look around. If I find something you need to see, I’ll either come get you or call you on your cell. But if you don’t see or hear from me in fifteen minutes I want you to get the hell out of here and call the cops. You got it?”

“Wouldn’t it be better if I watched your back?” He looked around the farm, trying to see every place at once.

I reached into my weapons bag, pulled out another 9 millimeter and handed it to him.

“What am I supposed to do with this?” He held onto the grip with two fingers, dangling the gun.

“If you’re going to watch my back, you’re going to shoot whatever moves when I tell you to. Can you do that?”

He handed the gun back to me and replied, “I can’t. I’m sorry. But I can do other things.”

“Thanks, but no. I don’t want to have to watch out for you as well.” He started to get all pissed off when I raised my hand and said, “Look. I’m not challenging your manhood. But I do this for a living. You don’t. And I need you alive if we have a demon to kick out of its new home. You copy?”

He blew air out and took another look around. “Copy. I understand, I’m sorry.”

“Don’t sweat it. Now get moving. I’m going to check out the house.”

Father Colton stomped off in the snow to the car and did as I asked, getting the car started and turned it around. I went to the front door and tried the knob. It was unlocked and I opened the door slowly, pushing it open wide with my foot and then I ducked my head in for a quick look.

When no one attacked, I stepped inside and stood listening, my back pressed against the wall. The house felt empty, no sound of movement, no running water. A house with someone inside gives off a different vibe. I kept my gun out and ready as I eased into the kitchen. The place was a wreck, with broken dishes and the morning breakfast spilled over onto the floor. The table, made of white Formica, reminded me of my parents kitchen table when I was growing up. Blood, however, covered it and someone had used a finger to write a message:

I'M WAITING!

I knew it was a finger because it was still on the table, positioned above a smeared dot, making the tall portion of a macabre exclamation point. But there was no body, just a finger.

I quickly cleared the rest of the house, both upstairs and down, but found nothing. I stepped back outside and to the car, lifted the rear door, grabbed my weapons bag, and slung it over my shoulder. I slammed the car door shut, then walked up to the driver's side window. Colton rolled it down and asked, "Nothing?"

"No bodies. But there's a lot of blood in the kitchen. And a message that I think is for me. Makes me wonder what the buzzards are after. I want you to pull down the drive a bit and away from the house in case someone is hiding in one of the outbuildings or in a field watching us. Keep your eyes and ears open."

He nodded, closed the window and pulled off. On the other side of the carport a trail led off towards the woods. I could make out the occasional footprint and a distinct trail of someone dragging something behind them. The footprint was good-sized with the tread of a work boot. I followed the trail across a field towards the buzzards who were just beyond a grove of trees.

The blood and the finger left little doubt that at least one of the Suttons, if not both, were dead. And I had a good idea who the killer was. I bet the prodigal son returned, carrying extra baggage rolling around inside his mind.

I ducked under the branches of several pine trees and stepped up to the edge of a clearing and stopped to take in Hell on earth. The clearing was about fifty yards wide and spread around the entire area were body parts. The vultures on the ground closely numbered the hundred in the air. Featherless, black heads bobbed up and down as they pulled and ripped the flesh off of bone. More than a dozen bodies were scattered around the clearing.

And sitting in the middle of the nightmare feast was Charlie Sutton. He sat on a plastic tarp soaked in blood, sitting in a yoga meditation position. He wore black jeans and a blue hoody with the hood pulled up and over his head, shadowing his eyes. I could see tan leather where the blood didn't cover his boots. On the ground in front of him rested a very large machete. The Butcher of Crestwood. I once again had that sense of wrongness I experienced when I was up-close-and-personal to Studley down in Florida. Guess these guys gave off weird vibes.

"Well, Charlie. Looks like you've been busy. Get bored with school?"

He smiled. "We both know you're not talking to Charlie, don't we, Spear of Uriel?"

"Spear? Dude. I don't know where you got that name. I'm the Hand of God. Maybe you called the person who had my job that name in your day, but times have changed. Didn't you get the memo?"

"Chained in the darkness for millennia after millennia? No. I'm afraid not. But I'm making up for lost time. How do you like my work?" He gestured with one hand to the horror he'd wrought.

"That you can only get buzzards to hang out with you is no surprise to me. So, which one are you? Whose ass am I going to kick?"

"My name is Arkas." He stood in one fluid motion, picking up the machete as he did so, then bowed. "The Spears were forever sure of themselves. Most to their ruin. You are the one about to learn something new."

"What? From you? Dude, do you know just how many fashion fads have come and gone since you were buried in your shit hole?" I gestured to the bodies scattered around. "I'm guessing two of these were the Suttons. Who are the rest?"

"Some of the parents were getting to be . . . a problem. You were starting to get close and the word was spreading. So I had my host's parents invite them to the farm for a strategy meeting. Clever, huh? Seems a private detective has been involved as well. We had ten show up. One even brought her son."

I felt my heart tear apart as I looked quickly around the field and then saw a knit cap, green with two black snowflakes and two ear flaps, the same as Rose Mary's son, sitting on the ground not far away from where I stood. I yanked my gun from its holster and squeezed the grip so hard it's a wonder it didn't crush in my hand.

"You know, when I guessed you were here, I planned on just subduing you so I could have you cast out of the body you're in. Now, I'm going to find out how I can make an angel suffer before we do that. So help me, God, I will find a way to make you pay. Making the kid kill his own parents? And murdering a twelve year old boy? What type of sick fuck are you?"

"You ask such questions of me? When God chose you and your kind over *me* and *my* kind? You are no more than the cattle of the field to the divine. All those years watching over you, sharing our knowledge with the sons of men, and for what? So we could watch our own children murdered? Drowned, every last one of them? Then locked away for an eternity? You will begin to know just how we felt when we had our children ripped from us. When we are once again free, we will repopulate the Earth with our seed and replace the inferior race that is man." He once again gestured around him. "I consider this a good start."

It took every effort I could muster to stop from shooting the son of a bitch where he stood. I promised to return Ruth Anne to her mother. That wasn't going to happen—if Rose Mary was one of the victims of the massacre which surrounded me.

Charlie Sutton was another lost soul whose only crime was being in the wrong place at the wrong time. He deserved a chance—even if the demon inside him did not. I'd seen my share of horrific scenes during my time serving Uncle Sam, but never anything like this kind of butchery.

I breathed deeply, despite the smell of death heavy in the air, and let it out slowly. "You should've had some of your buddies come and help you out. It's just you and me and I'm about to shove that machete up your metaphorical ass."

Spreading both arms out to his side, he said, "Just you and me? For shame, Spear of Uriel, I have many friends here. They have thanked me for providing this marvelous meal."

"What? The buzzards? You are insane. No wonder they had to bury your ass deep in some frickin' hole."

I started to move towards him, my gun ready, waiting for the trap. I knew this had to be a trap. No one sits in the middle of a field and waits to get their ass kicked. He wanted me out here, unless he thought he and his weapon of choice were enough to take me down.

I took two steps when the buzzards on the ground, all at once, turned and looked in my direction: every last one of them, in unison. Then the ones flying overhead began to fly lower. I stopped in my tracks.

"Ah," said Arkas. "Are you starting to comprehend? Each of the divine have their own special knowledge, our own expertise. Mine is the ability to speak and work with animals. And I've told them about you and what we will do here today. And how they will feast when your carcass joins the others."

With that he threw his hands skyward and every buzzard still on the ground shot instantly into the air to a height of about thirty fee and then dove straight at me.

Holy crap. I fired off a couple of rounds, with several birds falling to the ground, but there were hundreds of them and I didn't have nearly enough ammunition. Soon I was lost in a flurry of claws and beaks ripping at my head and hands. I covered my face with my arm, thankful my bomber jacket was thick, but they were shredding it like tissue paper. Blood began to flow down my face as one beak ripped a gash across my forehead and attacked my exposed hands.

I lost track of Arkas, so I tried to move backwards and almost tripped and fell, stumbling over someone's leg. Nothing else, just the leg. I could feel the first tendrils of panic stir inside me, but I shoved the feeling aside.

I said to myself, think damn it, think.

The buzzards were trying to get at my legs. I kicked out at them and managed to clip Arkas who had moved within striking distance, knocking him back just as the machete sliced down mere inches from my head.

Think, think, think. Then it hit me. I reached into my bag, feeling urgently around and found what I was looking for: a tear gas canister. I'd never removed it from my duffle after the Florida trip.

Back during my time in Basic Training with Special Forces, a sergeant challenged a couple of us, those who he thought were the most bad ass guys in the unit, to a competition. Late one night the four of us met the sergeant in the tear gas training room with the sergeant the only one wearing a mask. The first three out had to clean all the latrines in our building for a solid week with a toothbrush. The last one got a weekend pass—one of the most treasured rewards you could earn during basic training. I held my breath for as long as I could. In the end it was just me and one other guy. When I could tell I was about to lose the last of my air, I slapped the other guy on both sides of his face. He let out his remaining air in a rush, and then ran out. I stayed a while longer after my own air had left me to prove I was as tough as I thought I was.

I did the same thing here, took a deep breath, then popped the top on the canister. An ugly brown smoke spewed out of the can as I began to wave it around my head and the birds scattered. They may eat carrion for a living, but they didn't like the smell of toxic smoke. My eyes began to sting, but I kept them open and resisted the urge to rub them. Good thing as I saw Arkas swing in an overhand arc with his machete. I raised my weapons bag, blocking the blow, then shoved him backwards and pointed the can directly into his face. Arkas started rubbing his eyes and when he did, I kicked him hard in the balls, putting everything I had behind it. Arkas doubled over, dropping the machete, then breathed in deep and began to retch. I'm not sure how tear gas would affect an angel, but it for damn sure affected a human body.

I hit him hard in the temple, and he crumpled to the ground, knocked out. I tossed the can of tear gas far away, trying really hard not to rub my eyes. All the buzzards had flown the coop. I reached into the bag, took out plastic cuffs and secured Arkas. Then I took out a roll of duct tape and put a large piece across his mouth. No more Dr. Doolittle for you, asshole.

I used a towel inside my bag to wipe away the blood from my forehead, then tied it around my head to keep the blood out of my eyes, watching to see if the buzzards would return, but they didn't. I slung my bag over my shoulder, picked up the unconscious Mr. Sutton and started back towards the farm. At the tree line, I stopped, dropped Sutton on the ground and said a prayer for the dead.

My heart ached for Rose Mary and her son. I should have felt the same way for all of them, but their deaths didn't affect me like the death of the little boy which really hit me hard. Arkas began to come around and I grabbed a fistful of hair, turning his eyes to meet mine.

"Remember how I told you I was going to make you pay? If I could find a way to torture you before we cast you out, without hurting the boy, I'd do it. I don't care if it's not the Christian thing to do. You are evil incarnate and I wish I could do more than cast you into Hell. But that will have to do. Your freedom is almost over."

He tried screaming things at me as I dragged him through the snow to the car, but the damn duct tape over his mouth kept me from hearing what he had to say. Ain't that just a bitch.

CHAPTER 23

I called Father Colton and he met me at the door to the house carrying his bag of tricks. I stopped in front of him, dragging the fallen angel behind me. Arkas thrashed around and continued to scream, despite the tape covering his mouth. I'm not sure, but I think he called me a bad name. I grabbed him under the arms, lifting him up. Colton grabbed his legs and we carried him kicking into the house and plopped him onto a big four poster bed in a back bedroom.

"Hold him down for a minute while I get ready," Father Colton said.

I was more than happy to help, using my weight to keep Sutton from moving around. I put my lips next to his ear and said, "You don't know how badly I want to choke you, over and over, until you're almost dead, then bring you back to life and do it all over again. But that only punishes the kid. Just think, in a few minutes you'll be spending the rest of eternity wandering through the desert until Judgment Day when you'll be cast into Hell with that other fallen angel, Lucifer. Guess you guys can start a club. And Sutton, if you can hear me in there? We're going to free you, son. Hang on a bit longer."

Arkas continued his muffled screams and it took every ounce of restraint I had not to pinch his nose and end it, right then and there. Finally, Colton said, "I'm ready. Let me get these restraints on him."

Colton took hold of one of Sutton's ankles and buckled the leather restraint. He then tied it off to one of the poster bed's large posts. He did the same thing with the other ankle.

He moved to the head of the bed and said, "Now comes the harder part. I need you to uncuff him and keep him still while I get these arm cuffs on."

"Screw that," I said. "Hold him down for a minute."

Father Colton relieved me, leaning hard on Sutton while I went back to my bag and took out a taser. I walked over to Sutton, flipped the dart cap off, revealing the bare contacts, then pressed it against his side and pressed the button.

Sutton bucked from all the juice, then was still. I quickly rolled him over, took out a knife and cut the cuffs while Colton buckled on the leather wrist restraints to the bed, securing him to the headboard.

With Arkas now immobilized, Colton went back to his bag and pulled a towel which he wrapped around his neck, then took out several items he sat on the nightstand next to the bed: a Bible, a funny looking shaker, and a large metal cross.

"Your version of a weapons bag?" I asked.

"Yes, my Jesus bag. Don't leave home without it."

"What's with the baby rattle?"

He picked up the shaker made out of ceramic and colorfully decorated. "Filled with holy water. O.K. Here's what happens next. I want you to take the tape off of his mouth and then I want you to stand over by the door. No matter what you hear, you must not respond to what the demon says. Do you understand?"

"No sweat. Would you rather me leave the room?"

"Actually, no. If he manages to break free of the bed, you'll come in real handy. But you must stay quiet. The demon will try and get you involved, to break my concentration."

"Dude, I've been trash-talked by the best of them. I'm good. You ready?"

He nodded and I walked over to Sutton, who was starting to come around. I ripped the tape from his mouth. "Ready for your one-way to ticket to oblivion, asshole?"

Sutton was about to respond when Colton picked up the cross and the Bible, and the reaction by Arkas/Sutton was immediate, as he pushed the length of his restraints, trying to move off the bed.

Colton started with a prayer, "Father, who art in Heaven, hallowed be thy name, thy kingdom come, thy will be done, on Earth as it is in Heaven."

As he continued, Arkas yanked and pulled at his restraints, rocking the bed and howling with rage. His eyes, wild and large, searched the room and found me.

He said, "Free me, Spear of Uriel, and I will make sure your loved ones survive the purge. I can make that happen. Free me!"

I responded with a wink and then scratched my nose with my middle finger. I knew it was a childish insult, but since I couldn't talk, what was a guy to do?

Colton began reading from different parts of scripture, then picked up the holy water shaker and began to rain holy water down upon the body of Charlie Sutton. Sutton's body arched off the bed so hard I was sure the restraints wouldn't hold him, but they did. Veins popped out on Sutton's neck, and he continued to shake back and forth.

Colton kept his voice in a slow measured cadence. In response, Arkas growled, low and harsh, then spit a goober the size of a quarter into Colton's face. The priest, never missing a beat, used the towel to wipe the spittle off of his chin. He began to call the demon by name. "Here me, Arkas. In the name of our Lord and Savior, Jesus Christ, I call upon you to leave this vessel."

"Never," screamed the demon. "He is mine. I will not leave."

"You will leave, in the name of the Father, the Son and the Holy Ghost." Colton emphasized his words with more shaking from the holy water shaker, moving up and down the boy's body.

The demon once again howled, and then looked straight at me.

"Do you want to know what we did to your woman, Spear of Uriel? Did she share with you the way she screamed with pleasure when my brother took her? The way she begged him to take her again and again? Baraquiel said he'd never had a woman who begged him not to leave her bed the way the red-haired bitch did each night when he finished with her."

I leaned off the wall in a flash of anger, my breathing coming in large heaves. The demon smiled and said, "That's right, Spear of Uriel, she begged him on hands and knees and pleasured him in all ways. Others will get their chance with her and we will pass her around from brother to brother before we kill her. You have my word this will happen."

Father Colton never looked at me, never said a word to me, only continued to admonish the demon to leave Sutton's body, but he did speak louder. I wanted so badly to pound on this warped piece of crap. I ground my teeth in frustration, my fists balled, and fought for control. Did the other fallen angel really do those things to Samantha?

Is that why she didn't want to talk about what happened to her down in Florida? Because she'd been raped by Baraquiel? I knew something awful happened down there. How much of what Arkas was spewing was the truth? Some of it? All of it? None of it?

I took another step. I had visions of strangling the truth out of the demon while banging his head against the headboard. Or maybe I could smash the truth out him.

Instead, I closed my eyes and calmed myself. What I wanted was what Arkas hoped I would do. He wanted me to interrupt the exorcism, as he fought desperately not to be kicked into his own form of Hell.

I reopened my eyes, gave the demon my best smile, and slowly shook my finger back and forth. Then I went back to my wall and continued to lean against it making sure it stayed in place.

Arkas howled and his thrusting became even more violent. That is, until Colton, his voice rising, issued a final command for him to leave.

"In the name of the Father, the Son and the Holy Ghost, leave this vessel!" Then he pressed the cross down upon Sutton's head. The demon's howl turned into a shriek and then the sound faded, as Sutton's body collapsed onto the bed.

Sutton, covered in sweat, closed his eyes and then reopened them. He looked around the bedroom, at Colton, and then to me and the most pitiful wail I ever heard from any man escaped his lips and he began to sob. Father Colton placed his hand upon the young man's shoulder and said, "You have been freed of the demon. He has been cast out. You are now free."

"Oh, God," he cried. "He made me kill my parents. I, I, I . . . cut them to pieces. I—killed others. Oh my God, what have I done?"

Colton motioned to me and we removed the leather restraints. Charlie curled up into a fetal position, hugging his knees and sobbed. Colton sat down beside the young man and then lifted him up into his strong arms, and held him, the whole time speaking in a low, hushed tone.

I walked out into the front room and called Brother Joshua.

"Down to one hundred and ninety-seven," I said. "But it was a close call." I filled him in on the events at the farm and then asked, "J, there's a lot of dead bodies out here. Several families have lost parents. How do you want to handle this? This kid is going to be blamed for being a mass murderer and spend his life either in prison or in an insane asylum. I hate to just turn him over to the cops."

"Bring him with you. What happens will be up to him. We all make choices, Victor, and his choice not to be one with God left him open to the attack."

"Give me a freakin' break. The kid had no chance. You know what, J, I'm all for the whole 'you make your bed you lie in it' point of view, but I'll be damned if just letting this kid hang himself is the right thing to do. This holier than thou attitude is really starting to piss me off."

Never in my interaction with Brother Joshua did I let my anger come out. I knew I crossed a line, but I really didn't care. Maybe what the demon said about Samantha clouded my judgment. Maybe it was the fact no one was there to protect a little boy and his mother. Sometimes I wondered what the hell was the point of what I was doing.

"As I said," Brother Joshua responded. "The choice is up to him. It's all about free will and choices, Victor. Have Father Colton do what he can there and then return to the mission, with the boy if he will join us or without him if he will not. There's no way we can avoid calling in the police on this one. Once you've brought them here, I want you to return to the farm and call the police. You can tell them the truth: that you were investigating the disappearance of several local college students and stumbled upon the scene."

I leaned my head against the wall and prayed for God to give me strength.

"Yeah. O.K. Fine."

I severed the connection. I closed my eyes, listening to the wailing which continued in the other room. I couldn't even imagine being forced to kill your own parents against your will. I thought about Mikey, but realized the situation was totally different. Mikey deserved the wrath of God to be rained down around him. This poor family was decimated for no other reason than a young man didn't make the right choices when it came to faith.

Father Colton came out and put his hand on my shoulder. The wailing in the other room had subsided.

"You able to put him at peace that quickly?" I asked.

He shook his head, a somber look on his face.

"No, I wasn't. That's the result of a heavy sedative I gave him. He's not out yet, but will be soon."

"For the best, all things considered. Father Joshua says we need to ask him if he'd like to come back to the mission. His choice."

"My choice and the answer is 'yes.' The man is broken and is in no shape to face the world on his own, especially considering what is to come next."

"Yeah. Mass murderer is going to be a hard tag to live with. I'm hoping there's something Joshua can do about it. But we will see."

"Victor," Father Colton said slowly, "about what Arkas said in there, you do understand that lying is what they do. He was just trying to get a reaction from you. You showed incredible restraint. I'm sorry I had to put you through all of that. Most likely what he said is not true."

I didn't say anything for a moment, but then replied, "She'll tell me in due time if it did. Something happened down there, but I'm not sure what, and I'm not sure how hard I should push her. I'm trying to give her the space she needs. But it's tough, ya know?"

"I do. For now, let's get Mr. Sutton to the mission and go from there. What are you going to do about what happened out there?"

"No choice. I'll have to call the cops and tell them as much as I can. There are too many dead people involved. I'm worried about what happens if the police corner one of these Watchers. They're like an infection. Being able to move from person to person is a real issue."

We went back to Charlie Sutton and helped the drowsy man to the back seat of my car, laying him gently down on the seat. "How long before the Watcher can try and return back to Charlie?"

"There's no set time, but it won't be soon. I have time to try and increase his faith. But his mind is broken, Vic. What he was forced to do? I'm not sure anyone can recover from such horror. I will do what I can."

And that's all any of us can do, I thought. Soldier on, do the right thing and hope it's enough. I was starting to have my doubts.

CHAPTER 24

Kurt was having a really bad dream. Like one of the worst ever. It started out great, he and Ruth Anne were in bed, she was wearing the kind of teddy he only saw in magazines, but never in person. Then she was all over him, pressing her breasts against his face. Pure heaven. But then the nightmare started when she handcuffed him to the headboard and got worse when Mikey McCain walked in. What a buzz kill.

He dreamed Ruth Anne and Mikey had an argument. They wanted something from him, but he couldn't remember what. Oh. That's right. Where Vic had hidden the money. Vic never told him, he explained to them. But Mikey wanted to cut off parts of his body until he told and that scared him. Kurt liked his body parts right where they were.

But Ruth Anne said Mikey told her she could do it her way, and Kurt was all for Ruth Anne's way, especially if it involved teddies and breasts. But it didn't. She reached into her purse and pulled out a large syringe and stuck him in the neck and he fell asleep.

Now he could hear her calling his name and he needed to wake up. He moved his neck back and forth a bit and then finally opened his eyes, but it was still dark. He went to sit up, but banged his head on something hard after moving only a few inches. He tried to raise his arms but they hit the hard thing, too. Slowly he felt around and then shot wide awake as he realized he was in a wooden box. No, he thought. Not a box. A coffin.

Panic seized him and he began to pound on top of the box, screaming to be let out. He pushed up with all his might, but the lid didn't budge. He continued to scream until a small hole opened above his face. He stared straight up through a small cylinder at Ruth Anne's beautiful eyes.

"Ruth Anne. Let me out. Please," he begged. "I'll do anything. Get me out of here."

A frown creased Ruth Anne's brow. "Anything? You'll do anything?" she said.

"Yes. I swear it. This isn't funny. You have to let me out. Please," he pleaded.

She smiled. "So will you tell me where you and your friend hid the money? You'll do that for me, Kurt?" Kurt closed his eyes and didn't say anything. "Kurt," she continued. "You said you'd do anything, didn't you mean it?" Her smile was gone, and so was Kurt's hope.

"I don't know where the money is. He never told me." He knew they would never believe him. The night before was coming back with clarity and they didn't believe him then either.

Ruth Anne's face was replaced by that of Mikey.

"*Bullshit*, Kurt," Mikey said, trying to maintain his temper. "My brother doesn't have the brains to hide that much money. Nor the skill, but *you* do. And he trusts you. Come on, man, tell us where the two of you hid the money and we'll have you out of there in a jif."

"Go screw yourself, Mikey. I don't know and wouldn't tell you if I did." Kurt tried to keep up a strong front, but inside he was terrified. He felt a chill in his soul, as he knew he would never leave this box in the ground.

"Have it your way, Kurt. But you *will* tell us. This woman is quite talented. I wish you all the best. I'll make sure and tell Vic you said hello the next time I talk to him."

And with that, Mikey was gone and Ruth Anne was back. "Here's what I'm going to do, Kurt. I'm going to give you a while to think about it, then I'll be back."

Her face disappeared and she placed some type of cover over the cylinder and his whole world went black. Kurt started to scream again for someone to let him out, pounding on the top of the coffin. The lid was removed and Ruth Anne returned.

"Kurt, listen to me very carefully. If you don't stop screaming, then I'm going to bring the water hose over here and fill the box to the brim. Do you understand me? Shh. Now," she said, putting the lid back on.

This time Kurt stayed quiet and tried to think about how to get out of this situation. He took stock of his condition. He was shirtless, but still had on his shorts. He felt around but found his pockets were empty, so nothing there. He remembered the warning call from Vic the night before and wondered if the big guy guessed he was in trouble and what he'd do about it if he did.

For a moment Kurt started to hyperventilate and it was several minutes before he got his breathing under control. He used what space he had to feel around the seams of his makeshift prison, but could find no finger grips or gaps.

He laid there for what seemed like hours when the lid was once again removed and Ruth Anne appeared.

"Ready to talk, Kurt?" Her voice was pleasant, like it had been during their date.

"It was all a lie, wasn't it? You never liked me, did you?" Kurt asked.

Ruth Anne snorted, "Not even a little. I'd tell you I'm sorry, but I'm not. Like every other man on the planet, you think with the wrong head. You might as well go ahead and tell me what I want to know, Kurt. You're going to anyway."

"Kiss my ass, bitch." He tried to sound defiant, but the words came out in a defeated tone.

"Kurt, Kurt, Kurt. You sound like the private detective my mother sent out here to find me. He's in a box a few feet to your right. He said he wouldn't talk either. But in the end, he told me everything I wanted to know, right up until the very end. You wanted to know what I was doing the last few days? Well, that was it. I was having fun. Now it's your turn. The only question is how long it takes with you, Kurt."

Kurt whimpered softly and this made Ruth Anne laugh. She replaced the lid and left him alone with his thoughts. Kurt wished he'd done more with his life. Found a nice girl, settled down. He thought Ruth Anne would be that girl, but it was all a bag of lies.

And here Vic was looking for Mikey only to have him show up in Hawaii. He wondered how they found him. He'd done a great job covering his tracks. At least he thought so.

Finally, the lid was removed, the face of his tormenter returned.

"Time to talk, Kurt. I've waited as long as I can to let you do this on your own. Will you talk to me now?"

"Not a chance. I won't turn traitor. Do your worst." He was proud he said the words. But he knew he didn't mean it. He didn't want her worst. He didn't even want slightly bad.

"Good," she said, and sounded down-right pleased with Kurt. "I was sure you wouldn't put up a fight. Michael McCain said you'd fold before the first hour was up. I'm very proud of you, Kurt. So let's get started, shall we?"

Kurt watched through the cylinder as she leaned out of view, then returned holding something which she dropped down the pipe and quickly replaced the lid. His brain roared out a word just before the object hit him in the face: snake. He turned his head and screamed as the snake landed on his cheek and then squirmed down his chest. Kurt trapped it against his stomach and could feel the thing wrap around his wrist, then felt its mouth close down on his hand, striking him over and over. Continuing to scream, Kurt grabbed the head of the snake in one hand, the body in the other, and pulled with all the adrenaline his body had left. He felt a small pop, as skin, scales, and cartilage ripped and the head tore loose.

He laid there in the dark, crying, and threw the lifeless body of the snake down by his feet. He went back to pounding on the lid, screaming for Ruth Anne to let him out. He continued to pound until he could no longer lift his arms. Exhausted, he gave up, closed his eyes and tried to sleep. Fat chance.

His eyes were still closed when Ruth Anne said, "Come on Kurt, be a real man. That was just a baby rat snake. I have others. I tell you what. I'll let you choose what I drop down next." His eyes opened to see a slice of clouds in a beautiful blue sky as Ruth Anne continued just out of site. "Let's see. I have a couple of scorpions, several rattlesnakes, and my personal favorite, several gallons of red fire ants."

Her face once again filled his vision and he wanted nothing more than to reach up through the opening and strangle her. But the pipe was several feet long and she was just out of reach.

"I had to order more of those. I didn't like the P.I. so I chose for him, filled his box with fire ants then sealed the lid shut so they couldn't get out. He screamed for hours. But I like you, so I'll let you choose. Unless you don't tell me what I need to know. If you don't, I might just dump them all down there with you. Wouldn't that be fun?" she was practically giddy. "So, Kurt, where did you and Victor McCain hide the money?"

"If I tell you, will you let me out of here?" Kurt asked.

"Count on it. You give me what I want and I'll have you dug up, then I'll make sure they let you go."

Kurt knew it was all a lie, but what else could he do? He always had visions of riding into battle, saving the day, and being the hero. But trapped in a box, underground, with a dead snake and likely more on the way, he wasn't sure he had it in him. There was one more thing he could try.

"Vic and I hid the money in two different offshore accounts. I will need my laptop to tell you which ones and the account numbers. Spring me and I'll get the computer and print out what you need."

"How about this," Ruth Anne decided, "I'll go get your computer, bring it back here and you can walk me through where the information is stored. Then I'll let you out."

"You promise?" Kurt put as much hope into his voice as he could.

"Absolutely. Now where will I find your computer?"

"Look in the second drawer of my dresser, beneath my underwear and socks. And be careful with it. That thing cost me a fortune."

"You got it. Take a little rest, Kurt. I'll be back later. Oh, and Kurt?"

"Yes?" He didn't like the tone in her voice.

"If the computer isn't there, or you're lying to me, then I will be very angry with you. You won't like me when I'm angry."

"Don't worry. I'm playing it straight up."

"Don't go anywhere, ya here?" She put the lid back in place, her laughter as black as the darkness.

CHAPTER 25

After dropping off Charlie and Father Colton, I drove back to the farmhouse and called Rusty. "Hey, Rusty. Remember when I said I'd call you if my efforts turned into anything? Well, they have, and I'm not sure you're going to like it."

An hour later, the farm was crawling with cops and forensics teams. Rusty, a state trooper not too far from retirement, stood next to me as we watched a coroner head towards the clearing with even more body bags. Rusty's face, pinched and pale, watched them for a moment, then turned back to me.

"You know, Vic, I've been doing this nearly thirty years and I've never seen anything like this. And you have no idea who's responsible?"

"Like I told you, finding missing teens wasn't really my focus. I found out about them as much by accident as anything else. When Ms. Huffman asked me to look into it, I said why not? I'd only been on the trail for a day when I found this."

"You say you spoke to Mr. and Mrs. Sutton?"

"Yes, yesterday afternoon. From the way they talked, I thought for sure they had an idea where Charlie, their son, was hiding out. So I came out here earlier in the day to try and shake some information from them. I knocked and when I didn't get an answer, I looked in the window and saw the chairs overturned. When I saw the blood and the note, I had a bad feeling about all them buzzards flying around and went to take a look."

Rusty glanced at my head and hands, and the condition of my jacket, and said, "Never known vultures to attack a human. Throw up on them maybe, but never attack. Why do you think they did that?"

"Rusty, I honestly have no clue." Of course I did, but I didn't think my friend wanted to hear about fallen angels who talk to buzzards. "I just walked out there and when I moved towards the tarp they attacked."

"And you just happened to have tear gas on you?" His frown told me he wasn't buying that part.

"I had my bag with me. I always keep tear gas in there in case I have to break up an unruly group of family members when I make a bust. Non-lethal force. Seems to work on birds as well as people. Good thing for me."

He grunted agreement and nodded back towards my car. The two of us walked together in that direction, away from the other investigators.

"Sorry you got roped into all of this, Vic. The report the private investigator produced will be a big help. And we found the parents' cars in the two barns."

He checked his list.

"I have one last question for you. That message on the kitchen table. Do you think that was meant for you?"

"I doubt it, Rusty. The only person who knew I was looking into this was me. Well, and I guess Ms. Huffman. My guess is it was meant for someone else, but I don't have a clue who."

He watched my face closely, but I'm one of the better liars on the planet and after a moment he let it go.

"So, what, you think this is some kind of cult? These are not the type of teens to be gang bangers."

"That would be my guess. It's all very strange. But now the problem belongs to you guys. Good luck with that."

He gave a laugh devoid of humor and said, "Gee, thanks. We'll be in touch."

With that he strode back towards the house and the nightmare that waited beyond. I pulled out my phone and tried calling Kurt for, like, the tenth time with similar results: voicemail.

It was approaching five o'clock and Winston should have arrived in Hawaii, so I called him next. On the second ring, he answered.

"First Florida, then Hawaii. I'm really getting used to working for you. How about next you get me a gig in Europe. I've always wanted to see London."

"If we live long enough, I'll see what I can do. What's your status?" I fired up the Ford and headed out and soon left the Stephen King scene behind, even if I carried the images with me.

"Got booked into a room down the hall from Kurt. I'm going to start the search right away. I have the print out you gave me of the girl and pictures of Kurt he messaged out a few weeks ago."

Kurt had gone to his first luau and sent us pictures of him wearing about a dozen leis and doing his best not to look scared sitting there while hula dancers did their thing.

"Hit me up as soon as you know something, alright?"

"You got it boss man. I'll find him and bring him home. Count on it."

I told him about the farm and the successful exorcism of the fallen angel. He asked, "What's your next plan? Just in case you get hit by a bus and I have to take over for you?"

"I should only be so lucky. I think we need to stop chasing the tail and find the front of the dog. For the fallen angels to possess someone, they have to be close enough to touch them. If they'd been buried deep enough and they didn't make it to the surface, then someone found a way down to them. Add in the fact all the people possessed, so far, are from this area, then I think the Watchers were buried somewhere nearby. I'm going to try and find out where. Find the source and maybe I'll find the rest of them."

"You're gonna need a small army if you do find them. These are some bad ass mofos. Make sure and wait until I get back before you hit them. I'll find Kurt and high-tail it back. Be careful."

Winston hung up and I tossed the phone on the seat next to me. Don't worry, I said to myself, I will.

I sure hope I wasn't sending Winston into even more danger than he was in here. I pounded the wheel in frustration because I couldn't be in two places at once to help Kurt and to take care of things with the case here. Instead of riding the wave, I'd spent the last few days being swept under. I needed to talk to Charlie to see if he could add to what I'd learned from Mal McGeorge. Then J and I would talk, too. He and I were going to have a "come to Jesus" talk. Time to get back on top.

****

Winston resisted the urge to constantly scratch at the bandage on his side. He lied to Vic. Despite sleeping like the dead on the two plane rides to Hawaii, he woke up feeling weak. Thank God there was a Starbucks in the airport because he needed a caffeine jolt. But there wasn't much else he could do but get to it and find Kurt, and soon.

He first went and talked to the clerks at the front desk to ask if they'd seen Kurt. It took some convincing to prove the two of them were really friends. But after a few minutes they checked and confirmed that, aside from the cleaning crew, Kurt's door had not been opened since yesterday morning. Since Kurt had been staying there for the last three months the staff knew him pretty well. One of the desk clerks remembered seeing him eating breakfast with a pretty blonde woman the morning before. Winston showed her Ruth Anne's photo and she said that Ruth Anne was the girl he was with, but she didn't see them leave. Both of the desk clerks said Ruth Anne, however, was definitely not staying at the hotel. He gave them his card and asked that they call him if Kurt came back or they saw the girl again.

Winston thanked them and then walked down towards the beach. Now he knew Kurt was in deep trouble, having hooked up with a fallen angel. If they got wind Vic was closing in on them in Kentucky, having spoken to

Ruth Anne's mom, they may have made a move on Kurt. But to what end, Winston had no clue.

There were several different kiosks just before you hit the sand and Winston repeated the inquiries. A newsstand guy named Melvin said Kurt and Ruth Anne were at his stand the day before, early in the afternoon, and he saw them sitting down by the water. He remembered because the girl was super hot, but neither one passed his stand today. Again, he would've remembered. Hot, hot, hot.

Winston thanked him and decided to walk down the beach and talk to the people there to see if anyone else knew Ruth Anne and where she might be staying. He was walking and talking to people along the beach for about forty-five minutes when his phone rang. His caller ID showed a Hawaiian area code.

The person on the line said, "Hi. This is Susan Harover. You left us your card here at the hotel in case we saw Kurt or the girl come back."

Winston turned and began jogging back up the beach, but stopped almost immediately due to the pain it caused in his side. "Is he back?"

"He's not, but she is. She just walked through the lobby and took the elevator up."

"Thanks. I'm on my way there now."

"Would you like us to detain her?" The clerk sounded excited.

"No. Don't try it. She may be very dangerous and I don't want any of you to get hurt. Just keep an eye out."

He hung up and tried to pick up the pace, but fatigue quickly overtook him. He thought about the offer to have her detained, but as deadly as these fallen angels were turning out to be, he didn't want to put innocent people at risk. Not only that, but if she found out someone was here after her, she could just hop to another body and then he'd have no clue what the person he was searching for looked like.

He finally made the turn up the beach to the front of the hotel when his phone rang again.

"Tell me," he said.

"She just walked out the front door carrying a laptop. You better hurry." Susan replied.

Winston arrived in time to see a blonde matching his picture hop into a cab and pull away. Instead of trying to catch up with her, he slowed down, walked over to the parking lot, unlocked the door to his rental car and got in.

He pulled out his phone and opened a particular app, plugged in the car charger and went in the general direction the cabbie had taken. He could feel the anticipation building inside because now he knew he had her.

CHAPTER 26

Kurt heard the cover being removed and opened his eyes. He wasn't sure how much time had passed between Ruth Anne's departure and return, but it wasn't long enough to suit him. He'd tried in vain to once again push up on the lid of the coffin box he was buried in, but didn't have the strength to move that much dirt. Hell, he didn't think even Vic could muscle that much earth out of the way.

Resigned to his fate he considered his next course of action, a plan which might save him or might not. Then he spent a few moments praying. Before long he knew he'd have the answer to whether there really is a Heaven and a Hell.

"O.K. I have the laptop and it's powered on. What's your sign on password?" Ruth Anne said.

Kurt gave her a long string of numbers and he heard keys tapping. Then she said, "Crap. That's not right. Give them to me again. This time, Kurt, it better be right or there'll be consequences. You hear me?"

"Yeah, yeah, don't get your thong in a knot. I can't help it if you can't type."

But inside Kurt felt pretty damn good about himself, as his preparations months earlier were about to pay off.

****

Winston drove slowly up and down the residential streets not far from the beach. The cab went by him a few minutes earlier and he knew he was close. Then the app, open on his phone, beeped.

Yes! Winston said to himself.

He picked up the phone and looked closely at a map with a little blue dot a few streets over from where he now was, a spot right on the ocean. Someone tried accessing Kurt's laptop and put in the wrong password, which then sent a signal to the app on his and Victor's phones, showing exactly where the laptop was and, with any luck, right where Kurt was being held.

"Hang on buddy, I'm on my way." he said aloud.

His phone rang and the caller ID showed Vic's name. He pushed the answer button and before he could even say hello, Vic said, "You see it?"

"Yeah, man. I see it. I'm about two minutes away. Now let me do my job and stop botherin' me."

Winston hung up and watched the blue dot as he turned down Kauai Palm Lane, with the blue dot on the app matching up when he rode by number 116. A "for rent" sign rested against the house. A fence surrounded the back of the property, with the front facing the ocean with a gorgeous view. There was no one in sight and the curtains on the front window were pulled shut.

Winston drove down a few houses and found a public parking spot for those wanting access to the beach. He pulled into a spot, got out and locked the car. He wasn't sure what he would do once he reached the house, but he'd come up with something. He was always good that way. Being a linebacker meant you needed to react to what the offense did. There were times you could blitz and force the issue, but most times it was observe and react. Time to do some observing and then some kick ass reacting.

****

"I'm in," Ruth Anne said. "Now what?"

Kurt knew they now reached the tricky part.

"Vic and I put the money in two offshore accounts. The information is in two encrypted files. You can't just open them up and read them."

The truths was, these two accounts didn't have much money in them at all. They were there in case someone stole his laptop and then managed to break his encryption. The real account numbers were stored someplace else and numbered five in total.

"Not a very trusting soul are you, Kurt?" He could hear the snicker in her voice.

"Well, duh. Looks like I had it right, didn't I? What type of idiot do you think I am?" Kurt had no illusions as to what would happen once Ruth Anne and Mikey got into the accounts. Whatever the P.I. got he was surely to get even worse. He could only hope the signal the laptop sent out would alert Vic or Winston and for them to figure out he was in trouble and send the police to where ever he was being held. He programmed his own app and had them download it to their phones.

"So asks the man buried in a box. Do you really want me to answer that question? How do I un-encrypt them? Come on, Kurt. I'm on a deadline here."

No, he thought, I'm the one on a deadline, emphasis on dead.

"On my desktop you'll find a program called Wham. Click on it, then open the files and it will un-encrypt them. I designed the software myself. It's pretty neat. It uses several different algorithms which I don't even think the

N.S.A. could crack. You see, first I—"

"Uh, Kurt, shut the hell up, will you please? Please be quiet until I get these files open."

"Whatever. Sure. It's not like I'm going anywhere." She leaned over the pipe and started at him until he shut up. A few minutes passed.

"Got them," she said. "O.K. I see a listing for two accounts with links. One moment." There was a pause. "Got the first one up. Putting in the account number. Now, what's the password?"

"I don't have it."

Her face returned with lightning speed.

"What do you mean you *don't* have it? You set the accounts up, so don't hold out on me, Kurt. You can't imagine the ways I can make you suffer."

"Honest. I don't have'm. Never did. It's a failsafe built into the system. I set up the accounts and Vic puts in the passwords. The only way you can access the accounts is to have both of us in the same place at the same time."

For the first time since he was put underground he was smiling.

"Take that, bitch. No money for you or Mikey. Oh, and those account numbers change every day. The only way you will ever get that money is if you manage to capture Victor McCain, the Hand of God, and then make him talk. You are so royally fucked. Good luck with that." He crossed his arms, feeling smug.

"How do we reset the passwords? There has to be a way to recover them in case you forget them." Unconvinced, Ruth Anne continued to re-enter the data on the computer.

"There is. You have to show up at the banks in person, present the proper I.D. and they re-set it there. But again, with it being a dual account, both Vic and I have to be there. Kill me before you have the passwords from Vic, and no money. You have to keep me alive if you want a chance at the money."

She sat up out of view and he heard the laptop slam shut.

"It's me," she said a moment later. "No. I don't have the money. He—" There was a pause in her phone conversation. "Will you . . . will you shut up for a moment and stop screaming and I'll tell you. We have to have the Spear of Uriel as well to access the money. The idiot has the account numbers and the Spear the passwords."

Idiot. Obviously he wasn't an idiot. No idiot could ever design a program like Wham. That takes brains.

"Tell Mikey I said he'll be dead before he can ever get a word out of

Vic," he shouted.

"Fine. I agree. I'll take care of things here then catch the next flight back."

He heard her get up and leave and the brief burst of satisfaction he felt from screwing them over fled his body and was replaced by a gnawing fear of what was coming next. He prayed for snakes. At least a rattle snake bite would be quick. Or so he hoped. Fire ants were his biggest fear. Thinking of all those things crawling over him, stinging him thousands of times, made him start to shake.

Finally, she was back.

"As much as I'd like to send some of my pets down to visit, I don't have the time to enjoy it. So it has to be done another way." She sighed. "Goodbye, Kurt. You're a lousy kisser, by the way."

"Hey—" he started to protest, but stopped as a burst of water hit him in the face and he had to turn his head sideways to avoid the torrent of water pouring into the casket.

Oh my God, he thought, she's going to drown me.

He pounded on the lid of his coffin and scooted a few inches up, allowing him to get his nose away from the stream of water. He screamed over and over, but the water rose quickly in the confined space.

****

Winston eased into the carport and moved up next to what he assumed was a door into the kitchen. He started to turn the doorknob when he heard a loud slam from the backyard. He let go of the door handle and instead went to a gate in the fence, and listened intently. He heard a one-sided conversation by a woman he assumed was Ruth Anne discussing bank accounts.

"I'll take care of things." she said.

Winston looked around the carport for a weapon, settling on a shovel as his best bet. He lifted the latch to the gate. Thankfully, it wasn't locked. He cracked it open and saw a woman in the middle of the yard holding a water hose stuck into a pipe in the ground. One hand rested on her hip and she looked bored.

Despite the pain, Winston took off at a dead sprint.

"Excuse me!" he said.

The woman turned, her eyes wide with surprise as the flat of the shovel connected to the side of her head, sending her tumbling. Winston reached down and yanked the hose out of the pipe. Ruth Anne struggled to her feet and tried to run towards the house, but Winston was on top of her before she made it two strides and slammed the shovel into her legs, sending her to the ground. Before she could stand up, he struck her again in the head with the shovel. When she fell to the ground this time she didn't get up.

He pulled her into the house by her feet, watching to make sure she didn't pop back up like Jason in the *Friday the 13th* movies. He ripped the phone cord out of the wall on the counter and tied up her hands. He did the same thing with the phone line in another room and tied her feet. Then he carried her outside and dropped her next to the pipe in the ground. He looked down and could see the tip of a nose poking up and into the pipe.

"Kurt, if you can hear me, it's Winston. I'm going to dig you out," he yelled.

While keeping one eye on Ruth Anne, Winston used the shovel for the purpose it was designed for and began to dig.

****

Kurt's arms were starting to get tired. He propped up his body to keep his head above the level of the water and breathed in the air he needed so desperately. Strangely, he began to smell a difference in the air with the aroma of dirt drifting down to him. Taking a deep breath he turned his head sideways and put his ear to the pipe, and listened. Through water-clogged ears, he heard the sweetest sound he ever heard in his life: the smooth baritone of Winston singing a Gospel hymn, accompanied by the sound of a shovel striking the ground and the occasional grunt from digging in the dirt. If he wasn't under water he would have cried.

From time to time, Kurt pushed up on the lid, and after one huge heave the lid moved upward a few inches, then a few more, and suddenly he sat up as the lid lifted into the air and was thrown to the side. Standing at the edge of the muddy hole and casket which had entombed him was his friend Winston Reynolds, shirt off, covered in dirt, sweat, and blood streaming from a bandage on his side.

Winston smiled, offered his hand and pulled Kurt up and out of his graveyard-style dungeon. Both men, weak and tired, hugged each other and began to laugh.

Kurt stopped laughing when he turned and saw Ruth Anne on the ground, bound and glaring at him. The side of her head was covered in a growing bruise, her hair matted with dried blood and mud. He went and knelt beside her almost too tired to hold his head up, but there was something he needed to say to her.

You're a liar," he said. "I'm a great kisser."

CHAPTER 27

I sat back in my car and nearly wept after Winston called to give me the word that Kurt was safe, if a bit wrinkled, from being submerged in water for several hours. Hearing they caught Ruth Anne and she was still alive was another plus. I pushed my way into the mission and headed to Father Colton's room and found him inside lying on his bunk reading an autobiography. He put the book aside when I came into the room. I told him about Ruth Anne.

"I'll call a friend I have on the big island," he said. "It will take some time for him to get there, but he'll be able to help. Your friend is O.K.?"

"Yes, he is. Thank you. Look, I need to talk to Charlie. Where is he?"

Colton motioned me to follow him and led me to the room next to his. He knocked and then opened the door. Another priest sat in a chair reading his Bible, while Charlie laid on his bunk facing the wall, the mission's version of a suicide watch. Colton motioned the other priest out and he left with Colton taking the now vacated seat.

"Charlie, my name is Victor McCain, we, uh, met earlier today."

He turned over and looked at me. "You're the guy he was waiting for. The demon in my head. He did what he did just to get you to come to him."

While it wasn't exactly an accusation, it wasn't said without meaning. I couldn't even begin to think what type of thoughts were going through this kid's head.

"Yes. I'm afraid so. It's my job to stop them and, well, they are ramping up the pressure. I'm so very sorry for what happened to your parents. But you understand, there was nothing you could do to stop it?"

He laughed, but without humor.

"And you think that makes me feel any better? It was my hand that held the machete, Mr. McCain. I did it and I couldn't stop it. I murdered my parents, and all those other people—as surely as the monster did."

I wasn't about to spend the rest of the night debating right and wrong with the kid. I had more pressing concerns.

"I need to ask you some questions. I'm trying to figure out where they're coming from, where they're buried. They're here somewhere in Kentucky and someone has found the spot they were put in back in the day. Is there anything you can tell me which might give me a lead on where I can find where their bodies are buried?"

Charlie contemplated. "Maybe. It's not like we shared thoughts or anything. But we met with another one of the possessed people the day before I went home. He told Arkas that plans were under way to begin the dig. Arkas said the sooner they were freed from the cave the better. But he never said what cave or where."

"That's at least a start. Did he say anything else? Anything which might help us?"

"Not really, other than they really want you dead."

With that, Charlie flipped back over on his side again. Father Colton motioned for me to leave and he stayed behind. I closed the door and left.

I called Winston back. "Colton will have a guy headed your way, but it may be a bit. Rest up. I gave him the address and your cell number. Don't let her get away."

"I won't. But there's something else you need to know," his tone serious. "Mikey was here. In Hawaii."

"Is he still there?" I stopped where I was, stunned by the news, and waited for the answer.

"Nah, man. He flew out last night. The chick has no idea where he flew to. They didn't really get along, know what I mean? Your brother and the Watchers may be working together, but it's not one big happy family."

"Hell, he's been my brother for my entire life and I've never really gotten along with him. So yeah, I do. Keep me posted, alright?"

"Will do. Kurt and I will take shifts until the priest arrives." And with that he hung up.

I continued down to Brother Joshua's office, but before I stepped inside, I heard Samantha's voice and stopped to listen for a moment.

"You can't honestly tell me you believe the world was created in seven days and seven nights. You and I both know that's not possible," she said.

Brother Joshua responded, "With God, all things are possible. Does it really matter how long it took to create the universe and all that is in it? Isn't the creation itself wonder enough?"

Samantha barked a short laugh. "I'm not the one selling the book as gospel. You guys do that. Why not just tell the truth and let people decide for themselves?"

"The truth is told in the Bible, yet you refuse to believe it. Victor, won't you join us?"

How he did that I have no idea. I rolled into the office to see Samantha sitting in one of the chairs across from J, her legs folded beneath her. Yet again my heart soared when she looked at me and offered a small smile. But then her eyes changed to concern as she flew out of the chair and came to me.

"What the hell happened to you?"

She ran her fingers across the cuts on my hands, then up to my face and forehead.

"Are you O.K?"

"Yeah. Some birds went all Alfred Hitchcock on my ass, but I survived."

I gave her a quick rundown, and then turned my attention to Brother Joshua. "We found Ruth Anne in Hawaii. Kurt and Winston have her tied up in a villa she's renting. I already talked to Father Colton and he'll have a priest over there to perform an exorcism. So one more fallen angel kicked to the curb."

"That's great news."

"It is. I have a few questions of my own, if you don't mind." When J nodded for me to continue, I said, "Riddle me this, oh Wise One. How is it Satan gets a free hand, these days, but not a peep from God? J, that scene at the farm, it was . . . it was . . . a little boy was murdered there, J. If Satan can answer the prayers of Mikey and Samantha's father, why in the world would God not stop something like what happened out there?"

"There are several things wrong with your premise. Starting with Michael and Cyrus Tyler. I would suggest to you they did not have prayers answered. They made a trade, their soul for material wealth. God does not offer things in trade. If you believe in him, when you die you will find peace for an eternity in Heaven. It's a simple proposition, but with profound consequences both for those of faith and those without. God does answer prayers, just not in the way of Lucifer. I think when the final accounting is rendered, Michael and Cyrus will not feel they had their prayers answered when they are spending eternity in Hell."

"Fine," I said. "I won't debate the point. How about these fallen angels? He sent them to their prison in the first place. He was their jailer. If they were truly that evil and deserved their punishment, then why doesn't He take the steps to put them back in their place?"

"He is. Through you." Brother Joshua said. "God does what he does through the people of faith. You are doing God's work. And through you the threat will be stopped."

"While innocent people are murdered? He was only a boy, J. What did he ever do to deserve what happened to him?" I said, slamming my fist down on his desk. I stepped back a few feet and ran both hands through my hair, trying to get control of my temper.

"We've had this discussion. He did nothing to deserve it. The race of man makes their choices. Not all of them well. You must continue to have faith."

I shook my head and paced the room.

"It's not right. It's not." I began to wonder if my frustration was at God or at my inability to keep a young boy alive. It felt like I was running a race, going backward while everyone else was sprinting ahead.

"Read the book of Revelations, Victor. Things will be getting much worse before the end comes."

I threw my hands up in the air.

"Then what's the point of it all?"

Samantha watched the two of us, staying quiet, but she stared down Brother Joshua, waiting to hear the answer.

"Because it is what good people do and will continue to do until the end. Stopping Arkas means he will not be murdering other children. You must continue to fight those who are truly evil until your end comes."

"Which will come much sooner, thanks to you," Samantha said.

He shook his head no. "Victor made his choices. And his choices have consequences. He is paying for his sins and atoning for the wrongs he created."

Brother Joshua was right. I was responsible for my own actions. No one else. I thought I could save Mikey when all evidence told me I could not. It was my pride doing the talking. I was about to say something more when the feeling of wrongness hit me like a ton of bricks.

J closed his eyes and then snapped them open and called my name, but my gun was already in my hands.

"Get down behind the chair and stay there." I told Samantha.

I flipped the light switch off, sending the room into darkness. I heard Samantha get up and move as I requested. I glanced into the hallway. Light from a street lamp outside streamed through a window about twenty feet from me and I saw a shadow outside dart quickly from one side to the other.

"I thought we were safe here because of the Chapel?" I said quietly.

From right next to me, Brother Joshua replied, "You are safe in any house of God, as the Hand of God. Others are not as fortunate."

I cursed under my breath. "When I head out, you close and lock the door behind me." With my eyes now adjusted to the darkness I could pick out his form standing next to me. "Keep her safe, J. If you don't, it won't be pretty."

Moving into the hallway, I didn't hang around to see if he was ticked at my threat, and quickly made my way towards the front door. I knew it was near midnight and most of the homeless in the shelter were in bed. I didn't have to worry about bumping into one of them inside the mission. I eased up to the window and glanced outside. Standing across the street under the street-lamp stood one of the missing college students. I racked my brain and finally came up with the name to match the face. Kyle Beaumont.

He stood there with his arms stretched out to his sides, palms up, watching the mission, obviously making no attempt to hide. I made my way to the door, cracked it open enough to slip outside, with my gun raised to the ready.

He looked at me and then screamed, "Uriel. It is I, Shamsiel. Do you not remember me?"

"Hey, dickwad, I'm not Uriel. When are you guys going to get my name right? And no, I don't know you."

I heard the door open behind me and glanced over my shoulder. Brother Joshua stepped outside.

"He's not talking to you." Brother Joshua replied.

"Get back inside. Now." I hissed. But he ignored me and stepped towards the fallen angel. I snagged his sleeve and tried to pull him back, but he gently took hold of my hand and removed it from his arm.

"I'm in no danger, Hand of God. You may relax."

What the holy hell? Relax? After the last few days I'd been through and he wanted *me* to relax? Screw that. I watched as the body of Kyle Beaumont fell to his knees, his hands now reaching out to J, and tears streamed down his face. For my part, I pointed my gun directly at a spot between his eyes and got ready to blow him away if he so much as sneezed.

"Uriel, please forgive me. I have come to you to beg forgiveness for my sins."

Brother Joshua and I crossed the street together and I scanned the area trying to find other threats, but none appeared. Joshua went to Kyle and took his hands in his.

"I am sorry, old friend, but you are asking that which is beyond my power to grant." Brother Joshua answered.

My head snapped around to Joshua. "Old friend. Wait. You know this guy? How is that . . ." I stopped and I could almost feel my jaw hitting the pavement. "Uriel. You're Uriel, the archangel?"

"Much like the fallen, I, at times, manifest myself with Brother Joshua. Unlike what Shamsiel has done, however, I am accepted willingly." Returning his gaze to Shamsiel, he continued, "There was a time when Shamsiel helped me with different tasks. But he strayed, as did the other of the Watchers, and is sentenced to prison until Judgment Day."

"You spoke on our behalf before God," Shamsiel said. "You could do so again. I am pleading with you, Uriel. Go before God and ask for our forgiveness."

The face of Kyle Beaumont shone with a desperation one rarely sees. And looking into his eyes, I could see they were raven black with stars falling in them. I rubbed my own eyes and looked again, but the sensation of falling stars remained.

Brother Joshua placed his hands gently on either side of Kyle's head, then bent and kissed him on the forehead. Kyle closed his eyes and wept. Then J straightened, placing his hands on top of Kyle's head and said, "You have been judged, Shamsiel. You and your brothers sealed your fate the moment you turned from God. I command you, leave this body, and return no more!"

When Father Colton performed his exorcism, he worked at it for several minutes. I guess when you're an archangel you pack a bigger punch. Kyle's body arched back, his hands once again thrown out to his side and a high-pitched wail escaped his body, forcing me to cover my ears with both hands. The moment quickly passed, however, and Kyle slumped to the ground, his eyes rolling back in his head. Joshua knelt beside the young man and brushed his fingers gently across his forehead. As he did this, he muttered something softly. Kyle's eyes first closed, then opened again to reveal the black of the fallen angel now replaced by a much more normal green of the man he was before.

Joshua offered Kyle a hand and pulled him to his feet.

"I know you will have many questions, but for now may I offer you a place of rest?" Brother Joshua said to Kyle.

The boy nodded a very sleepy yes and J led us back across the street and into the mission. He asked me to wait while he took Kyle down to the room next to Charlie's. A few minutes later he came out and closed the door, and then stood in front of me.

"He will sleep soundly for the rest of the night. I will talk with him in the morning."

"That's how you know where to send me. Uriel is one of the angels allowed in the presence of God. You get your orders directly from the Big Man, right?" I may not know my Bible overly well, but I do know some of the more kick butt angels and Uriel stands near the top of the list. Knowing I was standing in his presence was more than a bit intimidating.

"The process is not exactly as you state, but close enough. When needed, Brother Joshua calls my name and I come. Most of the time you are dealing with him, but I come when needed."

"And tonight, you were needed. Back in the office, was Samantha arguing with Joshua or you?"

Brother Joshua smiled and walked by me. "Does it matter?"

"He said you argued for them before God. Is that true?"

"It is as Shamsiel said. I did argue for God to spare them, but He did not. I mourn for my brethren, but even for us, choices have consequences. Lucifer and the Watchers pay an eternal price for their defiance of God."

"And there is no chance God would change his mind?" I thought hard, trying to wrap my brain around the concept of redemption and salvation, or damnation and eternity.

"None. The judgment against the Watchers is final and there will be no reprieve."

"You know where they are, don't you? You could tell me where they're buried and allow me to end this, couldn't you?"

"I am sorry, Victor. It is not allowed. This is for you to deal with. I have faith you will do so."

"You know that's bullshit as far as I'm concerned. You guys upstairs play these games and we are nothing but pawns. God could end this in an instant, but he won't."

Once again, if Uriel was perturbed at my insolence, he let it slide.

"Things are the way they are and it's up to you and your fellow man to find your way until the end."

I slapped the wall hard with my hand in frustration, but reigned in my temper. After all, I watched as Uriel kicked a fallen angel out of a body the way I knocked a piece of lint off my shoulder.

"They keep calling me the Spear of Uriel. What's up with that?"

"From the time of the first Hand it has been my job to help them find their way in life. You are the Hand of God, but the divine have forever called them the Spear, as I use you to hunt down the most evil of your fellow man, then eliminate them. One of my jobs is to send people to Hell. You are the instrument I use."

"Great. I'm the Black and Decker tool of choice for God's handyman."

We walked together into his office and he flipped on the lights. Samantha came to me and took one of my hands in hers. "Everything O.K.?"

"Yeah. For the moment. Seems the Watchers are down another man."

I turned my attention to J. "I learned they were found in a cave. There are a lot of caves in these parts, starting with the mother of all caves, Mammoth Cave. Charlie says Arkas and another one of the fallen talked about digging out a cave. That must be why Mikey needed the construction equipment. I think that rules out a place like Mammoth Cave. Not exactly the kind of place you can do major digging without raising suspicion. I'll go back and talk to people to see if I can find out who may know anything about a cave."

Pointing at Samantha and me, he said, "Fine. I think it's time the two of you get some rest. In separate rooms, please."

We left him alone and walked out into the hallway together.

"Still worried about Brother Joshua?" I asked.

Once again she gave me the half shoulder shrug. "I don't like the fact he's the one responsible for choosing your assignments. I mean, you have no idea what his motivations are."

I debated how much to tell her about what I just learned, but decided now was not the time.

"Well, his motivations really don't matter much to me," I said. "The people I've killed have all deserved it. I appreciate your concern, but I'm really O.K. with my situation. I think Montoya was as well."

She leaned in and kissed me. "Doesn't mean I have to like it."

I watched her turn and go inside. I made it to my own room, stripped down, climbed into bed, and thought about the investigation. I always had a sense of when an investigation was coming to an end. I felt that about this one. I was close enough to the fallen and to Mikey that I could feel it.

It was a surprise to me that Mikey was in Hawaii. But it also meant he came out in the open. And to coordinate things with the Watchers this meant he must be somewhere very close. As exhaustion and sleep overtook me my mind began to wander and I thought of the many times Mikey and I were young and actually enjoyed being together. Like the time . . . I let the thought trail off.

Damn. I was now wide awake. Mikey was back in Kentucky and I knew exactly where he was.

CHAPTER 28

Michael McCain was pissed. He pushed the Bluetooth button on the steering wheel to end the phone call from Hawaii and then grabbed the wheel so hard he wanted to break the damn thing off in his hands. The fallen angel bitch failed. Not only was Kurt Pervis still breathing, but he was saved at the last minute by Winston Reynolds. And they arranged for yet another exorcism, sending one more of the fallen to wander in the arid abyss. He should have cut on Kurt the first night they had him instead of letting the fallen angel play with him. Note to self: tell the fallen angels to fuck off the next time they get in his way.

This meant he was no closer than he was before to the thirty million dollars stolen by Samantha Tyler, and a golden opportunity was wasted. If he was allowed to handle it his way they'd have the money. One royal screw up after another, all because people wouldn't let him do his job. Cyrus Tyler would regret the day he kept his daughter alive. Wait and see. The whole Florida operation blown. He snickered at that one and gave his brother credit. Never even considered he'd use a bomb to break her free. Good one, Vic. Let it not be said the McCain brothers weren't resourceful.

He pulled up to the security gate at the front of his driveway, punched in his code and watched it swing open. He could see the snow on the drive remained unbroken since the last snowfall. With Victor and others looking for his ass it helped to be cautious. He made sure no one was following him.

He pulled up to the old cabin he was refurbishing with all the creature comforts of home, got out of his car, hit the fob key on his keychain, and locked it. Bone tired, after all the travel he'd done in the last few days, he couldn't wait to get into bed.

He unlocked the front door, stopped to turn off and then re-arm the house alarm. He tried to change his dark mood by whistling a bluesy *Feeling Good* song he heard on the radio. Before he hit the sack, however, he needed to check on a few business items. He went to his study first, stopped at the wet bar and poured a double of Jameson Irish Whiskey, neat. Ice was for sissies. He sipped the whiskey and moved to his desk, but nearly jumped out of his skin when he heard a familiar voice.

"What, not going to pour me one?" Vic said.

****

"Come on, Mikey. I know you're a better host than that."

Mikey almost dropped his glass, but recovered and sat heavily into a leather swivel chair which was big enough to fit my large backside and two of his. Mikey took a long pull on the whiskey, and wiped his mouth with the back of his hand, setting the glass down on the large antique desk made of gorgeous cherry wood.

"Jesus, Vic. You scared the ever lovin' hell out of me."

His hand dropped low and out of site as I stood from a corner chair I was sitting in and walked towards his desk.

"You know, Mikey, I don't think that's possible. If I've learned anything over the last few months it's you have enough Hell in you to go around."

I didn't make it more than a couple of steps when Mikey raised his hands, pointing the business end of a Glock 19 at me.

"That's far enough, little brother. Take one more step and I will keep my promise I made to you back at the warehouse and shoot you where you stand." He stood and moved around his desk. "On your knees, if you please."

I did as he asked, slowly going first on one knee, then the other, laughing, and Mikey didn't like it. "What's so damned funny, eh brother? I'm the one with the gun and you're the one on your knees."

"I'm laughing because even on my knees I'm still almost taller than you are."

I kept laughing and he struck out, hitting me in the side of the face, the gun ripping a line across my cheek. I could feel the blood running down my face, but I ignored it. Between the damn buzzards and Mikey, my face was taking a beating.

"So here we are. The mighty Victor McCain on his knees. I've always been better than you, Vic. Always. There's nothing you don't want I can't take. I am curious. How did you figure out where I was hiding?"

"When dad died and mom had to sell this place, you threw a fit. It's one of the few places you seemed to actually care about. I thought back to that time when we came out here with dad, just the three of us, on a guy's weekend. Hunting, fishing, we all had a blast. Then a few years ago, I heard the old place had been purchased by some corporation who planned to use it for business retreats. It sounded like something you'd come up with so I did a property search first thing this morning. Then called up Kurt and had him track down the owners of the corporation. Low and behold, your name came up. So I figured you would run to the one place you loved. And here you are."

"Guess I shouldn't have used the same alarm code either, huh? Dad's birthday is one of the few things I can remember. Well, good job on hunting me down. But you should've shot me when I came through the door. Gun still in its holster?"

I slowly lifted the flap of my coat and showed him he was right, then let the coat flap fall back into place. "You're not going to shoot me, Mikey. You don't have it in you."

"Oh, really? Hmm. We'll see about that. Tell me, Vic, there were no car tracks. Did you really walk all the way into here from across the mountain?"

He tried hard to keep his eyes on me, but he couldn't help glancing around to make sure I didn't have someone else with me.

"Yep. I parked down at old man Hobart's place inside his barn. It really isn't that hard of a walk. Well, it isn't for real men. For pussies like you who don't even like to get their shoes wet, you'd never make it."

"Keep mouthing off and I'll shoot yer trap closed. I mean it, Vic."

His face contorted into one of barely contained rage and the gun began to shake a bit in his hand. Mikey always hated it when people questioned his manhood.

"Fallen angels? Really, Mikey? Let those things loose and what will your patron, Lucifer, do? Everything here will belong to them?"

"That's your problem, Vic. All muscle and no brains. Think about it. When the Lord of Light makes his move to reclaim his spot in Heaven, don't you think having two hundred pissed off fallen angels in your debt would be a good thing? Earth is only the first battlefield. Heaven is next. And when the war comes, the two hundred will be itching for a little payback for having all their children drowned like rats."

"So you're willing to kill everyone on the planet to get what you want?" I knew Mikey was evil, knew him to be certifiably nuts. But this far? "Mikey, you go down with everyone else. You realize that, don't you?"

"Like I said, all muscle and no brains. You keep thinking in this life. I'm working for a better position with the winning side in the next life."

"Always have a back-up plan, right Mikey?" Mikey used his other hand to make a pretend gun and pretended to shoot me. "How did you find them?"

"I didn't. Some poor college schmucks found them. One of them had a cave on a family farm down in Edmonson County and took some chick cave diving and got more than they bargained for. They possessed the girl and ate the guy. Guess the only one of them not shackled down was damn hungry. Then when they made it to the surface, the Lord of Light became aware of their presence and I made contact and we struck a deal."

"Which is why you needed Tommy Spenoza. You plan on digging them out, don't you? I figured as much. Well, plus you wanted that parchment. Sorry about that."

He waved it off. "Don't sweat it. I have others. I was never sure which one would work anyways. So, I tried to collect them all. All you did was slow me down. Was it you who whacked him?"

"I was. One less child molester in the world."

Mikey began to calm down, the usual sneer back in place. He always loved to run his mouth, so I let him.

"What about mom?" I asked. "You let these things out and she's as good as dead."

"Nah. You worry too much. I made a deal with the Watchers. A handful of people get to live. I mean, they will need people to help run things until their new children grow up. I'll see to it mom makes it. You have my word. I'll make you another promise, Vic—even though you don't deserve it. When I tell mom about your death, I'll tell her you died a hero, trying to save someone. I'll make up something good."

I let out a short bark of a laugh. "Thanks. You're still a prick, Mikey."

His smile, large and full, was sincere. "Yes. Yes, I am. Ain't it grand?"

"Where's the lap dog, Preston? I thought you two were best buds?"

"He's on loan to Cyrus Tyler in Washington, D.C. Changes are coming, Vic. Too bad you won't be around to see it happen. I wish I could say I'll miss you, brother, but you know how it is."

I shook my head. "Goodbye, Mikey."

His smile vanished. "Goodbye, Vic."

Pointing the gun at my head, he pulled the trigger. Then he pulled it again and again. In one swift motion, I stood, snagged the gun from him with one hand, and seized him by the neck with the other, forcing him back and onto his desk.

"Mikey, Mikey, Mikey. You think I'm going to come into your place and not look for weapons? I found the gun and removed the striker, then put the gun back. You should have thought about it, Mikey. You think I'd sit here and wait for you to blow me away? You know me better than that. Always have a back-up plan, right?"

I tossed the gun to the floor and started using both hands to choke the life out of my only brother. He clawed at my hands, but his fingernails couldn't do much damage to my already battered skin. His face began to turn a deep, purplish red.

"This is for Dominic Montoya, for the people you've allowed to be murdered in the name of the sick son of a bitch you follow. In a few seconds, you're going to be delivered to Hell. I've been given a taste of what awaits you. You are so royally screwed."

I tried keeping my emotions out of this, but I couldn't. I flashed back to when we were kids, fighting in the backyard, and I yelled to Mikey, "I'm going to kill you!" I didn't mean it then, but that was my intent now. The last three months set the two of us on this collision course with my hands around his throat. And in a few minutes it would be over. Eternal torment awaited.

"And I won't tell mom you died a hero. I'll tell her you were on the run from the law, that you were caught up in some type of scam you couldn't get yourself out of and were on the lamb. There will be no fond memories of you, Mikey."

His eyes bulged and his hands slapped at my arms to make me stop. After a few moments, his useless efforts at fighting me slowed. And finally, all movement ceased, my brother's body sprawled across the beautiful antique desk, lifeless. I kept the grip tight a little while longer to be sure he was truly gone. Then I let go, walked back to the chair I was sitting in earlier and thought about the last time we were in the cabin with my dad. I thought about all the laughter we shared when our innocence was still intact. Now it was all consumed by the flames of Hell.

I swallowed hard a couple of times, staring at my brother's still body, then I put my head in my hands and wept.

CHAPTER 29

I wiped down the few places I touched when I entered the house, threw Mikey's body over my shoulder, and headed across the mountain to my car. On the way there, I stopped at a deep sinkhole, tossed Mikey's body over the side, and watched it disappear into the darkness. I knew the sinkhole didn't go all the way to Hell, but at least it was now a bit closer. I said a short prayer for Mikey's soul, though I knew it was pointless. Mikey would spend the rest of eternity paying for his Satan-financed reign of terror.

I drove back to Louisville and thought about the story of Cain and Abel, one of the first lessons I learned when I was a kid. Now, as an adult, it seemed I was living my own version. The original Cain killed his brother and was condemned by God. I killed mine because I was told to do so, but by a higher authority. What did this mean for my own soul? One of the Ten Commandments is "thou shall not kill" yet that was practically my job description.

My brain bordered on exploding trying to reconcile the incongruity. There's no doubt God spent plenty of time punishing the wicked. The Watchers were directly responsible for God drowning every person who walked on the Earth not on Noah's boat. It was my job to track down and eliminate the worst evil the human mind could ever conjure into existence.

But this one, well, it differed from all the rest. It was my only brother. I had no clue how I would be able to sleep at night without Mikey's bulging eyes haunting my dreams. Mikey deserved his fate as Cain deserved his. But it didn't make it any easier to deal with. When Brother Joshua put me on the path to killing Mikey it had been an abstract kind of thing. Sure, I can do it. But actually choking the life out of him? Different matter.

I would like to say I will miss him. But we grew up to be very different people and were never very close. The best I can do now was try to remember the Mikey from my childhood and not the cold-blooded killer he became at the end of his life. The person I truly ached for was my mother. She would never know what happened to her first born, that he was killed by his brother. I would never be able to offer her closure without confessing my own role in his death.

I decided to spend the rest of the night at a motel in Lexington. After paying the clerk, I walked slowly to my room. Once inside I locked and chained the door and then put a chair under the door knob. I took a long hot shower and laid down naked on the bed and, to my surprise, fell into a deep and dreamless sleep.

I awoke refreshed the next morning and at peace. Mikey's fate— and mine—were intertwined. Only my death would answer the question of whether or not I'd join him in Hell or with my dad in Heaven.

The temperature climbed into the mid-thirties and the snow was starting to melt. It felt as if the world surrounding me was beginning to cleanse itself after a long cold spell steeped in near total darkness.

Time to get back to hunting fallen angels.

I called ahead and was greeted by Rob McGeorge. He shook my hand and invited me in. "Evelyn is at the market picking up a few things. Do you have any news for me?"

"I do. The individual responsible for what happened to your son will no longer be able to hurt anyone else, ever again."

McGeorge closed his eyes and gave a small shake of his head. When he opened them again, the fierceness and intensity of the man showed through.

"Thank you. I'm sorry it wasn't me who did it, but that it's been done will have to do." He seemed truly relieved. "You said you have a question for Mal? Then come on upstairs."

I found Mal McGeorge still in his bed, but looking better. He sat leaning against his headboard with ear buds in his ears and an iPod on his lap. His father called his name, he pulled the ear buds out and pressed pause on his player.

"What's on your playlist?" I asked.

"I'm listening to an audio version of the Holy Bible. Makes my mom happy and I have some catching up to do. I never paid much attention back when I went to Sunday school. So, you know, there's a lot I don't know," he replied. "Dad said you have a question for me?"

"Yes, I do. Did Ruth Anne ever mention anything about a cave? I'm thinking she must have been in one recently."

"You know, she did. She was really hot for this guy at U of K. Jason something or other. His family has a farm with one on it and she was invited to go with him. You think that's where they first made contact with these guys? Father Colton told me they were imprisoned somewhere deep underground."

"I think you can guarantee it. And I think I know which Jason, too." The P.I's report included the name of Jason Mueller. He was the only one of the missing students not to show any credit card activity. "Thanks, Mal. That really helps."

"Sure. Whatever. Happy to help." He put the ear buds back in and hit play on his iPod. Robert McGeorge and I left the room and he showed me to the front door.

"Do you really believe in this fallen angel stuff? I mean, I know Mal does and so does my wife, but do you?" he asked. I could read the skepticism on his face and couldn't blame him. To say it out loud sounded fantastical.

"Mr. McGeorge, yes, I do. They are very much real and before this is all over, I'm going to send them all to Hell. Just like the one who did this to your son."

I left him there, considering the existence of fallen angels, and returned to my car. If he didn't believe me, I couldn't blame him. Tell a man his son is the victim of a fallen angel and what would you expect? Our world is one of science, the real and the proved. Fallen angels were the stuff of legends. If I couldn't keep my promise to send them all to Hell, then everyone would soon learn how real they are.

Before I pulled out of the McGeorge's house, my phone rang. It was Winston. "We just landed at Louisville International a few minutes ago. Think you can come pick us up?"

"Sure. We? You bring Kurt back with you?" The fact Kurt survived his ordeal in Hawaii removed a huge drag on my emotional well-being.

"Him and the girl, too. Ruth Anne Gardner." Winston lowered his voice. "And man, you should see these two. They're all over each other." I could hear the laughter in Winston's voice.

"Really? Wow. So it took a girl possessed by a fallen angel to get Kurt a girlfriend? Why am I not surprised? See you in a few."

I drove up to the curbside pick up area and found the three of them waiting under the Delta sign, but I could tell something was wrong. Winston had a grim look on his face, while Kurt held Ruth Anne. The girl gripped him tightly, crying hard into his shoulder. I didn't have to be a rocket scientist to figure out what happened. She must have been contacted by the cops about her mother and brother.

I opened up the trunk and tossed in their luggage, while Kurt and Ruth Anne got into the back seat. The girl was a real looker, but the real shock was the look on Kurt's face. The man had always been, for a better word, soft. Not now. His eyes had a hard look and his jaw set with steely determination. Getting into the car with Ruth Anne, he gave me a tight, small nod in greeting. I expected him to start spitting out nails any minute, that's how tough Kurt looked. And Kurt *never* looked tough.

I walked up to Winston before he got in and asked, "She got the call, didn't she?"

"Yeah. She'd been trying to reach her mother. When she couldn't, she called a family friend and they told her. All of a sudden, her closest family is all gone. Doesn't help that they were done-in by the same group who hijacked her mind. Man, she's going to have a tough row to hoe, know what I mean?"

I did.

"Mikey's dead," I said. I worked to keep my emotions off my face, but there was no fooling Winston. He opened his arms and gave me a hug. I could feel myself tear up, but managed to keep the flood from springing forth.

"Lord's will be done. Ashes to ashes, and dust to dust. Your brother made his deal and now he's paid in full. I'm sorry for you, but you did the right thing."

"Yeah. I know. It's still hard." I glanced around to make sure no one was close by and then asked, "What about the P.I.? How did you handle it?"

"Wasn't easy. The first night Kurt and I took turns digging him up. I used my rental to dump the body in the middle of a thick wooded area. I don't think the body will be found anytime soon. Then we broke up the coffins and threw them in a dumpster behind a shopping center. When the next renters move in they'll be able to tell there was digging in the back yard, but not what for. Then we wiped down the entire house and checked out. She was paid up until the end of the month, in cash. So we're safe for a bit, at least."

"Good job. I understand the exorcism took most of the night before the fallen angel was kicked out. Did you guys get a name?"

"Yeah. Kokabiel. Where do they get all these silly ass names, anyway?"

"I have no clue. How did she seem when it was all over? Charlie had a real tough time adjusting to life once the freeloader was kicked out and dealing with the fact his body had been used to commit murder. How about Ruth Anne?" I asked.

"She kind of blew it off. Mainly because she never saw the guy die. She was forced to pour fire ants down a tube and could hear the guy's screams, but she never saw anything."

"Got it. Let's get these lovebirds back to the mission. I think I have a line on where the Watchers were hidden and she's the key. Time to devise a game plan."

Ruth Anne cried the whole drive and I didn't blame her a bit. Death had touched everyone in the car, one way or the other. When we got to the mission, Samantha waited inside the door, pacing back and forth. She hugged Winston first, then grabbed Kurt and held him for a very long time, whispering something softly in his ear. And, amazingly, Kurt hugged her back and kissed her lightly on the lips.

Wow. The old Kurt would've been frozen like a deer in the headlights. The events of Hawaii really had changed the computer geek. Samantha introduced herself to Ruth Anne, and then finally turned her attention to me. I took her in my arms and told her Mikey was dead and did my best not to cry. She kissed me, then told me to hold on a moment. She ran back to her room and returned with her winter coat.

"Let's go for a ride. I need some fresh air." She took me by the arm and tried to lead me out the door, but I didn't budge.

"I can't, Samantha. There's some things I need to talk over with Joshua. It's really important." I tried not to look her in the eyes, staring down at my feet, but she lifted my chin so we were eye to eye, my blues to her green.

"He can wait. Let's go," she insisted.

I didn't have any resistance left in me. I told Winston to fill in Joshua and to ask him to get Ruth Anne squared away and that I'd be back later. With that, Samantha and I walked out the front door of the mission and over to my car. I opened the door for her and then got in on my side.

"Where to?" With red hair framing a face to die for, I would have driven her through Hell itself if she asked me to. But she made it easy for me.

"Know of any good sword shops? I think it's time I get myself back in the game. But take the long way. We need to talk."

I did know of a sword shop over off Frankfort Avenue, where I previously bought one for a birthday gift. I pointed the Ford towards Market Street, then turned right, taking the side streets through town over to Frankfort Avenue.

She reached out and took my right hand in her left, lacing our fingers together, and covering it with her other.

"Tell me about Mikey," she said.

And so I did. About figuring out where he was holed up, about waiting for him, and about choking him to death. I told the story as if it happened to someone else. I told her about the weekend we spent at the cabin with my dad. And how I didn't know what I'd say to our mother, if anything. She listened to me without interrupting, squeezing my hand tightly between hers.

When I ran out of words, she said, in a very small voice, "John raped me down in Florida. More than once. I tried to fight him off, but he was so much stronger than I was that I couldn't stop him."

Tears of her own started falling from her beautiful green eyes. I pulled the car over, undid my seat buckle and this time it was my turn to hold her.

Over and over, she kept repeating, "I'm so sorry, I'm so sorry," as if what happened to her was her fault.

"You have nothing to be sorry for. I'm to blame. If I'd stopped them at the warehouse, then they would never have taken you to begin with."

She shook her head violently back and forth, "No, no, no. You did the best you could. I don't blame you for what happened."

I wasn't sure I believed her. Samantha's anger when I rescued her down south was very real. She was pissed as hell at me. I could still remember the left cross to the jaw.

"Look, we are two flawed human beings," I said. "Neither of us has lead a perfect life. How about from this point forward we do the best we can. Together."

I felt her nod into my chest. "It may take some time before I'm ready for intimacy. I hope you understand."

"I've waited my whole life to meet a woman like you. I'll wait as long as you need. And when the wait is over, I'll be here for you."

I kissed the top of her head, got back behind the wheel, snapped on my seatbelt and took us to the medieval weapons store. The woman knew her blades, and quizzed the guy behind the counter, as she picked out a new katana and carrying case. I damaged her old one when I took down a hell hound, so I paid for the new one. Seemed like a romantic gesture.

We returned to the mission.

"You go talk to Joshua. I want to go to my room and practice." she said.

"No worries. But you're safe here. You won't have much need for it."

Some of the fire I remembered returned as anger and flashed in her eyes.

"Look, I won't be staying here much longer. I'm owed some payback of my own and I plan to collect."

I thought about telling her no, that she was going to stay put and be safe. I couldn't stand the thought of losing her again, but I didn't. For the last three months Samantha was kept imprisoned by her dad. She was raped, emotionally battered, and no telling what else. If I tried to make her stay here, how was I any different than those who hurt her?

"Don't cut yourself practicing."

She gave me one of her patented Spock raised eyebrows, turned on her heels and strode off, a purpose in her step. Heaven help the person on the receiving end of her katana. Eamon tried taking her on when she held one in her hand and it sent him packing back to Hell. My guess is a few more would be doing the same before long.

CHAPTER 30

Buck Wilson was having one hell of a bad day. He continued to stare at the production schedules scattered across his desk, but no matter how he tried, he couldn't make them work. That meant the bonus he deserved for finishing the new bypass out in Shelbyville wasn't going to be his. The damn snow and cold kept his guys off their equipment and the dollars out of his pocket.

He and his top supervisor, Wendell Peters, were in the office doing their best to make the complicated schedules, and profit numbers, balance out. Perhaps they needed to hire another work crew or two? But that would eat into the profits. But no extra crews meant no bonus and no profits at all. So he asked Peters to work the phones trying to find warm bodies they could hire in case they got lucky and the weather broke.

He stopped what he was doing when he heard a truck pull up outside the double-wide work trailer. Glancing out the window he saw his cousin Bill get out and head towards the door packing his Dakota rifle. Hell, it wasn't hunting season, so what in the Sam Hill was he doin' lugging that thing around?

He didn't have to wonder long. The door opened and Bill came in, stamping the snow off his feet.

"Howdy, cuz. You doing alright?" Bill said.

"You know how it is, Bill. Could be worse, could be better. What the hell you doing out here?"

"I need you to do me a favor, Buck. I need you to give me some of that dynamite you keep in your storage shed, along with some blasting caps."

Buck laughed, a bit nervously. He looked over at Wendell who put the phone down, licked his lips and his face paled.

"Come on Bill, you know I can't just give away that kind of thing. You have to have permits to carry it and the state regulates that stuff. You come up missing even one blasting cap and your ass is grass. Whatcha need dynamite for, anyways?"

"Buck, if I told you, you wouldn't believe me. But I do need it, ya hear? So get your sorry ass up out of that chair, get your coat and get on out to the shed and get it for me," Bill insisted.

Wendell picked up the phone and began dialing. Bill turned to him, raised the Dakota to his shoulder and put a bullet right through Wendell's breast pocket, knocking him out of his chair—the phone still in his hands. Bill took a few steps and put another one in Wendell just for good measure. Buck peed his pants. He saw Wendell's feet twitch a couple of times, then stopped.

Bill turned his attention back to his cousin.

"Like I said, Buck. I need you to get up and get me what I need. Now, if you would be so kind."

Buck got unsteadily to his feet, and slipped on his old Army jacket, snatched the keys off his desk and eased by Bill out into the cold winter air and over to the metal storage shed. It took him a few tries to get the key into the padlock, what with how bad his hands were shaking, but he got it and slipped the lock off the door. He pulled it open and flipped on the single bulb light.

"How much do you need?" Buck asked.

Smiling, he replied, "All of it. Just pick it up and put it in the bed of my truck. Go on now, get moving. The daylight's a wastin'.'"

Several trips later, Buck leaned against the truck and said, "That's all of it, dynamite and caps. Tell you what, Bill. I'll just tell the Staties I had a break in. I won't tell no one it was you who stole the stuff."

Buck could feel the pain begin in his chest, his breath coming in wheezes. His doc had been on him about his weight for a couple of years and he knew he was having a heart attack.

He fell to one knee and looked at Bill. "Heart. Heart attack. Help me. Please."

"Be happy to, cuz. I wouldn't want ya to suffer." He raised the Dakota up and took aim down the barrel, the muzzle a few inches from Buck's nose. The last thing Buck thought before he died was, "That's not the kinda help I meant."

****

I entered J's office and found Kurt seated and typing away on his laptop he had balanced on his knees while Winston was leaned back in a chair, his feet propped up on J's garbage can that he pulled up in front of him. Since there were only two chairs in the room, I closed the door and leaned against the wall.

"Winston told me about Michael. I know it can't be easy for you. I'm sorry for your loss," Brother Joshua said.

"I don't really want to talk about it. Let's move on. Mikey did run off at the mouth a bit before the end and he told me the first contact with the Watchers happened in a cave between two college kids. I stopped and talked to Mal McGeorge and he said Ruth Anne knew a guy who had a cave on his family farm, which means Ruth Anne knows where they are. She's first contact."

Joshua picked up his phone and punched a couple of buttons. "Lisa, would you bring Ruth Anne to the office, please? Thank you." He hung up the phone and we waited.

When Ruth Anne entered the office, Kurt closed his laptop, stood and offered his chair. I'll be damned, I thought. I began to wonder if Kurt had been possessed and replaced by a tough but chivalrous fallen angel, but knew it was impossible. Kurt's faith in God was strong—stronger than mine, truth be told. Don't get me wrong. I know God exists, but faith? That's another matter and the events of the last few months were going a long way in testing mine. Still for Kurt, what a change. If a pretty woman walked into his presence like this before Hawaii, the hives would have already started.

I said to Ruth Anne, "You went with another student, Jason Mueller, to a cave on some property his family owns, right?"

A shudder shook her entire frame. "Yes. They have a farm down near Mammoth Cave. He invited me to go spelunking." Her eyes filled with tears and her bottom lip started trembling. "The guy we found down there," she hesitated, "ate him. Just ripped him to pieces and then . . . well, you get the picture. I don't have to go back there, do I?" She squeezed her hands between her knees and started to rock back and forth in the chair.

Before I could answer Kurt stepped beside her, bent over, and put his arms around her.

"Of course not," Kurt said. "We'll take care of it. Do you know the address?" When she shook her head no, he said, "Not to worry. I can find it." He sat his laptop on top of a file cabinet, flipped up the lid and started his search.

"We'll take care of it? You're not a field guy, Kurt," I reminded him. "Winston and I will handle it."

"No way, dude. I'm in. They tried to kill me and I won't let them get away with it. And after what they've done to Ruth Anne, I want in. Besides, you're going to need everyone you can get. Sounds like they're down four of them, but that leaves no telling how many more of them out there. You and Winston won't be enough if you go out to the farm and find them all there waiting on you."

"The man's got a point," Winston replied. "Especially if you plan on trying to take them out without killing them. If you want to sneak up on them and shoot'em all in the head, that's one thing. But otherwise, man, they're a little hard to bring down. I've got the stitches to prove it. And that one down in Florida nearly drowned your ass," he reminded me.

They were both right. But it didn't mean I had to like it. Kurt's only brush with danger prior to Hawaii was driving the van the night we sprung Samantha from the Church of the Light Reclaimed on a farm in the middle of nowhere. To put him in harm's way where the bad guys would like nothing more than to gut him and put his head on a spike would not be wise. I would have to try and find a way to convince him to sit this one out.

"Found it," Kurt said. "They own a farm in Edmonson County."

He got a post-it note from J's desk, wrote down the address, and then handed me the paper. I folded it and slipped it into my pants pocket.

"The person I met the other night, is he available to help out with this?" I asked Brother Joshua.

"He is not. He is not allowed to take a proactive role in what happens."

Both Winston and Kurt shot questioning looks my way, but I ignored them.

"How'd I know you were going say that?" I pushed off the wall.

"Alright then, here's what we do first. Winston and I will drive down to this farm and take a look around, and survey the place. Kurt, while we're gone, you pull up a map of it and any details you can about the topography, so we can make a battle plan. And Winston, do you think your uncle can get his hands on some tranquilizer guns?"

Winston scratched his side and said, "I doubt it. He deals in military grade stuff. Not much need for militias when it comes to tranquilizer guns. When the government comes to take all the guns away, they'll be shootin' to kill, not shootin' to snooze."

"Huh. Worth the thought." I turned to J. "We can try and use tasers, but when push comes to shove, we might not have any choice but to shoot them. I don't see how we can afford to let them get loose. The needs of the many over the needs of the few, or the one." I raised my left hand in a Vulcan V, but Brother Joshua ignored me. Again.

Brother Joshua replied, "Agreed. You do the best you can and—"

I interrupted, "Lord's will be done. Yeah, I know. I think I'll get that tattooed on my forehead."

"Now that'd be an improvement," Winston said.

I thought to myself, it might be the Lord's will, but it's my ass that will end up done.

CHAPTER 31

I plugged in the address into the GPS and before long Winston and I were on I-65 heading south. We drove in silence for a bit then I asked him, "Do you ever have any trouble sleeping at night with what we're doing?"

He shook his head. "Nah, man. I sleep just fine. Why? You tossing and turning? I would have thought this wouldn't bother you. Hell, how many guys did you burn overseas?"

"Dozens, I'm guessing. It's not the killing that bothers me, it's that we don't seem to be getting ahead. I mean, here we stop the Church from killing a bunch of kids and their teachers, and I'm thinking it doesn't get much worse than that, only to be faced with a bunch of former angels who would like to kill everyone drawing a breath. And if we stop them, then what's next? I thought I saw the darker side of man as a bounty hunter." He paused. "I really had no clue."

"Vic, bad guys have been around since the beginning of mankind. There will be bad guys after the Rapture comes. You have to keep plugging along and do the best you can. They didn't choose just anyone to be the Hand of God. They chose you for a reason. Seems to me you're doing a damn good job."

I drove the next few miles in silence. I bet if someone asked Rose Mary and her son Tim, they wouldn't agree with Winston. I should have been quicker clueing into the danger the Watchers posed to the parents of the kids who were taken. I knew hindsight was twenty-twenty vision, but I had to wonder if the stress of the job was starting to affect my judgment. If I wasn't careful, Winston and Kurt, and everyone else close to me could get killed.

My thoughts turned to Samantha. The words of her father stuck in my craw. If Samantha stayed with me she would always be a target. I remembered watching one of the Spider-man movies where Peter Parker told Mary Jane he doesn't love her, driving her off to try to protect her for her own good. I always thought it was a cop-out, but now I wasn't so sure. I loved Samantha and it ate me up inside when she was taken. Now, learning she was raped, it made me feel even more guilty. What if something happened to her again?

Winston shoved me in the shoulder. "Snap out of it, man. You look like someone kicked your dog and then shot it. It'll work out."

I laughed. Winston's sunny outlook on life was as constant as the smile on his face. With a faith damn near unshakeable, he made a good counterpoint to my increasing disillusionment. "Yeah, whatever. Let's talk about the farm. When we get off at the exit and start heading into the countryside, I'll find a spot where you and I can load up. I want you to have an MP5 locked and loaded. If things start to head south, shoot anything that moves."

"You won't have to tell me twice. I'm not really up to having a toe-to-toe with another one of those guys if I can avoid it. The guy I fought at the reservoir put up a damn good fight. With as much trouble as these guys are to take out, you may need to increase my insurance policy."

An hour and a half later, we left the interstate behind and followed the directions down a lonely country road. I eased off to the side of the road and the two of us went to the rear of the Ford and accessed the hidden compartment. Winston carried an MP5 with several magazines up to the passenger seat. I got into my weapons bag and attached a taser to my belt under my coat. I snagged one for Winston and passed it over when I got in. He sat it on the floorboard.

"Time to go up and ring the doorbell. Maybe we'll get to clip a few angel wings before the day is done."

"Wings, hell. You shoot for the wings if you want. If I need to pull the trigger, I'm hittin' center mass."

We found the driveway for the farm and after a quick weapons check, I nosed the Ford onto the gravel drive. The snow was packed down into a couple of wide ruts by more than one vehicle coming and going; several of the tread marks were wider than the driveway. We rounded a curve and the house appeared. It was an old but well cared for white vinyl-siding farmhouse with a wide front porch which wrapped around one side. A Dodge Ram pickup sat in front. I unsnapped my holster, pulled out my nine, and slipped it into my coat pocket.

Short of the house, the larger tire tracks split off and disappeared around a huge weathered dairy barn and into a wooded area some distance from the house.

"You hang here in the car, locked and loaded," I said. "If you think it's going down, terminate with extreme prejudice."

"You got it. I'd tell you to watch your ass, but yours is so big, you can't miss it."

"Baby's got back," I replied.

I parked so Winston's door faced the porch and he rolled his window down. I opened my door and slipped out into a beautiful mid-winter's day. The temp was around the mid-thirties and the sun shown down from a bright blue sky. I started towards the house and hadn't taken more than a couple of steps when the front door opened. A man stepped out wearing camouflage hunting clothes and matching hat with a large U of K emblem on the front of it. A feeling of wrongness hit me. Damn. Found one right off the bat. I wondered if they felt the same thing when I showed up.

"Go Big Blue,." I said.

The man, who appeared to be around fifty years old, smiled and replied, "Go Cats. What can I do for ya, mister?"

I stopped a few feet short of him, my hands in my pockets, one around the grip of my nine and my finger on the trigger. The buzzards had done a number on my bomber jacket, but the fact I didn't want to shoot a hole in one of the pockets didn't mean I wouldn't do it. I'd rather have a hole in the jacket than in me.

"I've been hired to look into the disappearance of the Mueller's son, Jason. You haven't seen him, by any chance, have you?"

I watched the man slip his own hands into the pockets of his hunting jacket. I wasn't sure, but I thought I detected a bulge in the right one.

"Can't say that I have. The Mueller's called me a few weeks ago, in case Jason went down to the old cave on the far-side of the property, but no one's been here in weeks. It'd been snowin' the day he went missing, and the drive was covered in unbroken snow and his car wasn't here. So," he shook his head, "I don't think he was out here. I went and checked the cave, just in case, but same thing. No one's been in or out of the cave, unless they found a way to walk in the snow without leaving a trace."

I glanced over at the tracks disappearing into the distance and nodded at them with my chin, keeping my hands in my pockets.

"The cave out near where those tracks are going, you mean?"

The man followed my gaze and said, "Yep. Same direction, but not to the cave. We had some trees fall out that way and loggers came in and cut'em up and hauled'em out. That's one of the ways the Mueller's make money off the farm, ya see, is by sellin' some of the old growth trees."

"Huh. Go figure. Would you mind if I went out to the cave and took my own look?"

I sensed movement in one of the upstairs windows and could see the face of a young lady looking down at me. I got the same sense of wrongness when I looked at her as I did the man.

"Actually, I would. I need permission from the Mueller's to let you wander on the property. If you really are working for'em, have them call me and I'll be happy to give you free range out here. Otherwise, I can't let a stranger roam around on the farm. Sorry."

Something we both knew wasn't going to happen. Rusty said a car with Fayette license plates was one of the cars found in the barn out in Crestwood which meant they were buzzard food and wouldn't be talking to anyone this side of a séance.

"I'll do that. I'm sure you'll be seeing me again. And soon. Who do I have them call?"

"The name's Bill. I look forward to it. Be sure and tell the Mueller's I said howdy, because I'm sure you'll be seeing them—soon." He nodded goodbye.

Veiled threat. Well, not so veiled. Then again, neither was mine. I don't know if he knew who I was, but I really didn't give a rat's ass. Direct confrontation was something I was good at handling. Truth is, I loved it. With all the things I dealt with, having someone to pound on made me feel good. And Bill, or whichever fallen angel was playing around in his head, had thrown down the gauntlet. I planned on picking it up and smacking him around the farm with it.

I went back to my car, walking backwards and keeping the man where I could see him. I offered him a short wave with my left hand, got into the car, put it in reverse and headed down the driveway. The man stayed on the porch and watched until I was out of sight.

Winston rolled up his window and said, "Did you see the chick in the upstairs window?"

I gave him an "oh, please" look and he laughed.

"I just wanted to make sure you did. You and the farmer were having such a pissing contest I wanted to make sure you didn't miss it."

"Yeah. And she's one of the missing teens. I think her name is Rexena. Looks like one of them traded up to an older model. I can't picture Bill hanging with a bunch of teens unless one of them is his and I don't remember any parent named Bill."

Winston shook his head. "You saying this Bill-guy is one of them?"

"Yep. When I'm around one of the fallen angels I get this weird feeling. Kind of like having a Spidey sense. You don't feel anything?"

"Nope, not a thing," Winston laughed again. "Guess there were more perks with the job than you thought. I wonder if it works with Vamps as well?"

"No clue. But the next time I run into one I'll let you know. Let's get back to the mission and decide on how we're going to hit this place. I think there's no doubt we've found ground zero."

By the next morning, with any luck, the Watchers would be planted firmly back into their cage. If not, I would know if I'd done enough to demand a few answers of God or would now keep Mikey company. If I was a betting man? Toss up.

CHAPTER 32

There wasn't enough room in J's office for the entire Scooby Gang, so we moved the meeting to the cafeteria, now empty with the evening meal finished. Everyone joined in: Brother Joshua, Winston, Kurt, Samantha, Father Colton, and Ruth Anne. The meeting started off with some somber news.

"Charlie Sutton decided to turn himself in and face the charges against him," Father Colton said. "While you and Winston were on your reconnaissance trip, the local news went with a story he was a person of interest in a murder at the farm. The police are keeping a tight lid on what went down out there, but they're on to Charlie. He said he would tell them the truth. That voices in his head made him do what he did. I told him we could find a new life for him, if he chose, but he declined. He said he would keep Victor and my involvement out of it."

"*Jiminy Cricket*, you guys should have done more to convince him not to do that! His life is over. The best he can hope for is life without parole, but we still have the death penalty in this state and you can bet to high holy Heaven he will get the needle," I replied. I was so frustrated, I wanted to break something.

"As in all things, the choice was his and his alone," Brother Joshua reminded me. "We did offer him a new life and he refused. There was nothing more we could do." Changing the subject, he glanced between Winston and I and asked, "What did you find out at the farm?"

I shook my head in disgust, but moved on. It's the place we're looking for. There are at least two fallen angels there and my guess is there are more. Kurt, did you pull up the maps of the farm?"

"Come on, dude. Easy-peasy." Kurt passed around several color printouts of the farm and the surrounding area. "The farm itself is several hundred acres. They mostly have corn fields and timber. Another farm backs up to this one and the house is down a really long driveway. We can start up that drive and then cut across the first field we come to. If we go late enough at night the people living at that place will never know we're there."

"Good work." I studied the maps for a bit and continued, "Even better, the second farm is nearer to where the cave is located. We can check it out before we hit the house. O.K. Here's what we'll do. We'll split into two groups. Kurt and Samantha will go with me. Winston you'll have Father Colton with you. If we encounter an unfriendly then we'll take them down with tasers, if possible, with lead if not. We can try and wound them, but that's really hard to do. If you need to shoot, unless you're really close, shoot them center mass. Everyone but Father Colton goes armed. Kurt, you ever shoot a gun before?"

"Paintball with my bro's, but how hard can it be? Point the thing at something and pull the trigger." Kurt pantomimed pointing a gun at me and pretended to shoot me, mouthing the word "pow."

"It's a lot harder than that, especially since you've never killed anyone before. If you hesitate, you're dead. And I've seen you cut up your food. Hell, you close your eyes if your steak even bleeds a little red. You close your eyes when you shoot tonight, they will close them permanently." I hated to be so harsh, but this was my friend, so I continued. "There's no shame in saying you'd rather stay here. You have nothing to prove to me or anyone else."

"Dude, they tried to kill me. They killed Ruth Anne's family. And if they aren't stopped, they will kill everyone on the planet anyway. So fight them now, or fight them later if you fail. I'd rather kick some angel butt now. Don't worry about me. I won't let you down."

I knew the man meant well, but all I could see in my head was Kurt going down with a bullet in his brain. But he was right. The choice was his. If someone tried to kill me I'd sure as hell want to take a piece of their hide. So be it.

I looked at Samantha and before I could say a word, she said, "Stuff it. I'm going."

I stared at the top of my shoes and chewed on my lower lip. I could do like her father and lock her in the basement to keep her from harm's way. After losing her twice before and considering what happened to her down in Florida, I had every right to try to protect her. But it would also be wrong. Like Kurt, Samantha needed to get some payback. She was not the "hide in the basement" kind of woman at any rate. I looked up and into eyes full of strength and determination. If only the two of us could have met under different circumstances because the two of us made one hell of a fierce team. Yet the longer we stayed together the greater the chances she would never see her thirtieth birthday and I wasn't sure I could live with myself if she died. But I couldn't tell her no.

"I wouldn't dream of it, honey. But this time, the only the way they get to take you is over my dead body."

She blew me an air kiss. "That's why I'm going, to make sure your body stays upright. They say behind every great man is a greater woman dragging his ass around."

The group laughed at that one, even J. "Whatever helps you sleep at night, sister. It's 9 p.m. I want everyone to get a few hours rest and we'll leave around 1 a.m. We'll hit them around three. Even angels have to sleep. At least their bodies do."

"I'm sorry I'm not going. I wish I could, but the thought of going anywhere near that cave again makes me want to throw up," Ruth Anne said.

I gave her my best high wattage smile, "No worries, little lady. You've done enough already. Right, Kurt?"

Enough of the old Kurt remained to send his face flushing red, but he said, "Damn straight. You've been through enough." Our little Kurt was growing up.

I looked from person to person and felt a great measure of pride in my friends. Despite knowing they were about to do something which could end in their deaths, they were going anyway, to help me. It didn't remove my concern for Kurt and Samantha, as they were stepping out of their element. But it was their choice. Brother Joshua always preached that our lives are about the choices we make and the good and bad consequences from those decisions. At least all of them knew the score and they chose to go anyway.

"Alright. Go get as much rest as you can. I will need you sharp, not bleary-eyed."

"I'm sleeping here tonight," Kurt said. "I'll just walk Ruth Anne to her side of the building then hit the hay." He helped Ruth Anne to her feet and the two of them left the office, hand in hand.

"Same for me. I'll be ready at the appointed time. See you guys in the morning," Father Colton said, and he also made his exit, leaving just Samantha, Winston, Joshua and me.

I asked Winston, "Think your uncle will mind us purchasing two more flak jackets? We have an extra out in the Ford, which Father Colton can use, since the two of you are about the same size. But we also need one for Kurt and Samantha. And I think we only have four com links, so we're going to need at least one more of them. Might want to get a couple more, just in case one or two don't work. And a couple more night vision goggles."

"Got it. I know he won't mind. I'll head his direction and call him on the way. I'll bunk down at his place and see you guys back here at one." He pushed himself up and out of his chair, kissed Samantha on the cheek, and left.

When he was gone, Samantha asked J, "Are you going with us?"

"No. I'm not. That's not the role I play." He folded his hands on top of the table and looked back at her calmly, knowing her well enough in their short time together to know what was coming.

"Another king sitting on his throne, asking others to do what he won't because either he can't or he doesn't have the balls to get involved." She looked at me. "Doesn't this bother you?"

Yes, it did actually. Having the archangel Uriel beside us walking into battle would be much better for our continued existence. But I also knew it wasn't going to happen, so bitching about it was useless. Trying to figure out why the Almighty did things the way He did was turning out to be more than my poor brain could handle.

"Doesn't matter if I do or I don't. He's out. It's my job to prevent them from getting loose and ending life as we know it. I'm guessing Moses, or Noah or Jesus, for that matter, didn't have all the answers either. We do what we are asked to do. Besides, with you watching my back, what could happen?"

She gave me a sad smile, stood, took me by the hand, and we left the room. She never looked back at Brother Joshua.

We made it down the hallway, but instead of crossing the lobby to the dorm area she pushed open the front door and led me out into the cold night air and down the block, where our breath mingled and made little clouds. She stopped and turned into my arms, kissing me, then wrapped her arms around me as far as they would go and buried her face into my chest. I squeezed her tight, pulling her close to me. We stood this way for several long minutes, neither of us talking, merely living in the moment.

Eventually she looked up at me and asked, "Do you think we will live to see the morning?"

I shrugged. "I honestly don't know. Most times, I know what I'm up against. the goals are clear and the objectives easy to figure out. This time, I'm supposed to kill the bad guys without killing the bad guys, stop them from taking over the world without knowing if it's even possible. There's a lot about this which is unknown."

I paused for a bit and glanced around at the other buildings surrounding the mission, the hustle and bustle of daytime activity given way to a quiet peacefulness. Most windows were now dark and silent.

"But, I'm good at these types of operations," I said, trying to reassure her. "Winging it is a strength. See what the bad guys do, react and then punch them in the mouth as hard as possible. The next few hours will decide not only our futures, but perhaps the future of mankind. And the fate of the world will come down to two bounty hunters, a computer geek, a priest and the most beautiful woman I've ever known. Maybe the angels will take one look at you and stand still watching you long enough for us to take them out."

She slugged me hard, but the smile which made my heart soar had returned. "Lord knows it won't be *your* good looks they'll be watching. You need a shave."

I rubbed my chin, feeling the several days growth of a beard. "I've been thinking of growing a big beard. Maybe it will give me a more ferocious look."

"I've seen you in action. I don't think you need anything else to make you look ferocious. You probably scare women and children by just walking down the street."

Funny thing was? That thought made me feel happy. I offered her my arm, she slipped hers around mine, and we returned to the mission. I didn't know what would happen a few hours from now in the darkest part of the night. But for right now, for this moment, I found joy walking with the woman I loved. It sure would be nice to be alive the next night to do it again.

CHAPTER 33

When the alarm went off at 12:30 a.m., I awakened and felt surprisingly rested. I wasn't sure if I'd be able to nap, with Samantha on my mind, but years of military training had taken over and I went right to sleep. As for dreams, if I had any, I couldn't remember a single one.

I padded down the hallway to the bathroom, hopped into the shower, turned the hot water up and let the water pound any residual soreness from my muscles. I used a towel to wipe the steam from the mirror and examined the face staring at me. The beard and mustache were coming in a dark black and my hair was growing long. I looked a lot like the Viking down in Florida. I picked up my razor, twirled it in my fingers and then set it down on the sink. I kind of liked the look and decided to keep it another day. If I lived long enough to take another shower then I might shave it off. Then again, I might not.

In my room, I put on a T-shirt and jeans, slipped on my flak jacket and finally a long sleeve shirt. Sitting on the edge of the bed, I tugged on my old Army boots, laced them up tight and pulled my jeans down over them. Picking up my beat-all-to-hell bomber jacket I held it up to the light. Fashion statement it was not. When this was all over, I decided I needed a new one. This one had been to Hell and back, almost literally, and was way too beat up to keep wearing. Bummer.

I slipped my wallet and keys into my pockets, my holster and Glock onto my belt and left my room for what I hoped would not be the last time. I'd grown fond of living like a monk. Not.

I found the others waiting in the cafeteria. Kurt was next to Ruth Anne, arms entwined, while Joshua, Winston and Father Colton talked in low tones. Samantha stood by herself, looking out the window at the night, her sword case leaning against the wall next to her. Three flak jackets were sitting on one of the tables.

"About time you got up," Winston said. "I thought we might have to come getcha moving."

"Yeah, yeah, yeah. You that anxious to start killing people?"

I aimed for light banter, but the words caused everyone to stop and look at me. I asked, "What?" When no one answered me, I continued, "Samantha, Kurt and I will ride in the Ford. Winston, you and Father Colton will follow in the van."

They all nodded. I walked over to the flak jackets and handed one to Father Colton, one to Kurt and one to Samantha. "You three put these on when we get in the car. They're not all that comfortable, but they may just save your life."

Kurt lifted his up and down a couple of times. "Man, these things are kind of heavy."

"Tough. You don't put it on, you ain't going. Simple as that."

"Dude, quit busting my balls. Never said I wouldn't wear it." Ruth Anne looked at Kurt, then reached up and patted him on the cheek, smiling.

"Good. There's an all night convenience store right off the exit. We can stop there for some coffee and a late night snack. They have a parking lot around back with no camera. Winston and I checked on the way back. We will arm up there. Let's get after it."

Samantha picked up her sword case and walked to me, slipping her hand into mine. Kurt hugged and kissed Ruth Anne goodbye right in front of us. I was guessing all those blow up dolls in his apartment would have to go before she came over for the first time.

Kurt, Samantha and I hopped into the Ford while Father Colton joined Winston in the church van, an older model white panel van. I lead our two car convoy out of the parking lot to I-65 and then up to cruising speed. I asked Kurt, "You and Ruth Anne seem to have hit it off. Are you sure that's wise? I mean, she did try and drown your ass."

"No, that wasn't her. That was Kobiashi, whatever his name is. Dude was all messed up. She said even though she didn't have anything to do with her body when the fallen angel tried to seduce me, that at least I was hot and she really dug me. When you consider what we've both been through, at least we can talk to each other about it."

Well, that was true.

"I think the two of you make a cute couple. I'm happy for you, Kurt," Samantha said.

"Thanks, gorgeous." They blew each other kisses. I wasn't sure I would be able to take the new confident Kurt.

I reached over and clasped Samantha's hand in mine. It felt warm and comforting, a lifeline in a sea of chaos. We drove on through the night, the three of us lost in our own thoughts, staying silent until we were off the interstate and into the parking lot of the convenience store. The store closed at midnight and with nothing else around for miles we could arm up with little chance of interruption.

I told Kurt and Samantha to stay in the car, went and opened the rear hatch, pulled up the rubber mat and punched in the digital code to unlock the secret compartment. Winston got out of the van and joined me with a bag of his own. We took a few minutes to sync up the com links, then divvied up the weaponry.

Winston selected an MP5, night goggles and a couple of concussion grenades.

"You know, Father Colton doesn't want a gun, but maybe you can talk him into keeping a couple of concussion grenades with him. If he accidently gets himself in the fight, he can at least stun the bad guys, too," I said.

Winston nodded. "We were talking about that on the way up. He really doesn't want to hurt anyone, but he gets that he might not have a choice when it comes right down to it."

I got an MP5 for both Kurt and myself, and a Glock 21 for Samantha as well as the two last concussion grenades and my own pair of night goggles. I closed the gun safe and heard it relock. I put the mat in place and shut the door.

Opening Kurt's door, I handed him the MP5s and his com link, showing him how it worked. "Here's where the safety is located. Don't even play with it until we're at the farm and out of the car. I don't want you shooting me in the back on accident."

"Yeah, right. Dude, I got this. I've watched all the *Rambo* movies. I'm good."

Huh, I thought to myself. I tried to decide if he was joking or telling the truth. I gave up and closed the door then opened Samantha's handing her the Glock.

"Don't worry. I know how to use one of these. I'll have my sword, too," she said.

I smiled. "You know how sexy that sounds? Beautiful woman with a sword in one hand and a nine in the other?"

She kissed me and said, "I always wondered how you pictured me when you dream of me. Now I know."

I kissed her back and shut the door. Then I climbed in on my side, started up the car and we returned to the road. Kurt's maps showed the driveway we needed to be on was about three quarters of a mile past the Mueller's farm and I found it easily enough. The driveway snaked through a wooded area and I stopped well short of the house with the van pulling up behind me.

We both turned off the engines and sat there for a few minutes. I used my com link to contact Winston. "Let's sit here and see if anyone pays us any attention. Use the night goggles."

"Roger that."

I slipped on the goggles, pulling the harness over my head, and looked towards the Mueller's farm. The night transformed from a deep black to a ghostly green through the goggles viewer.

I saw three deer walking slowly through the woods between us and the entrance of the cave, but saw nothing else.

I pushed my com link and said, "Clear. Agreed?"

"Unless you think them angels are running around as Bambi, we're good." Winston replied.

"Alright, let's get this show on the road."

I slipped off the goggles and Kurt said, "Where's my pair? I want one of those."

"Hold your horses. Look in my bag and get out a pair for you and for Samantha. The power switch is on the side. If we use a concussion grenade, don't have your eyes open if you have the goggles on. Your eyes won't like you very much if you do."

I spent the next minute watching Samantha get her harness adjusted, watching the way her brows pulled down in concentration, the movement of her long, nimble fingers. She must have felt me watching because she glanced my way, her eyes shining in the dashboard lights with a heat which bore deep into my soul. She stretched out her hand, brushing the stubble on my cheek with the back of her hand. I snagged it and pressed her hand to my lips.

Over the com Winston said, "We're ready to go. How about you, old man?"

Kurt snickered and I turned to glare at him, but he had his goggles on, the one central eye staring back at me which made me laugh. I pushed the button on my com and said, "Yeah, yeah. We're ready. Remember to turn off your dome light."

I switched my dome lights off, then got out of the car quietly, making sure Samantha and Kurt did the same thing. The moon, what was left of it, stayed hidden behind a thick covering of clouds. The weather gurus at the local news stations said we could get a couple more inches of snow. Or none. I was betting on snow.

I pulled the goggles into place, slid the safety on my MP5 to the off position and motioned the gang to come in close.

"We will need to spread out about ten yards between each of us in a staggered line," I said softly. "No chatter on the com's unless it's unavoidable. Sound carries a long way at night and we don't want them to know we're coming until we put the barrel of a gun next to their heads. Everyone understand?"

Each person nodded, their breath mingling as we huddled together. I stuck my hand out and each of them placed theirs on top of mine. I raised my fist in the air and then lead my little band of heroes across a field covered in a blanket of white to begin the hunt.

Before we left I memorized the map of the area and knew about where the cave was located. I took point with Kurt to my left and Samantha to my right. Winston and Father Colton fanned out further to the other side of Samantha.

I could feel the excitement level in me rising. This was what I was built for, to hunt down and deliver justice to my fellow man, sometimes killing them. And I was damn good at it. Winston was right. They picked me for a reason to be the Hand of God, just as they picked Dominic Montoya before me: killers who did what was needed with no remorse, no regrets.

I always wondered why I didn't feel at least some remorse when I found someone in my sights and pulled the trigger. In Iraq and Afghanistan, I killed people who asked for it. You take a swing at Uncle Sam and you better damn well know we're going to put a boot up your ass for the trouble. I knew every man I killed over there would have slit my throat in my sleep if given the chance. On one mission I shot and killed almost a dozen insurgents and that night I slept the sleep of the righteous.

In my fight with Satan and his minions, I was responsible for the deaths of over a dozen people and never lost one iota of sleep, no self recriminations. Like the Taliban, they declared war on the world and I was happy to bring the fires of Hell right to their door.

Tonight, I didn't know if I would kill anyone or not. But I knew if called to do so, I'd pull the trigger and start looking for the next target. Which begged the question, how did stone cold killers like me ever make the trip up instead of down? In moments like this, I not only didn't know, but I didn't care.

Off to our left, the trees were thinned out and I could see construction equipment lined up around a mound of dirt. I got the attention of the others, raising my hand for them to stay put, then ran low to the edge of the dirt. I belly crawled the rest of the way up the mound and slowly looked over the top.

All the trees in the area before me were gone, with a large section of dirt removed and pushed to the side, creating a semi-circle of dirt, open at one end for trucks and equipment to move in and out. All that remained in the middle was the hard surface of a rock shelf.

Sitting upon the rock like two alien insects ready to pounce were two Furukawa hammer drills. I'd seen them over the years used by road crews building new highways in the rockier part of the state. They'd already begun to make little rocks out of big rocks with a pile waiting to be hauled away by the trucks. Now I knew what the fallen angels were up to, via a host of hijacked bodies, and that was digging a hole down deep enough to allow them to escape.

I was turning to crawl back down when I saw movement in the cab of one of the dump trucks and I froze. Colored by the green lens of my goggles, a face searched the night through the front windshield of the truck and I saw Maxwell Neunen, a foreign exchange student from Belgium who came to this country seeking a degree in engineering only to now find himself huddled in the front seat of a dump truck in the middle of B.F.E. with a fallen angel riding around shotgun in his head.

I surveyed the area and the equipment, but found no one else. Looks like Maxwell drew the short end of the stick and got the graveyard shift.

I eased my way down the hill, gathered everyone close, and explained the situation in a hushed tone. When I finished with the recap, I said, "Winston and I will circle the wagons and close on the truck." I pointed to Kurt, Samantha and Father Colton. "I want the three of you to do as I did, slowly crawl up the hill and watch us. If you see anything, use the coms to warn Winston and me. The MP5 has a night scope in case you need to let loose with it. Got it?"

Once again everyone nodded. I said to Winston, "You come up on the passenger side of the truck and I'll come up on the driver side. He's in the front truck. When I click the com, we hit him from both sides using tasers."

He gave me a thumbs up and we trotted off into the night, with me circling around the pit to the right as Winston went left. We made it around to the back of the dump truck without anything untoward happening. I could pick out the rest of the group watching from the top of the hill.

I clicked my com and said, "Go," then raced for the driver's side door, taser in one hand, my MP5 on a sling around my chest.

I jumped on the door runner and yanked the door open. Winston did the same on the other side. The cab between us was empty except for a small cooler and a McDonald's bag wadded up next to it.

"Well, this sucks," I said.

Before I could turn around, Samantha's hissed in my ear, "Vic, behind you!" Her warning wasn't needed. The feeling of wrongness hit me like a mental whip.

I spun on the truck running board as Maxwell and another man sprinted from the hammer drill, his mouth drawn in an angry scowl. The new guy held a machete and Max held a knife long enough to be just this side of a short sword in his hand, raised to plunge as deep in me as he could shove it. I, of course, took exception to this, and dove into the cab, pulling my legs up with inches to spare. The knife whistled by my foot, struck the side of the seat, and ripped a long tear in the fabric. The other guy came sliding to a stop when I pulled the door half-closed and blocked him from getting a swipe at me.

Max readied his weapon for another swing when I aimed the taser at his face and pressed the button. I'm guessing they didn't have anything like tasers during their day. I did feel a bit guilty hitting him in the face and neck, but he wore a heavy winter coat and I went for exposed skin, not wanting to take a chance the layers would lessen the jolt. His body jerked in a spasm and he began to fall. I kicked the truck door all the way open, and he clipped the other guy squarely in the chin with the edge of the door, knocking him over.

I followed Max's body down, holding onto the taser—as the body, fallen angel and all—convulsed on the ground. I put a boot on his wrist, and kept the voltage going. Then I aimed the MP5 at the machete-wielding wild man's direction when I heard a quick three shot tap of a machine gun and watched him as he did a weird stilted dance as the shots hit their mark and he fell to the ground, landing flat on his back.

I quickly looked to the dirt hill and saw Samantha, eye to the night scope of Kurt's MP5, scanning for other targets.

Winston joined me and I let off the trigger of the taser. Max twitched a few more times and then was still. Winston unwrapped the stunned man's fingers from the knife handle, picked it up and tossed it into the darkness. We rolled Maxwell over and cuffed him.

I could see a walkie-talkie in his pocket and it was on. Pulling it out, I slipped it into my coat. I used the com and said, "Kurt and Samantha, stay in position and keep scanning in the direction of the house. Nice shooting, Samantha, but I had him. Father Colton, meet us at the dump truck, if you please."

"Maybe you did, maybe you didn't, but I didn't want to take a chance. I did promise to keep you upright," Samantha said.

"Roger that."

Winston and I picked up Maxwell, lifted him into the cab of the truck, and cuffed him to the steering wheel. I stood on the driver side door runner until Father Colton climbed into the cab on the other side. Winston did a quick check of the other equipment to make sure we didn't have any other surprises waiting.

Colton took a few items out of the bag he brought with him and prepared to do an exorcism on the spot. "Any idea who the dying man is?"

I glanced over my shoulder at the man bleeding out on the ground, his blood mixing with the snow and dirt.

"I think it's Bernard Rollins. He went to school with Charlie."

Rest in peace, Bernie, I said silently to myself.

I shook my head, saddened by his death, wondering which way he went, to Heaven or Hell? The poor guy went from worrying about finals to dead in a field nowhere near family and friends.

Father Colton crossed himself. It took a few minutes to bring Maxwell around. When he came to, he pulled hard on the steering wheel and only stopped when I put the muzzle of the MP5 to his head. "Settle down or I'll send you to the abyss faster than you can say, 'Ah, Hell.' Comprende?"

He started shouting things in a language I never heard of until Father Colton raised the cross in his hand and started the ritual which would kick out whomever was using Maxwell for a roaming Motel 6. The walkie-talkie in my pocket chirped. I jumped down from the cab and pulled it out.

"Armaros, what's going on? I heard gunshots. Answer, please," a voice said.

There were several ways to play things out. I could stay quiet and let them stew about what was transpiring out by the cave or I could engage the target in conversation. If I stayed quiet there was a chance the rest of them could load up and head out before we got there. Then again, he already knew we were here and one thing I learned in my brief encounters is these guys took arrogance to a new level. What the hell.

"Hey there, Bill. Hate to break it to you, but you're down a few more brothers in wings. They now know the answer to the eternal question of just how dry it is in Hell's desert. How's your night going so far?"

There was the briefest of pauses, then Bill replied, "The Spear of Uriel. I knew you would come sooner or later. Seems you picked sooner. Why don't you come on up to the house and stay awhile?"

"First off, dipshit, I'm the Hand of God. When are you guys ever going to get that part right? I know it's hard to teach an old angel new tricks, but get real. Secondly, we'll be there in a bit bringing the wrath of Heaven which will rain down upon you with the finality of Judgment Day." I delivered the last line with the cadence of a soap box preacher. Father Colton never faltered in his exorcism, but he did shoot me a quick glance. I smiled and shrugged my shoulders.

I waited for another reply, but none was forthcoming. I added the "we" to give him something else to worry about. He had no idea if it was me or several hundred guys coming down on his helmet, but why make it easy for him?

Winston came jogging into view from behind one of the rock breakers and waved me over. After making sure Colton was O.K., I followed Winston to one of the hammer drills where he had the lid of a storage locker open. He nodded for me to take a look. Inside, stacked neatly in a large pile, was stick after stick of dynamite taped in groupings of five. Holy crap. My skin began to itch being this close to that much TNT.

He shut the lid on the locker and we rejoined Colton at the dump truck, Winston on one side and me on the other. We guarded our friend until, at last he called for me to join them in the cab of the truck. The feeling of wrongness had vanished, so I slipped a knife out of my pocket and cut the young man free from the cuffs. He rubbed his neck and face where the taser darts struck him and I could see fear on his face.

"What's going to happen to me?" he asked. "I didn't mean to attack you. The demon made me do it. I swear it."

"Relax, kid. Don't sweat it. We know you didn't have a choice. But you do now. Did Father Colton explain to you why you were possessed and how it can happen again?"

"Yeah, he did. Aw, man, I mean, I've never believed in all that Jesus crap, but now? Man, I don't know."

"Hey, up to you. But if you don't believe it, the fallen angel will return. And this time he'll bring friends. And each one will be worse than him. What can you tell me about the rest of them? How many are at the house?"

Max was shivering, despite wearing a coat, and kept rubbing his hands for warmth. "There are four more at the house, not including the leader. His name is Samyaza."

"Any idea how they plan to defend themselves?" I thought about the bulge I'd seen in Bill's pocket. "Any of them using guns?"

He pursed his lips. "Only Samyaza has guns. He's forcing the others to use knives and machetes. He seems to think only he should have the power to use guns. He's one warped asshole."

Colton said, "This is not really surprising. They didn't have guns when they were imprisoned and Samyaza, being their leader, would want the most power. Back in their day, the sword and spear were the weapons of choice and I'm guessing the ones they feel the most comfortable with using."

Max said, "Something else. I see you guys have night vision goggles. These guys don't need them. They can see in the dark. That's how my guy was able to see you coming."

I let out a string of expletives. I was hoping the night vision goggles gave us a tactical advantage. Now I find out not only didn't they give an edge, they were no better than breaking even.

I motioned Max to get out of the truck and I helped him down. Pointing back the way we came, "Head that direction and you run into our cars.

Wait there until we're done. If we don't return by morning, make your way up to the other farm and call the cops. Understand?"

He nodded. "Yeah. Sure. Good luck. Whatever you do, don't let these guys in your head. It really sucks." With that, he lumbered off into the night. I could only imagine what it would be like to have some whacked out fallen angel rolling around in my head. Then again, as I glanced at Bernard's body on the ground and his sightless eyes staring up into a starless sky. There were worse things that could happen to you.

I waved for Samantha and Kurt to join us. I knew of a few more fallen angels who needed to be introduced to Mr. Worse.

CHAPTER 34

My band of fallen angel hunters and I crept along the edge of the woods with no issues—other than Kurt tripping on the roots of two different trees. With no crops in the field during winter, there was little in the way to mask our approach as we silently moved forward.

Gazing towards the farmhouse, I could see the back of an old dairy barn between us and the house. And to the right there was nothing else but wide open spaces. There was no way to sneak up on the house: with or without individuals possessed by divine beings with great night vision. Damn.

All the lights were off in the house. The *Night Before Christmas* verse kept running through my head, *and not a creature was stirring, not even a mouse.* Things were looking very quiet as Winston and I spent several minutes watching for movement. I started to worry they'd packed up and flown the coop when Bill appeared in an upstairs window, smiling a night vision green tinged smile and motioned for us to come on over.

I promised not to kill any of the possessed unless I absolutely had to. I understood the people the fallen angels took over were just innocent bystanders, not much more than kids in most cases. But if I got a clear shot at ol' Bill, I told myself, I would shoot the son of a bitch and wipe that grin off of his face without giving it a second thought.

I pushed my goggles up onto the top of my head, raised the MP5 to my shoulder and took aim at Bill through the night scope. As soon as I did, he ducked down out of view. I lowered the gun and moved my goggles into place.

"You see all that?" I asked Winston.

"Yeah. Seems he wants us to come out and play." His head swiveled towards the barn. "How much you wanna bet there's a few of them bad angels waiting in the barn?"

"No bet," I said. Figures it'd be a barn. Things didn't go so well for me the last time I got into it with bad guys on a farm. My mind did a quick rewind on my torching several members of the Church of the Light Reclaimed the night I met Samantha using Molotov Cocktails and hay soaked in gasoline. I'd be rotting somewhere in the woods, most likely, if not for being bailed out by Dominic Montoya, the last Hand of God.

"I hate barns." I mumbled.

"O.K. Here's what we'll do. Winston and I will hit the barn and make sure there are no hostiles inside. We'll slip through the rear door. Kurt, you take one corner, Samantha, the other. If anyone comes down either side, don't ask questions, just shoot'em. Father Colton, you stay between them and do whatever you think needs to be done. Everyone got it?"

They all nodded yes and I lead our small force to the other side of the barn where Samantha and Kurt took up their positions watching our flank. After Father Colton flattened himself against the barn, Winston and I pulled doors apart just far enough for us to slip in.

The barn was two stories tall. The ground floor had a main aisle flanked with old dairy cow stocks. The farmer put hay down in the troughs on one side of the stocks and as soon as the cows stuck their heads through the slats to get the hay, the farmer would squeeze the two sides of the stocks together, keeping the cows in place. Then milking equipment would be fastened to the udders of each cow with the milk flowing up to and then down a pipe to a collection tank in the front of the barn.

The equipment appeared ancient and rusted from disuse. It was obvious this farm hadn't seen a dairy cow in quite some time, but it still smelled of old hay, manure and dust. I took the left side and Winston the right and we moved silently down the main aisle. I scanned the ceiling as I moved. The second floor was normally where the hay was stored and could be accessed from the main floor. I saw a ladder leading to the above floor at the far end of the barn.

Winston raised a fist, bringing me to a halt. He stood still, looking through one of the stocks at something on the ground. Slowly he squeezed through the opening, gun first, barely fitting, and squatted down out of sight.

From the com in my ear, I heard Winston say, "There's a body here. Young girl, beat all to hell. I'm checking her now."

I heard Winston grunt and then nothing. I called his name and when he didn't respond, I started in his direction. I took a step, but heard a sound above and behind me. I glanced over my shoulder in time to see a trap door open, the kind farmers used to drop hay from the top floor down to the first, and a figure hurtling through it.

A man landed on top of me, planting two feet smack dab in the middle of my back, and we tumbled to the ground. I tried to roll into the fall, but didn't quite make it and instead slammed my head into the stocks. My goggles smashed on impact, twisting and breaking, and for a moment the world moved in and out of focus from the force of the blow.

I started to push my way to my feet, but a length of twine, the kind used to hold hay bales together, looped around my neck and was pulled tight. The rough material bit into my neck and began to cut off blood flow to my carotid artery. The man pulled savagely, trying to keep it taut. My fogged brain reminded my body I had about ten seconds to do something about the situation, but my gun was trapped beneath me.

He leaned forward and said into my ear, in a voice more suited to a horror film soundtrack, "Time to die, Spear of Uriel."

I reached quickly behind me, using all the brute force of my six foot six inch frame, and seized the man's head in my hands. I pressed my thumbs hard into his eye sockets and squeezed his head in an attempt to crush it with my bare hands. He tried jerking his head free, but I held on as if my life depended on it. And it did.

With a howl of pain and rage, he let go of the twine, grasping my wrists and tried to pull them apart. Good luck with that, asshole. The twine loosened enough for the blood to flow freely and my anger to flow with it. I yanked hard, trying to pull his head from his neck, and the man flew forward as I drove his head into the same wooden beam I'd hit my own head. I heard a loud crack and wood splintering. Blood began to trickle down where I must have split his head open on the beam.

I heard another set of feet land behind me. I flung my first attacker off and rolled to the side as something slammed into the ground where I'd been laying. Without my goggles things were now cloaked in a deep darkness and they had the advantage. They could see just fine, but I couldn't. Before the new attacker raised his weapon again, I reached out and wrapped one of my big paws around the handle of what might have been a pitchfork or shovel, held it in place and struck out with my foot, smashing it into the side of the next attacker's leg. I could feel it buckle and he fell to the ground near me.

As he landed, I lashed out again with my foot, trying to kick the crap out of him, but his reflexes were good and I missed. With my head pounding from both my fall and the garrote, I needed some help. I wondered what had happened to Winston when the mystery was solved, as a woman screamed at me from where Winston had disappeared.

Sensing movement, I raised the MP5, using the side of the gun to block off her attack, and took the blow of something heavy that jolted my arms down to the elbow, then rolled over several times, putting distance between me and my attackers.

I hated to shoot them, but since I didn't plan on dying any time in the near future, I didn't know what else to do. If I started shooting wildly into the darkness, I was just as likely to hit Winston or another from my team standing outside the barn with one of the rounds as I was one of the fallen angels. Then I felt like an idiot. My night scope.

I managed to get to my feet, raised the rifle to my shoulder, and I sighted down the scope. The view was limited, unlike the wide angle view of the goggles, but it worked. I swung the gun around just in time to see a woman, her face a mass of bruises, one eye nearly swollen shut, and her lips pulled back in an expression of pure rage, swinging a sap at the side of my head.

Ducking, I heard the sap wiz by, brushing the hair on the top of my head. I lowered my shoulder and lunged forward, swinging the stock of the gun at her midsection and felt the blow connect. She howled in pain. I followed the blow with another quick strike to her kidney and she fell to her knees. I hustled back a few steps in case it was a ruse, but a glance through the scope showed her writhing in pain on the ground.

Before I could decide what to do next, I heard duel battle cries from both Samantha and Kurt. Using the scope, I watched Samantha rain blows down on the man who tried to strangle me driving him back to the ground. Blood flowed from the wound on his head and there was no way a normal human being could have continued the fight after the blow I'd given him, but he was trying.

A multiple black belt in Tae Kwon Do, I'd seen Samantha use her sword and her martial arts fighting skills. Both beautiful and deadly, she followed one strike after another until the man was knocked unconscious.

Kurt had his hands full with the pitchfork attacker. Wielding a two-by-four he found somewhere in the barn, he slugged away on the other guy who was hobbled from where I slammed his leg. It took a moment for Kurt to be victorious, but in a spin move Samantha and I would be proud of, he feinted left, then spun around quickly in the other direction and clubbed the man on the head. The attacker fell to the ground as if someone had reached inside him and hit the off switch.

When all three fallen angels were cuffed, Kurt started shouting, "I'm the man, I'm the man!" at the top of his lungs, and in an imitation of Samantha's fighting style, kicked a nearby post. Unfortunately for Kurt, it dislodged a loose board from overhead which crashed down and hit him on top of the head.

Kurt sagged to the ground. I walked over, reached down and removed the goggles from his head and put them on.

"Taken out by an inanimate object. Great goin', Kurt. Samantha, keep a look out, I need to check on Winston."

I looked on the other side of the stocks and saw Winston sitting up with his back against the wall, cradling his own head in both hands. He had a nasty welt running down one side of his face.

"She sucker punched you, didn't she?" I asked.

He moaned as he got to his feet and picked up his MP5. "Damn. I have to remember just because they're women don't mean they ain't dangerous. Man, when I saw her on the ground, all beat up and shit, I thought she was out. I went to roll her over and bam, she pops me upside the head with a sap. Sorry. It won't happen again."

"Don't sweat it. I took my own beating out here. Nearly got myself strangled to death and aired out with a pitchfork. Come on."

I cleared the rest of the barn, leaving Samantha to guard Kurt and the captured fallen angels. I went to the rear door of the barn and motioned for Father Colton to follow me. We managed to capture all three without killing them, although the one with the split head would be hurting once his divine host was forced to flee.

"There ya go Father, three of them. The guy with the split head is Julio Railoa, the other guy Michael Peko and the girl is Angie Newman. Three more college students who had gone missing. Can you do the exorcisms here in the barn? And can you do all three of them at once?"

"I can try here, but I can only do one at a time. Exorcism is a personal thing. Casting out one is difficult enough. Three would be impossible to do at the same time."

"O.K. Do what you can." I reached into my jacket, pulling out a small flashlight. Kurt was coming around and rubbing his head where he got thwacked. I tossed the flashlight to him and he caught it after fumbling it a couple of times.

"Kurt, you and Samantha stay here and guard the good Father. Winston, you and I need to take the house. You feeling up to it?"

He gave me a quick smile and said, "Even after the beating I've taken, I can still kick more ass than you can." He took a couple of steps and then went down to one knee.

When he tried to get back up, I pushed him down to the ground and he didn't resist. I pulled away his coat and saw a trail of blood down his side. The knife wound must have split back open.

"Damn. Man, you're not going anywhere. Here, let me help you over to Kurt. You can help guard the fallen until I get back."

I got him settled and he said, "Vic, you can't take the house by yourself. You're going to need someone to go with you."

Samantha stepped next to me. "He won't be alone." She reached up and pushed my goggles back up on my head, did the same to hers, and kissed me long and deep.

I wrapped my arms around her, squeezing her as tight as I could. After a moment I said, "I love you, but you're not going into the house with me."

She tried pushing me away, but I held her tight. The fact I didn't have my goggles on and couldn't see her face gave me the courage to continue.

"I can't worry about you while I'm inside. I'm trained on urban assaults and you aren't. I can keep you updated via the comlink."

"But—" She tried to object, but I cut her off, adding some steel to my voice.

"No but's, Samantha. Besides, I'm not cutting you completely out. If I don't take down the two fallen angels inside, and they make a break for it, I need someone to take them down. I need you to do this for me. Stand at the barn door and if anyone but me leaves that house then cut them in half. Do you understand me?"

It took her a moment to respond, but she finally responded, "Fine."

Her body remained rigid and after a minute I broke our embrace.

I slid my goggles into place and said to the others, "I'll be back before you know it. Winston, if you or Kurt so much as see a nose, shoot it. There are at least two more so don't take any chances."

"Then you better make sure and let us know before you stick your nose back in here. As dizzy as I feel, I might get confused and blow your ass away," Winston replied.

Something told me that was the least of my troubles. Time to go cut the head off the snake.

CHAPTER 35

Samantha and I moved to the front of the barn. "You ready?" I asked her. I couldn't read her expression with the goggles on, but she seemed calm.

"I've been dreaming of getting revenge on these sons of bitches ever since . . . since . . . well, you know. Doesn't matter. I should be going in with you, but I get it. How do you want to do this?"

I took a quick glance through the crack in the two barn doors. Before I could answer her, a shot rang out, blasting the wood next to my head, sending splinters into my cheek. "Shit!" I pulled back and removed a sliver of wood nearly an inch long from the side of my face. I was starting to get really pissed at Bill. "I'm going to throw this door open then you're going to unload on that house with everything you've got while I cross to the house. Ready?"

She gave me a quick nod and raised the gun up to firing position. I kicked the door all the way open and tore outside. Samantha rocked the MP5 laying down a line of fire for me. There was only one brief shot from the upstairs window which missed, thank the good Lord, as the glass and wood of the window exploded and Bill was forced to dive for cover.

Miraculously, I made it to the porch without any extra holes in my body. I reached out and tried the knob on the front door and was surprised to find it unlocked. I reached into one of my coat pockets and took out a flash bang grenade. If they had superior eyesight, and perhaps hearing, then a flash bang might have even more of an effect.

I pressed my comlink and said, "I'm going to use a flash bang. When you see me open the door, close your eyes for a moment. Understand?"

"Yes. Be careful, please." I could hear the worry in her voice and I didn't blame her. Taking on someone on their turf is never optimal, but I didn't have much of a choice. Time to get moving.

I swung the door open and tossed in the grenade. I turned my head to the side and closed my eyes. A moment later a loud explosion rocked the night. I entered right behind the explosion into a living room. A long couch stretched out before me and I darted behind it, seeking what little cover it offered.

Plaster fell from the ceiling, but otherwise, there was no movement. The room had two open exits: one leading to a room off to the right, the other to a hallway. I duck-walked over to the room and took a quick look. The room looked like what my grandmother would have called a sitting room with all the furniture covered in plastic. No one was in it.

I then moved across the room to the hallway. Glancing in, I saw a kitchen off in one direction and stairs going up to where Bill was shooting in the other. I edged my way towards the kitchen to make sure no one was coming up behind me while at the same time I kept an eye on the stairs. I took another two steps when someone began taking pot shots through the ceiling above me, trying to put one through the top of my head.

I dove into the kitchen and landed on my stomach next to a freestanding island in the middle of the room. The shooting stopped and I resisted the urge to return fire, not wanting to give away my position just yet. I laid there listening, reaching out with all my senses, my MP5 pointed towards the stairs. I thought I heard footsteps above me. I wondered if their hearing was good enough to hear my breathing through the floor between us. Screw it, time to take the fight to them.

I started to push myself to my feet when, with a yell, Rexena hurtled the island and tackled me, stabbing down with one long ass knife. I managed to roll onto my side, deflecting the strike from my chest, but the knife still sliced through my coat and shirt biting into my shoulder.

Gritting my teeth against the pain, I reversed my block, and slammed my fist into the side of her head, banging it off the kitchen island. She started screaming at me in the same ancient language the other fallen angels used.

She raised her knife to strike again, but I seized her wrist in my hand, stopping the blade a few inches short of my nose.

"Didn't your mother ever teach you not to play with knives?"

I managed to get my other hand around her throat and tried pushing her off me, but she was stronger than any woman had a right to be. Seems having a fallen angel inside you was better than any fitness workout program.

She started clawing at my eyes with her free hand. I turned my head to the side and her fingernails clawed my cheek, drawing blood. I used every ounce of strength I could find to sit up straight and threw her off of me and across the room into the door of the refrigerator hard enough to release a torrent of ice from the icemaker.

Good thing, too. Just then Bill appeared at the bottom of the stairs and aimed his gun in my direction. I dove to the side and tried to put Rexena between the two of us. I raised my gun and let loose a few shots in his direction as he did the same. Parts of the kitchen counter exploded around me, but I went unscathed. I, on the other hand, hit pay dirt when Bill howled in pain.

Rexena, who was gathering for a new assault, her knife raised in both hands, froze and her eyes widened when she heard Bill cry out. Bill began shouting in the same alien language I heard before. Rexena quickly turned and ran to Bill. He dropped his rifle and blood flowed from his now shattered elbow. Lucky shot, or perhaps divine intervention. When she reached him he put his other trembling hand on top of her head and closed his eyes.

It took every ounce of control I possessed not to let loose with a hail of bullets, killing both of them. It's what I wanted to do, to end it here. I'd killed dozens of people in my life. If I lived long enough as the Hand of God, I would kill more. But killing the two fallen angels meant killing two innocent people and consigning both of them to Hell. I wanted to scream out in frustration.

Getting a hold of my blood lust, I got to my feet and raised the MP5 to my shoulder. "Move and you both die," I shouted.

Bill cried out again, but this time it was different. The sound he made was more human and he tried to shove Rexena away from him.

Rexena took off up the stairs, leaving Bill behind. Bill let loose a string of curses and then shouted up the stairs, "So help me God, I will hunt you down and kill you for what you've done to me! Do you hear me, you son-of-a-bitch. I will gut you and watch you bleed out when I get my hands on you!"

He laid back on the stairs, moaning in pain. I moved quickly down the hallway, my gun trained on the wounded man, but when I reached him, I knew the fallen angel had fled. The feeling I had when I was around the fallen was no longer present in him.

"What did he just do?" I asked.

Bill, eyes filled with pain, growled, "He moved from me to her. They're both in the girl now. We *have* to kill that bastard."

He started to get up, but I pushed him down to remain on the steps. "I'm on it. You're badly wounded. Stay here. Try and get your belt off and use it to make a tourniquet. I'll go after them. Anyone else up there?"

He shook his head. "No. Just her. Or them. Christ, this hurts," he said, holding his shattered elbow. He continued, "Don't hold back. He wants you dead in the worst kind of way. Shoot the fucker. If you don't, I will." And I knew he meant it.

"I would rather take her down without killing her, then kick them out of her body. After all, if I followed your advice, you'd already be dead." I said.

"Damn straight. But they would be, too. You should've taken the shot."

"Rock and a hard place, man. Rock and a hard place." I patted him on the shoulder and started slowly up the steps, my MP5 raised and ready. I reached the top of the steps when I heard a crash, the sound of glass breaking, and a thump on the porch roof. Then I heard footsteps of someone moving fast. Damn. Rexena was attempting to escape the house.

I ran back down the steps, sliding past Bill, and headed to the front door. Suddenly I heard the bark of a machine gun, then Samantha yelling, "Get down!" At least this time she did as I'd asked her.

Making it to the door, I saw Rexena turn and face Samantha, a contemptuous smile on her face. Samantha, the MP5 in one hand, her sword in the other, screamed, "On your knees, bitch, or so help me, I'll blow your face off."

Rexena did as she was told, going down to both knees in the snow. Holding the gun in one hand and her sword raised in the other, Samantha closed the distance between them and hit the kneeling woman in the face with the hilt of her sword, knocking her to the ground.

"Samantha, no!" I shouted, running towards the women.

But Samantha ignored me, stuck the sword in the ground, grabbed a handful of hair, and yanked the young woman back up, blood running from a gash on her forehead. Samantha then placed the muzzle of her gun against the side of the woman's head.

"I should kill you now," Samantha said.

Rexena took hold of Samantha's wrist and tried to break free, but Samantha's grip was too tight. Finally, Samantha let go and shoved her to the ground and took a step back.

Before I could yell anything else, Samantha pulled the trigger. The round took Rexena in the chest, blood blooming a deep crimson across and down the front of her shirt. She collapsed onto her side, her life drained away.

I was stunned. I stopped a few feet away, shocked beyond belief. "Samantha.Why in heaven's name did you kill her? We could've *saved* her!"

Samantha turned on me and said, "I told you, if given the chance, I would kill the bastard who caused all this to happen. And I did. The demon inside her didn't deserve to live another second."

Father Colton appeared in the barn door and began jogging our way.

I closed my eyes and said a silent prayer for Rexena. When I opened them again, I looked at the woman I loved and said, "No, Samantha. You just sent an innocent young woman to Hell. What you did was wrong."

"Whatever. You know why I did it. I won't lose any sleep over it. You shouldn't either," Samantha replied.

We both watched as Father Colton reached the dying woman and began saying last rites. Then Samantha pulled her sword from the ground and started walking towards the barn.

When she passed behind me, my world fell away, and the blood froze in my veins. The feeling I got when around the fallen moved with her. I pulled my Glock out of its holster and pointed it at Samantha.

"Samyaza, stop," I said, my throat choked with emotion.

Samantha turned to me with a look of confusion. Then the same sneer and contempt I had seen before on those possessed by the fallen appeared on Samantha's face. Father Colton stood and I could see realization in his eyes.

Samyaza spoke, "Ah. You must be able to sense us. Is that it?"

When I didn't answer, he continued, "I should have considered such a thing. In the past, before we were chained in the darkness, one had but to look at us to know we were of the divine. That the Spear of Uriel would know us, no matter the form, should be of no surprise." The alien sounding voice, coming from Samantha, made the whole scene seem like a bad dream.

"I'm called the Hand of God now, asshole. And before long, I'm going to send you to the pit of Hell."

Samyaza raised one of Samantha's eyebrows. "You mean by exorcism? I don't think so." And with a casual move of her hand, the MP5 rang out and Father Colton danced backwards a few steps before collapsing to the ground, dead.

"Oops. Scratch one priest. They sure don't make them like they used to." Samantha/Samyaza laughed and dropped the gun to her side.

I howled in anger, closing the distance between us, putting both hands on my Glock because with one, it was shaking too much. "Raise that gun again and I'll kill you where you stand."

A porch light blazed to life and Bill came out onto the front porch, the Dakota rifle held in his left hand, his belt strapped around his arm to stop the bleeding. Winston slowly came out of the barn, his own weapon up, taking in the scene. I shoved my night vision goggles off my head.

"You won't shoot me. I'm controlling the love of your life. When I take possession of a body, I instantly know what they know. And I can feel her love for you as well as how much she believes you love her. Dangerous thing, loving the Spear of Uriel. But there is a way out. Here's what we're going to do. You're going to let me go. In a few days, I will find a new host and I will let your lover go. You have my word on it. You should know, when one of the divine gives their word, they must honor their promise. She will be unharmed. But you *will* let me go."

Standing there, all the emotion left my body. It was as if all feeling, the anger, the frustration, the hate, rushed down a well buried so deep inside me it would never resurface, leaving a vast emptiness inside me.

"She can hear me, right? She's aware of what's going on?" I asked.

"Of course. She is aware of all that happens." She smiled at me, and I knew it wasn't her, but the demon.

"Then Samantha, I'm sorry. I'm so very sorry. It should never have come to this."

I could feel tears stinging my eyes as I lowered the gun a few inches and fired.

CHAPTER 36

I recalled Deveraux and Samantha in the warehouse, his gun pointed at her head. I thought about how, after rescuing her in Florida, she said, "How could you let them take me?" And here I was again, with one evil son-of-a-bitch planning to do it once again, to steal her away from me. And I wasn't going to let that happen.

The bullet struck Samantha in the right hip. I knew where the Kevlar vest ended and where I needed to hit her. She spun around, dropping her sword, took one step and fell to the ground. I crossed the distance between us and trapped her MP5 on the ground with my foot as Samyaza tried to roll over and blow me away. The demon howled in pain and frustration.

I bent over, yanking the gun out of her hand, and tossed it away. Bill and Winston both ran up as I turned her over. Samyaza continued to scream with pain. I planted the muzzle of my Glock on Samantha's forehead.

"Move and it's over." I asked Bill, "Are there any animals on this farm?"

He looked at me bewildered for a moment, not answering. So I shouted at him, "Are there any animals on this farm?"

He snapped out of it.

"Yeah," he said. "On the other side of the house, there's a small pig pen. There's a sow with a couple of piglets. I keep 'em fed and make sure they have warm bedding through the winter. The owner loves country ham, so he raises his own."

I looked at Winston, "Go get one of the piglets and bring it here. Bill, you show him where they are."

The two men left and I looked back into the eyes of the woman I loved. In the porch light I could see stars falling through iris darker than the night surrounding us. We waited this way, as the blood continued to flow from the wound I'd inflicted on the woman I wanted to spend the rest of my life with.

It seemed like hours, but it was only a few minutes when Bill and Winston returned, a piglet under Winston's arm. He knelt on the ground next to me, holding the squirming pig still.

I said to Samyaza, "New deal. If you transfer into the pig, I will let you go free. I will give you one week to try and find someone else to transfer into. After one week, I will hunt you down and plant you so deep into the ground no one will ever find you again. You have the word of the Hand of God."

He snarled, "I will not. You won't kill her. You won't." I could hear the desperation in his voice. And the fear.

"Look deep into my eyes. I love her. But I won't let you take her from here. It's this deal, or no deal. If you don't take the offer, when she bleeds out you will spend eternity wandering in Hell."

He swallowed hard a few times and let out another scream.

"You swear that you and your friends will let me go?" he asked.

"As God is my witness, neither I nor my friends will do anything to harm or stop you. For one week you will have your freedom. But both you and the other fallen angel inside her must leave. If I feel either of you still there, she dies and Hell is your new home."

The fear in her eyes was replaced with hate. Seeing such hatred coming from Samantha, even though I knew it wasn't her, chilled me. She reached out a hand, placing it on the piglet's side, and closed her eyes.

A moment later the piglet squealed and Samantha opened her eyes, as pain, unfiltered by a fallen angel, racked her body. She gasped in a deep breath and began to moan in pain. I pulled the gun away from her and stood up. I motioned for Winston to move away from her with the pig, and the feeling went with the pig. It had left Samantha. She was now free from the evil residing inside her.

I nodded at Winston and he let the piglet go and it took off. Before it ran more than a few feet, however, a shot rang out in the night, the piglet squealed, rolled over, convulsing on the ground a few seconds, and died.

I turned quickly, bringing my gun up. Bill lowered the Dakota.

"I told you I'd kill that son-of-a-bitch," he said.

"What have you done? I promised none of us would hurt him. You broke my promise. You don't realize what you've done!"

"Like hell I did. I was listening. You said neither you or any of your friends would hurt him. Mister, I'm not yer friend. I don't know you. So I'm not covered by yer promise. If he was too damn stupid to know that, then screw him."

I didn't have time to argue and hell, he could be right. I went back to Samantha.

"We have to get her to a hospital. *Now*!" I shrugged out of my coat, pulled my shirt off and pressed it to her wounded hip. Her eyes were starting to glaze over with pain, but was aware of what was going on around her.

She gripped my hand and gasped, "Thank you." And then her eyes closed and she slipped into unconsciousness.

Bill stuck his good hand into his jeans pocket and pulled out a set of truck keys. Nodding to his truck at the side of the house, he said, "That's my truck. We can take it."

I slipped my coat on, then I bent over and picked up Samantha as gently as I could and carried her to the truck while Bill unlocked the doors and opened the back door to the dual cab. I laid Samantha on the seat, ran to the other side and got in. I lifted her head and rested it on my lap.

"You sure you won't pass out on the way to the hospital?" I asked Bill.

"I'm a lot tougher than ya think. It won't be a problem."

Bill fired up the truck and I rolled the window down.

"Winston, what about the fallen angels in the barn?"

"Colton was able to exorcise the one with the busted leg. I left Kurt and him to watch over the other two. They're tied down and won't be a problem. I'll go get our cars and the other guy and we'll drive our vehicles back here. We'll wait until you return or we hear from you."

There wasn't time for more conversation as Bill took off, tearing out down the farm's gravel drive. I hit the speed dial button for Brother Joshua and he answered on the first ring.

"Samantha's been shot," I said, trying to stay calm. "We're on our way to a hospital. I *need* you. I need Uriel. You have to help her."

"I'm sorry, Victor. But it doesn't work like that. Uriel is not 'on call.' I will say prayers for her. Which hospital are you going to?" All said as if we were discussing what place to go to dinner. I nearly crushed the phone in my hand.

"Didn't you hear me? Samantha's been shot. She's lost a lot of blood. She needs you. I need you. You can't let her die." I said, infuriated.

"I will pray for her Victor. That's what I can do. The other thing I can do is have help waiting when you get to the hospital, but I need to know which one."

I stared down at Samantha, brushing the hair from her forehead, her breathing shallow and rapid.

"Please, Joshua. Please," I was desperate. I knew Uriel had made it clear how much involvement he was willing to provide, but watching Samantha cling to life, I just couldn't lose her again—I *really* needed him.

"Victor. I will do what I can. But I need to know the hospital."

I asked Bill what hospital was closest, and relayed that information to Joshua. He once again said he would do what he could and hung up. I didn't even tell him about Father Colton. I thought about calling him back, but decided, "screw it."

I don't remember much about the rest of the trip to the hospital. I zoned out, watching Samantha take each breath, afraid each would be her last. I prayed with all my might, trying to will the next breath to come.

We roared up to the hospital emergency room door. There was a team of medics waiting. Bill gave them some story about someone trying to carjack his truck when a gunfight ensued which injured Samantha and him.

True to his word, Joshua alerted the hospital we were coming in and they hustled Samantha onto a gurney and rushed her into emergency surgery. They took Bill, who by this time, was starting to fade in and out, into a different surgical room.

I sat in the waiting room, hoping to hear news soon, but I realized it could be hours. I wasn't there long when two cops showed up to talk to me about the shootings.

I began reciting the story about the carjacking, keeping it simple. I told them the men had worn ski masks and there wasn't much in a way of a description I could give them. I talked with my head in my hands, not looking them in the eye. They kept asking questions, but I told them I couldn't add any more and left it at that. They weren't very convinced and told me not to leave town.

A few hours later, a doctor came out and told me Bill would be fine, but would need to stay the night for observation. When I asked about Samantha, all he could tell me was she was still in surgery.

A few minutes later, Brother Joshua walked into the waiting room and sat down next to me. He laid a hand on my shoulder and asked, "How are you holding up?"

I stared at him for a moment before answering. "Great. Just frickin' great."

"You do what you have to do, Victor," Brother Joshua said. "She went with you willingly." He paused, then continued, "Tell me what happened."

And I did. It all came pouring out, slowly at first, then faster, as I remembered all of the events of the late night mission of my team at the farm. When I told him about the death of Father Colton, he didn't seem surprised.

"She's lying in there, near death, because of me."

"No," he replied, "She's in there fighting for her life because of you. If Samyaza had been able to leave with her, there's no telling what would have happened, but I can promise you it would not have been good."

"I can't believe he was able to possess her. I know she thought God was dead, but I thought I'd been able to change her mind about that, you know? But I failed her there, too."

Before he could answer, a very tired-looking doctor came out. He greeted Father Joshua by name, then turned to me. "It was close. But I think she'll be O.K. She will have to go through a lot of physical therapy following her recovery, and even then, I'm not sure how well her hip will function. The bullet did a lot of damage, but the surgery went well and I'm very hopeful for a full recovery."

I nearly wept at the news. I thanked him and asked how soon before I could see her.

"It will be some time. She's lost a lot of blood and will be in I.C.U. for the foreseeable future. I suggest you go home and get some rest and come see her in the morning."

I nodded my thanks and the doctor left us. I turned to Joshua and said, "We have unfinished business at the farm," I continued. "We need someone to finish the exorcisms. Care to help out?"

He agreed and we drove to the farm where we found Winston, Kurt, Neunen and Peko still watching over the other two fallen angels. They stepped aside to allow Brother Joshua to finish the job started by Father Colton. Newman and Railoa would need medical attention. Brother Joshua said he would take them to a clinic in Louisville where no questions would be asked.

"What do we do about Father Colton?" I asked.

"Bring his body back to the mission. I will handle things when I return from the clinic. We need to think about how to handle where the Watchers are buried."

"I already have a plan for how to deal with that. Let me make a few phone calls."

"Good. I will see you and Winston later. Get some rest."

Winston, Neunen and I helped him get the wounded college students into his car. Neunen said he would go with them, and I watched as they drove away.

"Man, being an operations guy instead of just a tech guy is rough." Kurt said.

I glanced at him and asked, "Ready to hang up your spurs there, Kurt?"

"Not a chance, big guy. I kind of like mixing it up in the trenches. Really gets the blood flowing."

Yeah, I thought. The problem is too often it's our blood.

****

I must have been more tired from our mission than I realized. Once Kurt and Winston were settled into spare rooms, I collapsed into my own bed and was sure I'd never be able to sleep with visions of Samantha and the way her hip exploded burned into my retinas. But within minutes of hitting my bunk, I was asleep and stayed that way until late into the morning of the next day.

I woke up, took a quick shower and went in search of Joshua, finding him in his office, naturally.

He waved me in and I took a seat across from him. "I'm going to head down to check on Samantha. Do you want to come along?"

"She isn't there." He stared at me serenely, hands folded in front of him.

"What? She's been moved to a different hospital? Where?" I felt my heart beat jump, my anxiety racing. "Is she O.K.? What's happened?"

"She's fine. But as for where she's at now I'm afraid I can't tell you."

"Why the hell not? That's insane. I have to see her." I didn't realize it, but I was no longer sitting. I was standing, my fists clenched at my sides. I forced myself to relax, breathe, and slow my racing heart.

If Joshua was upset by my body language he didn't show it.

"She's been moved to a private rehab facility at my request. As for you not seeing her, she requested I not share where she is."

"*Her* request? I don't understand. Doesn't she want to see me?" My chest felt as if a giant was holding me down and slowly squeezing me. "J, I have to see her!"

"I'm sorry, Victor. But it's for the best. She will get in touch with you when she's ready."

I couldn't breathe. Didn't want to see me? I paced back and forth in Joshua's small office, my mind racing through all the reasons. Who could blame her? I promised to protect her, to take care of her and what did I do? Not only did I not protect her from some of the worst evil the planet had ever known, but I shot her. My idea of saving her came down to me pointing a gun at her, the woman I loved, and pulling the trigger.

How many times had I thought, now that I'm the Hand of God, we can never be together, our relationship can never work, it's too dangerous for Samantha to be near me. And now that she didn't want to see me, why was I surprised?

I sat down, deflated. "Will she be O.K.? I mean, will she recover from where I shot her?"

He nodded. "All indications are, she will, at least physically. I will certainly pray that is the case. She will have a harder time coming to grips with what she did while possessed."

"You mean Samyaza shooting Father Colton. It wasn't her fault. She couldn't help it."

"All true. But the same could be said about you and the fact you had to shoot Samantha. Does the fact you had no choice make it any easier for you?"

Touché, Brother Joshua. I had no reply. I knew I'd never forgive myself for shooting Samantha. I could only imagine what she was feeling after shooting Colton.

"What about Father Colton? Will there be a funeral?"

"There will be a private service for him back in California. He served his faith well, Victor. He has moved on to a much better place."

I wondered, again, if I would make the same trip. I had my doubts.

"You said you had some ideas on what to do about the resting place of the Watchers. What did you have in mind?" he asked.

"I still need to make a few phone calls, but I have a plan."

I told him what I needed and Brother Joshua smiled.

CHAPTER 37

Paulie, the Viking and I watched as the old man walked out of the cave. He stopped, looking up at the sky, stretched his back, then walked over to us.

"Won't be a problem," he said. "You have enough TnT to close up this cave so that no one will ever climb down there again. The cost will be about what I thought it would be. You got the cash?"

"In the Ford. I added a bit for a tip. I appreciate you coming up and taking care of this personally for me."

The three of them drove up the day before. Winston's uncle was kind enough to put me in contact with the bombers. They'd been able to use the Florida action in a beneficial way and were happy to lend a hand—for a fee, of course.

"I'll get to it," the old man said. He glanced back at the mouth of the cave. "Damndest thing," he continued. "While I was looking around I could swear I heard somebody whispering. Made the hair raise up on the back of my neck."

"The cave has strange acoustics. Probably picking up our talking out here."

"We weren't doing no talking out here," the Viking guy said.

The old man gave me a long look, but said nothing more. I left them to their work and walked back to the farm house. Bill, Winston and Kurt sat around the kitchen table talking like three old women at tea time. Their drink preference was a bit stronger, though, than tea, something Bill called a Fire Pepper: Diet Dr. Pepper with a large portion of Fireball Whiskey mixed in for good measure.

"They going to blow the joint up?" Kurt asked, taking another swig of the cinnamon flavored whiskey.

I was still getting used to the "new" Kurt, the one infused with a gallon of testosterone. He insisted on coming along to meet with the bombers and I let him. After all, he'd done his part the night of the raid, so he earned it.

"Yeah. They're setting up the explosives now. In a couple of hours, the cave will be no more and the only way to get down to the fallen will be through solid bedrock. And that will take time. Not like you can do that in just a few days. They're hosed."

"Are you really going to buy the farm?" Bill asked.

He'd filled us in on Samyaza's plans, about the murder of his uncle, and the theft of the dynamite.

"Yes. The family had it for sale, quietly, before they were murdered and the estate is anxious to sell. I've hired a real estate lawyer to handle the purchase. In the next month or so this will belong to me. Then I'm going to donate it to the mission and we will build some type of retreat out here for kids. There will be no way to drill down to the fallen angels. Not any time soon."

"Too bad you're tearing down the barn, though," Bill said, with a hint of disgust in his voice.

"Bill, I really don't like barns. And this place won't miss it."

Winston laughed, but then turned somber, sipping his Fire Pepper, he asked, "Still nothing on Samantha?"

I shook my head in the negative. The more I thought about what Brother Joshua told me, the more I came to realize it was for the best. It didn't hurt any less, with Samantha not wanting to see me, but it didn't change the facts: the longer she was around me, the more likely she was going to get hurt even worse, or wind up dead.

Reading my thoughts, Winston said, "On a different subject, seems we got all the fallen angels, but one. Bill was telling us one of them had a huge knock down drag out with Samyaza."

"Ain't no doubt about it," Bill said. "And Samyaza was pissed to all get out. His name is Gadriel and I can tell you this much, Samyaza was afraid of this guy. When Samyaza told Gadriel his plans, Gadriel called him an idiot and said he wouldn't help. When Samyaza threatened to fight him over it, Gadriel spread his hands out to his sides and said, 'Give it your best shot.' Well, not in those words, but you get the message. It's one of the reasons he wouldn't let the others have guns. He didn't truly trust the other angels with them."

"What happened?" Kurt asked. He drained his drink, and motioned for Bill to fix him another round.

He handed Kurt a Fire Pepper and said, "Keep drinkin' these, it'll put hair on yer chest."

Kurt looked down his shirt at his still smooth chest. "Hmm."

"As fer Samyaza and Gadriel? Bill continued. "Not a damn thing. Samyaza backed down and the next day, Gadriel was outta here. Ain't heard from him since. So you still got one out there. And be careful. This one seemed smarter than the rest of them. He told Samyaza his problem was he was still thinking old school and wasn't keeping up with the times. Gadriel insisted on having a gun, but Samyaza forbid it. Gadriel just laughed. When this guy shows up, he'll be packing."

"Great," I said. "A gun-toting fallen angel with brains. Can't wait to meet him. You O.K. hanging out here until we can get a more permanent presence?"

"Shoot, since my old lady kicked me out, I need a place to stay anyways. Works for me. And with the salary you're offering, why the hell not?"

"Thanks, Bill. And sorry about the elbow. Hope it heals up alright."

He waved it off with his other hand. "Don't sweat it. Once you've had a prick angel in your head, everything else is a piece of cake."

I picked up the bottle of Fireball Whiskey and poured several fingers into a glass I found on the table. I leaned against the counter and downed half of the glass in one shot while I thought about Samantha and the bad ass angels she had in her head. I thought about a lot of things. I chugged the rest of the whisky, the cinnamon flavor adding a nice burn on the way down. And I thought about the future. At least I could now do the things I needed knowing she was safe from harm, wherever she was. For now, that was enough.

EPILOGUE

Elsa, the reigning Sports Illustrated Cover Super Model, followed Alex Dabney as he jogged up the steps of his private jet. She heard him leave strict instructions for the crew to take off as soon as they were ready—but under no circumstances, short of the plane about to crash, should they disturb him once in the air.

They made their way to the private cabin. He slipped off his sports coat and undid his tie, tossing them across a seat. Elsa walked to the wet bar and poured them both some Glenfiddich Janet Sheed Roberts Reserve 1955. He said the stuff cost him nearly a hundred thousand a bottle. But as one of the Fortune 500 richest men, he didn't care.

He told her after taking over his father's manufacturing company and turning it into one of the world's foremost weapons makers, he could afford just about anything, or anyone, he wanted.

She sauntered over with the drinks and handed him one. He sat down, then she sat on his lap and began nibbling on his ear. Life was very good. When she moved to kiss his lips, she hesitated for moment. Gazing into his eyes she swore she saw stars falling.

ACKNOWLEDGEMENTS

There are many people I wish to thank, starting with my own Scooby-gang who have no fear in telling me when my writing needs work: Wendell Farrar, Donna Krieg Monroe, Brad Stiles, Bob Dalton, Kurt Owen, David Deatherage and Tom McNeil. And, of course, Bob Fulks without whom this book would never have been written.

Thanks to Starbucks Store # 2464 in Prospect, Kentucky who kept the coffee flowing and for giving me a space I could escape to.

Thanks to my wife, Karin, who did the major edits on this novel in a way which didn't affect our marriage.

Thanks to Hydra Publications and all the wonderful authors with whom I share space on the shelves.

I would also like to thank cover artist Karri Klawiter for doing another fantastic job bringing the ideas in my head to life.

But most of all I'd like to thank you, dear reader, for making my first novel, *The Hand of God*, a success and for clamoring for the sequel. You've taken the characters to heart, and what more could a guy ask for?

ABOUT THE AUTHOR

Tony Acree lives in Goshen, Kentucky, with his wife, twin daughters, two female dogs, a female cat, and the way the goldfish looks at him, he's pretty sure she's female, too.

Visit his website at Tonyacree.com. You can find him on Twitter and Facebook, too. Email him at Tonyacree@gmail.com

CPSIA information can be obtained at www.ICGtesting.com
Printed in the USA
LVOW12s0208070514

384680LV00008B/36/P

9 780996 086714